HALF PAST NOON IN CUBA

MAXIMILIANO FEBLES

outskirtspress

DENVER, COLORADO

Half Past Noon in Cuba
All Rights Reserved.
Copyright © 2015 Maximiliano Febles
v3.0

Cover Photo © 2015 thinkstockphotos.com. All rights reserved - used with permission.

Outskirts Press, Inc.
http://www.outskirtspress.com

ISBN: 978-1-4787-6063-4

Library of Congress Control Number: 2015945185

Outskirts Press and the "OP" logo are trademarks belonging to Outskirts Press, Inc.

PRINTED IN THE UNITED STATES OF AMERICA

To my Cuban brethren;
The beauty of our land
Will always lie within.
Nobody can ever
Take that from us.

To my native land,
The United States of America;
The wonder of our country,
Lies in its governing structure -
May our democratic freedoms perpetually endure.

To Maria, my rock and the love of my life.

To my four children
Michael, Michelle, Angie, and Christy
I adore you all.

To my special lady, my mom, and my mentor, my dad.

Contents

Introduction

In early 1962 my mother boarded a plane in Havana, headed for New York City. She travelled pregnant and alone, unsure of her future. Leaving behind her husband and countless family members, along with the comfortable life she had treasured since birth in her native land, was the most difficult thing she had ever done.

Soon after arriving in her newly adopted country, one she has loved and defended at every turn for over fifty years, I was born. After many struggles attempting to finalize his emigration, my father joined us in New York.

My life has been blessed because of their courageous actions, leaving behind loved ones and all their material possessions to achieve freedoms that few countries could offer. They sacrificed willingly, never looking back with regrets.

My family's courage is multiplied many times over, theirs is representative of so many thousands of Cuban-Americans who experienced similar fates because of Cuba's date with destiny. Its tyranny was one brought on by heartless thugs who stole the dreams of millions, broke up families for life, and created perpetual misery for those who remained on the island.

I have written this novel, with heart and soul, thinking of all who have sacrificed seeking out ideals to which all humans are entitled — freedoms that the United States offers its citizens.

Cubans' struggles have been many, but not unique. Tyranny knows no borders, there are many governments around the world denying its citizens the freedoms that all human beings deserve. We are all brothers and sisters of the same race – the human race.

May this novel entertain and inform.

Here is to a world we have all envisioned, one that has been conceived with utilitarianism at heart.

May freedom ring worldwide for all to experience.

Chapter One
Differing Views

E ven though he did not regret the incident, Arsenio's confronta-
tion with an esteemed colleague was unfortunate. Those who
knew them well figured it was only a matter of time before it got
physical between them. His black eye had hurt, but he could live with
that. What bothered him the most, to the core of his being, was the
topic of conversation on that gloomy day. He was not a fighter, his tool
was language. His oratorical abilities were known beyond the reaches
of the University of Havana. Through his eloquence he could convey
messages, beliefs, and political ideologies in a way that left nothing
to the imagination. Sometimes this ability, coupled with his political
beliefs, caused problems.

The day of the discussion, Dr. Buendia felt that things were
about to erupt. Volcanic eruptions are harmless when proper pre-
cautions are taken, but he was not one to back down in the face
of adversity. Here he was, three weeks after their encounter, back
on campus ready to do what he loved best – attempt to change the
world.

The professor drove into the lot and parked the car. As he approached the decaying building where his office was located, he
took notice of the beautiful weather they were having this winter,
rainy season had not been too bad thus far. After passing by his office to welcome everyone back and to pick up his mail, he walked
to his favorite lounge on the other end of campus. This daily walk
became a ritual, he could just as easily park closer to the lounge, but
he enjoyed the exercise and the view. He spent a great deal of time
there, sometimes it felt like his second home. Two of his friends met

him there with great frequency, one of those "friends" was the one who had assaulted him prior to their holiday respite.

The lounge was less than a year old and Arsenio referred to it as the best kept secret on campus. There were chairs with ottomans, sofas, and dining tables – all so comfortable that when grading papers he would frequently fall asleep and wake himself up with his own snoring. There were times when grading assignments in the office was unproductive because of the constant ringing of the phone.

He entered the lounge, chose a table, and waited for his friends. His political views were well aligned with Dr. Diaz's; it was Dr. Rivera who would always clash with Arsenio when discussing politics. Both were friends, but he felt a special affinity with Dr. Diaz. He and Carlos had been close ever since they started teaching together twenty years ago. Adolfo was radical, he too wanted to change the world, but his views on necessary political changes starkly contrasted those of Arsenio's.

"Welcome to 1958 Arsenio, this is our year, my brother. How was your vacation?" inquired Carlos as he sauntered across the lounge.

"Great Carlitos, how did the Three Kings treat you?"

"Can't complain, Rocky!"

"Rocky?" responded Arsenio with a puzzled look.

"Aren't you the Cuban Rocky Marciano?"

"Carlos, don't kid around like that. Remember, he's the only one who took a swing."

"Arsenio, speaking of Adolfo, is he sleeping around with another student? Rumor has it that his restraint didn't last long, he'll never learn. Those are grounds for termination."

"I refrain from bringing up personal topics with him, he's married with three children and it breaks my heart," responded Arsenio.

Carlos discreetly pointed to the door across the lounge as he whispered, "Speak of the devil."

Adolfo swaggered across the room. The same man who had

vehemently denied there was even an infinitesimal chance of Arsenio being correct about his views on communism was joining them for their weekly reunion.

"Gentlemen, how goes all with the crème de la crème of our esteemed university?"

Adolfo constantly praised his two companions with a mocking tone, something that both Arsenio and Carlos intensely disliked.

"I didn't think anybody could possibly top you, especially in your political science classes," shot back Carlos, with an embedded message Adolfo was sure to decipher.

"Brevity is the soul of wit, my friend, and your statement lacks both," responded Adolfo with a forced smile.

"Gentlemen," interjected Arsenio, "this tension is giving me a headache. I'm the one who got punched in the eye. Remember? I'm more than willing to forgive the impudence that took place the final day of the Fall semester."

Carlos exploded, "Impudence? It was nothing short of assault! People have been arrested for much less."

"Maybe if Arsenio would not be so vocal about his elitist beliefs, I wouldn't get so boisterous at times."

Arsenio felt the need to get a word in, "Wait a minute, are you telling me that my defense of democracy is now relegated as a character flaw? That is the ultimate in both arrogance and ignorance, even for you, Adolfo. We are living at the foot of Vesuvius, any day we will wake up to an unrecognizable system, and I feel like, well like... Listen, if we are to remain friends, we must refrain from discussing politics. You have openly expressed your passion for communism, and Carlos and I must respect it. We ask that you respect our beliefs, let's end it at that."

Adolfo uncharacteristically acquiesced, without uttering another word. In all his years of teaching with Arsenio he had never seen him at a loss for words, a sure sign that his passion for that topic of conversation exceeded his zeal for most other things.

"Carlos, Adolfo, let's now forget this ever happened. We're not going to let one swing ruin a friendship of so many years."

At that point Adolfo reached out his hand. They all shook, it was understood this would never happen again. Differing political views were not enough to disband this loyal trio.

As he made his way back to the other side of campus, Dr. Buendia rehearsed his first lecture of the semester to himself. He visualized the opening speech he had given to his sophomore students so many times before. His job as a good professor was to be stern enough to draw respect from his students without sounding tyrannical, even though leaning towards a dictatorship with students sometimes worked best, especially with freshmen and sophomores. There were some educators he knew who attempted to be too friendly with their students, and that would usually backfire. The professor's new "friends" ended up coming tardy to class and handing in late assignments without fearing consequences.

Dr. Buendia's appearance demonstrated his attention to detail, he had the look that made heads turn. His physical traits along with his elegant wardrobe gave him that air of refinement. He wore elegant suits everywhere he went, and was born owning the innate understanding that looks, assisted by the choice of garments one wears, convey a certain message about that person.

His posture and demeanor added to the mystique of Arsenio Buendia, as people would see him and immediately understand the importance behind this authoritative figure, a figure who neither entered politics nor won any major battles as a general, but nonetheless exuded confidence and authority. He moved slowly and deliberately, knowing that others would wait as long as it took.

His students would sprint to class, knowing that being tardy was not acceptable under any circumstances. These traits catapulted him to the upper-echelon of respected leaders within his university and his community as a whole.

He took great pride in his institution, which was established in 1728. As one of the oldest universities in America, the University of Havana had been educating Spain's elite since colonial times.

It was a beautiful institution in need of some tender, loving care. Scaffold was up in at least half the buildings, proper maintenance lacked and there was some catching up to do. The university president was effective and ran things well. When it was time to create the yearly budget, he motivated his staff to work with great efficacy to perform minor miracles. But the well was dry, they included only basics in the budget, while overlooking needed repairs. Much needed maintenance had always been pushed off to "next year". They estimated it would take two years to complete the necessary maintenance. Arsenio was glad to see they were finally making the needed changes, he couldn't wait to see the final product.

The professor proudly passed by the statue of Alma Mater every morning on his way to class. When overwhelmed with work, Arsenio would take some time off to walk along Calle San Lazaro, breathing in the ocean air and clearing his mind.

His first class this particular morning was Nature of Politics (P 680-210), which was a course he relished because of the diversity of students and the numerous debates that transpired throughout the semester. The last few semesters in this course had produced many heated debates disputing pros and cons of different types of governments. Arsenio found it more difficult than ever to remain objective, considering the number of communist students who had signed up for his course the last few semesters.

He entered Room M319 and set down his suit jacket and leather briefcase as he scanned the students in the room. Thirty-one out of thirty-two students from his roster were on time.

"Good morning, ladies and gentlemen. I will teach Nature of

Politics P 680-210 for the next four months. Some of you have taken my courses before, I am Dr. Buendia. The first thing I do each and every class is take attendance. If you are late less than ten minutes, I will give you a T for tardy. Any lateness over ten minutes earns an A for absent, at that point whether you stay for that day is entirely up to you. And please save your excuses, I've heard them all before. All classroom policies appear on your syllabus, which this young lady will now distribute."

Dr. Buendia was more flexible than he let on at the beginning of the semester, but instilling a little fear in the hearts of his students usually resulted well.

He summoned the curly haired girl wearing the spectacles sitting front and center. He noticed she had filled almost an entire page of notes in less than ten minutes, serving as an indicator that the student was dedicated and possessed excellent study habits.

She walked up to the professor, looked him in the eye, and confidently stated, "It is good to finally meet you, Dr. Buendia. I am Lily and I'm looking forward to your class this semester."

"Lily, it is a pleasure to meet you. Kindly ensure that every student gets a copy of this. Thank you." He handed her the syllabi and waited a couple of minutes as Lily circulated the copies.

After completing her task, Lily sat back down, pen in hand, ready to soak up all the knowledge Dr. Buendia would impart on his students. His reputation preceded him, and she eagerly anticipated learning much in his class.

"Analyze the syllabus at your leisure, time waits for no one. Now, remember this — it is through posing questions that we learn. I will utilize the Socratic Method throughout this semester to uncover truths and ideologies about different types of governments. Socrates effectively utilized questioning techniques to extract information from his students, questions led to more questions, which in turn added to the fountain of information a drop at a time. Socrates never wrote, his student Plato diligently wrote down his life's work and had it published. That is where you come in, for your final assignment you will join forces and publish material covered this semester. For your efforts I will forward 1% of my royalties, to be shared equally among you."

Those lacking a sense of humor gasped, sensing a herculean task with little or no compensation in return. Most chuckled, as they had grown accustomed to professors with a dry sense of humor.

"Let's begin. Consider this straightforward question – What is the purpose of government?"

Allen, a stout youngster with an overabundance of hair, uttered, "Governments are established to run the country."

"Run the country? When government officials are elected, or placed into office, do we define their job as running the country, or can we more specifically define it to better ensure that efficiency is achieved?" inquired Dr. Buendia.

"A government provides safety for the people it governs," replied Gilbert from the back row.

"Young man, we can temporarily work with that. We must create a working definition of government in order to explore alternative methods when one doesn't sufficiently meet the needs of the people. In order to formulate a satisfactory definition, it must fully encompass functions and the nature of the government in question."

As the professor was about to continue with his lesson, a hand went up...

"Professor, I believe there are too many functions to name...if I were to summarily describe the most important ones, I would include the following..."

"A government's primary purpose is to defend the rights of those it governs. It creates legislature and properly interprets those laws. The government establishes justice, ensures domestic tranquility, and provides for the general welfare of its people. By establishing a common defense and following the previously mentioned functions, it ensures liberty of its citizens."

"Of course, Dr. Buendia, this is the ideal that many governments strive to achieve. It is not always obtainable," said the young man.

Dr. Buendia had to bite his tongue, he could not hint that this student had articulated his own beliefs, held dearly for all these years – a belief that was getting more difficult to defend in present day Cuba.

"Young man, that was an eloquent definition of a well functioning government. Throughout the semester we will return to your definition and consider others in order to hopefully agree upon an ideal government, a utopia of sorts. Tell me your name and a little bit about yourself."

"My name is Manny, I am studying political science hoping to achieve something with my degree. Studying for the sake of learning is noble, but I want to make a difference. Some of what I see around us is disturbing to my family. My father has built a company from the ground up and is afraid of losing it."

"Very good, Manny. I hope you gain much from my class, my goal is to get you all to think. Through brainstorming and contemplation much can be accomplished."

Another student interjected, adding to what Manny had said. It was Lily, the young lady who had introduced herself before class.

"Dr. Buendia, it is my belief that a key function of the government is to give its citizens what they want and need. Sometimes those two are not perceived to be one and the same, in which case government officials must make difficult decisions. For example, even though not all citizens may realize it, taxes are instrumental in providing people with certain necessities. Without those funds garnished by our country we would lack schools, parks, garbage disposal, etc. Government intervention in certain cases is necessary, but overall, individual companies should be left to create their own policies to compete in an open market," added Lily.

"Using the word garnish to describe how we are taxed is a bit harsh, don't you think?" asked Alyssa.

"Do you have an option, are we able to opt out and cease paying taxes altogether?" pointed out Lily.

"Not really, but the word has a negative connotation attached to it, taxes are used for maintaining parks, garbage removal, schools, and many other things that benefit the people who provide those funds," responded Alyssa.

"I believe in a democratic system, but I make no attempts to claim that it is perfect. It is through critiquing that we are able to improve its good points and fix what needs overhauling."

"Thank you, students. I can see we are embarking on a productive and stimulating semester," added Dr. Buendia.

After a day of classes and clerical work that always accompanied his teaching duties, Arsenio left his office eager to drive home to his wife and children. As he drove home, a whirlwind of thoughts entered his consciousness about the argument with Adolfo. He wondered whether his friend would ever act on his convictions. They had known each other for many years, each year brought Adolfo closer to communism. Arsenio believed that his companion had crossed the line last semester by preaching his political beliefs to his students. When educating, especially at the collegiate level, it is each professor's duty to teach students *how* to think, not *what* to think.

He discarded the thought about his friend's political convictions and focused his energy on his classes and his new students, it seemed like a promising semester.

Chapter Two
El Malecón

Ana and Arsenio had lived in their corner home for twenty years. They built it together, choosing everything from the tiles on the patio to kitchen appliances. Only a couple of years into his profession as an architect, everyone familiar with his project agreed that Aldo's work was splendid. Prominent ionic columns supported the balcony facing the ocean. The columns were meadow brown, matching the color scheme of the rest of the structure. One could hear the crash of the waves while sitting outdoors. Blue skies scattered with cumulus clouds served as a reminder that nature's beauty cannot be duplicated; the view of the ocean from the house was spectacular. The famed seawall could easily be seen, people would meet there to enjoy the tropical breeze and beautiful views.

As you entered the portico, your surroundings gave you the sense that you had been transported to another place and time. With 8 bedrooms and 5 bathrooms, Dr. and Mrs. Buendia would host parties with plenty of space to offer their guests overnight accommodations. Only the highest quality materials had been used in its construction. The house was nothing short of stunning; its physical structure combined with the picturesque landscaping created a grandeur admired by passersby.

Living less than half a mile from El Malecón, the family made use of it. They would go for long walks by the ocean, enjoy a bagged lunch there during the week, or go stargazing late at night.

El Malecón was the name of the street crossing east to west in the city of Havana. Well lit at night, the seawall extended 8 km (5 miles) with El Hotel Nacional at the end. The original purpose behind building El Malecón (the seawall goes by the same name as the street) was to protect Havana from stormy waters. It wound up serving as a promenade for tourists, lovers, and fishermen. Cubans who moved off the island reminisced about many things from their native land, El Malecón was always at the top of that list. It was a sight to behold.

After breakfast on a clear Sunday in February, the family got into their convertible, eager to drive through Havana with the top down. The weather was perfect, it was 28 degrees Celsius (82 degrees Fahrenheit). Spring weather in Cuba, especially early in the season, was irresistible.

"Daddy, are we going to pass by the wall that wets us?" asked Barbara.

"Yes, honey. That wall is called El Malecón, and the waves crash against it with such force that it splashes cars driving by. It's like an amusement park ride," added Arsenio.

"Pops, let's be daring and leave the top down," suggested Angel.

"That's the plan, my boy, I want to get soaked!" he responded with an evil laugh, as he laughed and looked at Ana.

"Arsenio, I don't want to get drenched. I just had my hair done yesterday morning," said Ana with a concerned tone.

"You'll be all right, honey."

The forecast for the next couple of days was not good; a huge storm was brewing and would soon enter the Caribbean. The family was driving down El Malecón on the perfect day, the waves would be powerful.

As they approached El Malecón their hearts started to beat faster. Barbara and Angel were the most excited of the five, Maria wanted to get wet but not soaked. She was at an age where looks are everything. She would crawl under a rock if friends from school would see her - especially male friends - soaked from top to bottom.

There were times when some passengers would get their fair share of water while others would barely get wet, it depended on the crashing waves as the car drove by.

Arsenio was driving with Ana by his side. In the back seat, Barbara sat to the far side of the ocean, Angel was closest to the seawall, and Maria sat in the center. Nobody attempted to get the ideal seat because there was no such thing, the waves were unpredictable.

They were approaching the section of El Malecón that was closest to the ocean, thus wetting the cars the most, many slowed down to 32 km (20 miles) per hour or less to get the full effect. Most were tourists, but a large share were lifelong citizens who never tired of this beautiful drive along the coast.

"Here we are!" yelled Angel.

"Get ready," added Arsenio.

They had barely finished their statements when a huge wave came crashing in, the seawall redirected it skywards. All eyes were on that wave, traveling in slow motion; what seemed like minutes passed by, and then everything sped up.

Swoosh!!

As Arsenio continued driving slowly, everyone looked around.

"I'm soaked," yelled Barbara in delight.

"Me too," said Arsenio.

"Thank goodness my hair is fine," sighed Ana.

"We're both bone dry," expressed Angel. Neither he nor Maria had received a drop of water. Maybe next time, thought Angel.

The wave had magically skipped over those closest to the seawall and completely drenched the passengers to the far side. They always had a blast driving by their beloved seawall.

They pulled off to the side and started to dry off. The car also got soaked. Malecón waves were rarely this big, but the anticipated storm was powerful, creating larger waves than usual.

"Daddy, you know what comes next," said Barbara with wide eyes.

"Ice cream!" yelled Dad.

The ice cream parlor they frequented was a small establishment near the National Hotel at the end of El Malecón, Ana swore it was the best chocolate ice cream she had ever tasted.

Everyone was in a wonderful mood, this Sunday routine was something they looked forward to all week. Today the Carnaval added to the excitement of the day, the entire family looked forward to it every year.

On those rare Sundays when the family decided to have lunch somewhere other than Guillermo's Café, they would dine at Casa Potin in Vedado. The restaurant was clean, well maintained, and it offered good food. Arsenio did not mind dining in modest restaurants, they needed to be clean with good food and good service. He never considered himself an elitist, there was just no need to have a little fork for the salad and a large fork for his steak all the time. He liked to loosen it up at times, never feeling above anyone else because of his economic situation.

This particular Sunday, all five were going to dine at Casa Potin and then attend the Carnaval by El Malecón. Every year, thousands of Cubans looked forward to the traditional festivities that took place every Sunday for a few weeks in February and early March. It was full of energy and conviviality, with an explosive show of colorful allegoric floats and dancers. The parade was a sight to behold, it offered entertainment for the entire family.

Organizations and companies decorated their floats; their employees dressed up in bright, matching dresses, and represented their companies on the floats.

Among the many companies represented throughout the years at the Carnaval were:

- *Winston Cigarettes*
- *Chesterfield Cigarettes*
- *Ace Laundry Detergent (Hace de Todo — It Can do it All)*
- *Cuban Pineapple Distributors*

- *Polar Beer*
- *Cuban Wine Companies*
- *Transporte Aereo (A Cuban Airline)*
- *Camel Cigarettes*

And last but not least:

- *The Float with the Queen of the Carnaval*

"Let's park the car and walk as quickly as possible, the parade starts in a little over an hour. You know how packed it gets, we want to get a decent view. I can't carry Barbara on my shoulders the entire parade like I did last year, I needed a chiropractor for a month," winked Dad at Barbara.

"There's our usual spot, Arsenio. It offers a great view and provides us with shade. We still have enough time to claim that location," said Ana, as she pulled Barbara out of the car and rushed the other two.

"Mom, this looks more crowded than last year," exclaimed Maria with a concerned look. Of the three children, she was the one who enjoyed the Carnaval the most. Maria was very conscious of new fashions and loved dresses. She always looked out for the floats with the exotically dressed women. Their dancing and wardrobes stole the show every year, Maria had heard that some of those women were the same entertainers who danced at Tropicana.

"Let's walk quickly, walk and talk," Ana demanded, as she finished locking the car. "Follow me."

Ana also enjoyed the Carnaval very much, she took the lead now. Every year they stood next to a little grocery store where the view was surprisingly good. At first look, that location seemed to have a partial view at best. People stayed away from it for that reason, it was Ana's little secret. She wasn't sure whether anybody had discovered her spot.

The Prado-Malecón intersection was the most heavily populated for the parade. Prado was a popular street known for restaurants such as La Floridita, frequented by tourists. The Capitol and Plaza Hotel were also on Prado. The family would strategically situate themselves eight blocks away, avoiding many tourists and unbearable crowds. It didn't matter much where you stood, the parade ran the course of the main strip.

"Mom, look over there. Our usual spot is empty, reserved for the Buendia Family," stated Maria, excitedly.

"Let's go," added Barbara as she made a run for their corner.

Arsenio looked at his watch, a watch that was over 15 years old and worn. It was time for a new watch, maybe someday soon. "It's now 1:50 pm, the parade officially begins at 2 pm. By the time it takes the first float to get to us, it should be approximately 2:30," mentioned Arsenio.

"There's the first float," shouted Ana.

As the float got closer, they were able to appreciate the colors and intricacy of its design. Ms. Cuba from the previous year was on the first float, wearing the *Ms. Cuba 1957* ribbon around her torso. In a few months she would pass the torch to Ms. Cuba 1958. Dancers performed on the float, with two policemen on motorcycles riding on each side. The fort, surrounded by clear blue water and white puffy clouds in a matching blue sky, served as the perfect backdrop for the floats as they came to view.

"Daddy, look at Ms. Cuba," said Barbara as she pointed to the young lady on the float.

"That's not Ms. Cuba, Babita. Ms. Cuba is standing right next to me," Arsenio exclaimed as he pointed to Barbara. He grabbed her by the waist and kissed her.

"Arsenio, look. Tropicana floats get better every year, there are so many dancers this year. I love it," remarked Ana.

"No matter how many times we go to Tropicana, it reminds me mostly of one thing," reminisced Ana.

"We dined there during our honeymoon, gorgeous," said Arsenio with a smirk.

The Tropicana float had two levels - the first level consisted of two tables with diners and servers, the diners were served three course meals as they meandered down El Malecón on their mobile restaurant. The dinning area was covered by a yellow canopy and tastefully decorated like the nightclub. There were red velvet stairs that led to the second level where dancers performed under a yellow, neon Tropicana sign. The dancers wore matching outfits, green and red with elegant headpieces extending a foot above their heads.

Each float had its own music; Tropicana played Mambo while the dancers performed and some of the diners would get up to dance as they waited for their next course. The float was all about detail, it did an amazing job of simulating an evening at Tropicana.

"Arsenio, what do I always tell you about your shirt when we go out to dine?" asked Ana.

"That the shirt usually consumes as much food as I do," replied Arsenio with a smile. "It's usually true, what made you think of that?"

"Look at the next float. Appropriate, right after the Tropicana float."

A sign with a three-letter word decorated the front of the next float: ACE. ACE Laundry Detergent was the most popular among Cuban housewives. The float had a makeshift laundry room, housewife and all. There were two washing machines, she washed one load with ACE and the other with the "other brand". Through the performance of a comical skit, she demonstrated how laundry washed with ACE came out clean, clothes washed with the competitor's detergent were an absolute mess. Roxana, a top executive for ACE, performed the skit every year, always fulfilling everyone's expectations. It was a very funny skit.

Floats got more elaborate every year, the dancing in the parade was spectacular. Those who wanted to drive or participate in the parade representing small organizations would have to register months ahead of time. There was food everywhere, from popcorn to cotton candy — every child's dream.

It was clear to those viewing why so many would drive from miles away to experience the Carnaval. Not everyone was lucky enough to live within the vicinity; this is something Arsenio never took for granted. He knew where he lived, he understood how lucky he was, he appreciated everything he had, and he prayed everyday that he would never lose it.

Chapter Three
Brandy and Cigars

Their lives of splendor had been achieved through indisputably difficult times, helping develop great success for their family. Having lived in economic comfort for many years, Ana and Arsenio could afford the luxury of discarding the banal aspects of day-to-day living much like Ana's wardrobe every spring when the new fashions were introduced. She, however, never took things for granted, always appreciating the simpler things in life, and treating everyone with the utmost respect. Her servant Ofelia, after all, was like one of the family.

Humility served Ana well, she wore it as elegantly as the many gowns that Arsenio had bought her throughout the years. Arsenio would come home and surprise her with gifts, no special occasion needed. That was the type of relationship they had, she served the role of queen as he tried to please her in every which way, his love for her and his need to keep her by his side for his remaining days trumped all.

As a sharp dresser, Arsenio displayed the pride he felt in his family, his accomplishments, and his country. With him there was also, as with his lovely wife, an extraordinary amount of meekness and empathy for those not as fortunate as they. Pride and humility are two traits often difficult to balance; Ana greatly admired her husband for the ability to equally exude both traits, letting others understand why he became the most respected professional in his neighborhood, as well as one of its most beloved citizens.

He was a man to be respected, both for his distinguished look as well as his actions. There were few, if any, who envied him for his position in society.

Distinctions were clearly made between the haves and the have-nots. Servants usually worked long hours, got paid on an hourly basis, and medical benefits were non-existent. When Ofelia became ill with appendicitis and needed surgery, Arsenio insisted on paying for the hospital stay and forwarded Ofelia her full salary as she recovered for a few weeks.

His generosity was frequently spontaneous, as instinctive to him as his own heartbeat or the involuntary shrinking of his pupils when his eyes were suddenly exposed to bright lights.

Driving home one day, the professor spotted a homeless man and couldn't help but wonder...

What occurred in his life that created such a dire situation for him? Where was his family? What was his life like before this?

And he wondered so much more...

Arsenio parked by the curb and observed the homeless man for a few minutes. He was invisible, the man recited his plea for money as some passersby dropped change into a tin can he had, most sped up when reaching the tin can.

"Money for food, money for food, please..."

Clickety clack, clickety clack.

"Money for food, money for food, please..."

Clickety clack, clickety clack.

Arsenio finally stepped down to listen to the disheveled stranger's story, he must investigate. His goal was to cure the world of its ills, little compelled him more than making a difference. Having experienced poverty as a child, he would always do his share to ease the suffering of others. He listened as the stranger addressed him.

"Excuse me, sir. Would you please spare some change? I haven't eaten in over a day and would greatly appreciate some money."

"My good man, what is your name?" asked Arsenio.

"I am Gerson, I've been out of work for four months. I lost my apartment and the little savings I had."

"Gerson, what did you do for a living?"

"I worked for a huge tobacco company, but when the layoffs came, I was one of the first to go. Without savings or any family in the area, I got hit hard, so I'm living in the streets due to these unfortunate circumstances."

"I too have been poor and have felt hunger pangs, not knowing where my next meal would come from. I would like to assist you, can you be trusted?"

Arsenio waited for the stranger's response.

"Trusted in what way, sir? I have already explained that the only reason I'm living on the streets is because of my unemployment and a streak of bad luck. It isn't due to drug use, lack of education, or laziness. I would do anything to get back on my feet again. Please provide me an opportunity to prove myself, I'll do anything to get out of this deplorable situation I'm in."

"Get in the car, you will dine with me at home today."

"Sir, I am touched! Whenever I get back on my feet I will repay you for your generosity, but most of all for taking the chance by bringing a total stranger into your home for lunch. That act speaks volumes to the quality of your character."

"My kind sir," Dr. Buendia replied, "seeing you enjoy lunch with me is payback enough. Let's go and enjoy, my good man. When you get back to work, repay the favor to someone who's not as fortunate as you, so you may experience the feeling of helping out a fellow countryman in need."

When Arsenio arrived with Gerson, he announced his visitor to Ana. There was no surprise in her look, as this was not the first time she had set an extra place at the table for someone her husband had invited over. Angel, their oldest, was not fond of the habit. He claimed that strangers exposed the family to potential harm. After all, dining at the Buendia home was an experience for the senses. Not only was the food memorable, but the entire experience of being pampered by

Ofelia, who was superb at what she did, was reason alone to want to return.

Items within the house, from fine china to modern electronics, would impress most. Television consoles were far from ubiquitous in the late 1950s in Cuba, the Buendias were one of the first families in the neighborhood to own one. Friends would gather around the set and enjoy picture quality that was unprecedented to that point. These were the things that drove fear into Angel's heart every time he discovered that his dad had invited another "guest".

Throughout lunch, Gerson took notice of Ofelia. Even through the loosely fitted servant's outfit, he liked what he saw. Only in her twenties, Ofelia could best be described as a plain looking young lady with an attractive figure. What took her over the top was a look about her, a look that was subliminal in nature. The message sent to those of the opposite gender was simple - I'm a self-confident woman who is up to the challenge, give it your best shot.

Gerson read the message well, he decided that he could not act on his impulses. In his present condition it would be comical should he attempt a move of some kind.

When lunch ended, Arsenio led Gerson to the library to sit, have a bit of brandy, and chat. There was no look in him that indicated alcohol abuse, otherwise Arsenio would not have offered the drink.

As Ofelia offered both gentlemen drinks and premium cigars, Gerson recoiled in shame. He wasn't ashamed of *who* he was, but his current situation was not representative of the man he had become throughout the years. This lovely lady, one he had noticed from the very beginning, was serving him. Serving *him*, a man dressed like a pauper, which was what he had become. Imagine that. He knew deep down that it was temporary, he would find a way out of these unfortunate circumstances. Regardless of his present situation, he still believed in himself.

After their brandies, they began discussing their country and its current state of affairs. Gerson was very knowledgeable and could hold his own in discussing politics with the professor. They were in agreement on some issues, but worlds apart on items regarding wealth distribution. They were from two distinct classes and their contrasting ideologies were clearly surfacing as the conversation progressed.

Dr. Buendia, Gerson interjected as Arsenio attempted to make a point, "Do you think that our current economic system is one which benefits our overall society, or detracts from it?"

"In what sense?"

"Well, I have been poor all my life, and unless there is a drastic change in my life I'm likely to die a pauper. There are people who, whether through luck, hard work, or a little bit of both, are wealthy beyond anyone's imagination. Could we ever find a compromise in order to curtail poverty?"

Arsenio, after this eloquent argument, could not help but think that Gerson was not your typical homeless person, who was lazy or lacked education. He knew that somewhere along the line Gerson had acquired a good education, formal or not - the man was able to hold an intelligent, well-articulated conversation.

In responding, Arsenio expressed his beliefs regarding that loaded question.

"My good man, that is a question that has been posed by many, including the Athenians in their attempts to form a just government thousands of years ago. I assure you that regardless of how much brandy we drink, the solution to such a complex question will still elude us at the end of the evening." Arsenio attempted to lighten the tension through humor.

Gerson smiled, he appreciated a good sense of humor, and felt warmly towards Dr. Buendia. He realized that most would never contemplate taking home a beggar for lunch, much less sit and discuss current events as his equal.

"Seriously, the discussion of wealth distribution usually causes me discomfort due to my fortunate situation. Even though I grew up very poor, sometimes not knowing if I was going to eat that day, I realize that not many have it as good as I do. I must respond honestly, however. Sharing wealth through certain government assistance is acceptable. There must be safeguards in our modern society to ensure that the poor have their basic necessities met. Roosevelt with the New Deal did much in the United States twenty years ago to create some of those programs to which I refer." Arsenio hoped this conversation would end soon, knowing that Gerson's views greatly differed from his.

"But sir, is that enough? Why should I live in poverty when others live in palatial homes with an overabundance of material wealth? Shouldn't the government take from the wealthy to give to the poor?"

"Gerson, not only have you assailed me with three questions, but they are of a topic that is near and dear to my heart. I will respond to you with the passion that accompanies my beliefs. Taking from the wealthy to create a comfortable lifestyle for the poor is a mistake. A move such as that would serve as a suction cup sucking the motivation from people living within that society. Sharing the wealth would alleviate the current situation by creating a classless society while creating problems that do not currently exist. Take the hypothetical situation of a doctor who has been a student for most of his life in order to achieve a prestigious position that pays handsomely. Would that doctor go through all that trouble with the understanding that when he begins to work 16 hour days in the hospital or his private practice he will get equal pay to all who have foregone higher education? Should the doctor get paid the same as a garbage collector?"

"Sir, medical doctors make too much money as it is, so when the poor get sick they can't afford to visit them. I don't see anything wrong with what I envision."

"Gerson, we have a difference of opinion. Let's end this day amicably. It has been a magnificent afternoon, I want to express my best wishes to you, and may you succeed with your future endeavors, whatever their nature."

Arsenio gave Gerson his business card wrapped in a $100 dollar bill. He opened up to him and offered a piece of advice that would live with the homeless man for many years.

"Gerson, not everyone is born with the same opportunities in life. I have scratched and clawed to get where I am now, Arsenio stated with a solemn tone. My mother passed away when I was very young and poverty has been at my doorstep most of my life. If you take anything away from our meeting, let it be this: make your own destiny, don't sit back and wait for it. Be firm and fair, respect others, and be true to yourself - the rest will follow. Here is some money to hold you over and my business card. Create a game plan that will help change your life around and give me a call. At that point I will do what I can to get you employment or connect you with someone who will. Good luck."

Gerson didn't know what to say, he had never experienced such generosity in his life. He took what was offered and walked out.

Having three children, Ana and Arsenio had their hands full. Between work and home life they were constantly busy, wishing to spend more time with each other, but understanding that leisure time was a commodity in low supply. With the exception of traveling to Miami in the spring most years, they didn't travel much. The children, two of them teenagers, were very close to their parents. They would never hesitate in approaching mom or dad with any concerns.

Every night at the dinner table, the family would discuss the day's events. Along with personal occurrences of the day, the conversation usually veered off to current events. The political situation in Cuba was precarious, to say the least. With the announcement that governmental winds were blowing in a certain direction, this family had reason to be concerned.

Teaching political science at Havana University, Dr. Buendia had shared many political theories with his students throughout the years. Just the thought that a door could be left ajar in order to permit entry to a Marxist regime was enough to send chills down his spine. Inevitably, dinner conversation would wind its way to that of many scenarios that seemed plausible for the future of Arsenio's country.

On his way home from the university, when Arsenio anticipated a late evening grading papers, he would stop at his brother's café for some strong Cuban coffee to keep him awake for a few hours. Ofelia's coffee would have sufficed, but he loved the excuse to stop by and visit his brother. Guillermo and Nora owned the café since getting married; for almost ten years they had been waking before sunrise to prepare breakfast, and remained open until 8 pm. They made most of their money on weekends when families bonded by going out for a meal, followed by a drive down El Malecón.

Cabaret Quarterly, a tourism magazine, once described Havana as "a mistress of pleasure", the lush and opulent goddess of delights. El Malecón was a must see for tourists visiting Havana, natives and tourists alike appreciated the beauty of El Malecón, the divider between ocean and land. The waves crashing against the man-made wall served as a thrill for any youngster driving by, as the Buendia family well knew, experiencing this many times over. The sound it made created an indelible memory for Cubans; one that would last as a reminder of how close Cubans had come to paradise.

At least that was the perception by those who were lucky enough to live on the right side of the tracks and who lived in houses that were envied by the needy. Havana was well known for extremes, both economic and otherwise. Many families ended up at both ends of the spectrum throughout the course of a lifetime, starting off living in poverty, then making something of themselves through sacrifice and hard work.

Every evening on his route home, Arsenio passed the same billboard without thinking much of it. The billboard read:

**Open Your Mind
Envision the Future
Pontiac**

Arsenio was a big fan of Pontiac and drove one himself, he owned a blue Pontiac Bonneville Convertible. Pontiac was a hot seller in Cuba in the 1950s, capturing the imagination of the public with its vivid colors, powerful engines, luxurious interiors, and reasonable prices.

Guillermo's Café was located just beyond that sign. On this particular afternoon, Arsenio parked his Pontiac in one of the assigned spots and got down. It was a day like any other, there were few things Arsenio liked more than routines, and his brother knew it.

"Guillermo, how are you, my brother?"

"Busy as always, Arsenio. Come here, give your older brother a hug. Wait a minute and I'll get your toasted bread and coffee. Late night tonight?"

"You've got me pegged, hermano. I've just given exams and have to grade them. I'll give myself a few minutes to have my bread and coffee and be on my way. How is business?"

"Business is good as usual. The only difference I've noticed within the past few months is that the number of homeless people getting food from me at closing has at least doubled. I'm concerned about the economic situation in our city, my brother."

"Guillermo, it's funny you should mention that. Just the other day I was discussing that with a homeless man I..."

"Please don't tell me you took another homeless person home to dine with your family! That will end up biting you in the ass someday, Arsenio. For crying out loud, think of your family!"

"Treat people well, and they will reciprocate. I have faith in this credo and will continue to live by it."

"Just be careful, that's all."

The brothers chatted a bit more as Arsenio ate his bread and drank his coffee, he was eager to get home to grade those papers and go to bed, it had been a long day.

"Thanks for stopping by, I'll say hello to Nora for you, she had to step out. Finish your coffee so you can go grade your papers, come back soon when you have time to sit and talk for a while like the old days. Get out of here!" Guillermo winked at his baby brother with a big smile.

Arsenio, also smiling, replied, "Love you too, brother!"

After getting home, Arsenio called Ana and hugged her. He had been thinking a lot about the future of his country and how certain changes could end up affecting his family. As a professor familiar with the intricate details involving governments and how they operate, he seemed to have a sixth sense about pending changes. As a sensitive person, all of his thoughts affected him in a way that was difficult to explain. He knew one thing, nothing was more important to him than his family.

"Ana, I'm home."

"Arsenio, how was your day? You must be exhausted. Do you want to go straight to bed or would you like a drink first? Ofelia has gone to sleep, I'll be glad to get it for you."

"No my dear, that's quite all right. I still have a few hours left. I wouldn't be able to go to sleep until all these papers have been graded. Have the children gone to bed?"

"Yes, they went to sleep a couple of hours ago. Angel took the girls for some ice cream and then went off to bed. Maria went to sleep without a problem, but Barbara fought the sleep until the very end. Sleep finally won the battle."

"That's good, honey. Love you, I'm off to grade papers."

"Love you too, baby. I hope you finish soon, see you in the morning."

"All right, I'll try not to wake you when I go to bed."

Arsenio went to grade the papers. Once he started, he didn't stop until the task at hand was finished, he wrapped it up by 1:30 am. As was customary with the professor, when he finished with the final paper, Arsenio poured himself a Brandy, and smoked a cigar. This was his time to relax, enjoying all three – the Brandy, the cigar, and his thoughts.

He couldn't stop thinking about his lunch guest and the conversation they had shared earlier in the evening. Gerson's stance on monetary issues in Cuba struck a chord with him, having experienced financial success, he did not concern himself with having to live day-to-day like many Cubans. What worried him was losing touch with reality, he would never want that to happen.

As he dozed off he couldn't help but think of the seemingly insignificant sign he passed by everyday.

Open your mind, envision the future.

Chapter Four

The Timepiece

It was one of the most famous nightclubs in the country and arguably the world. Cabaret Tropicana originally opened in 1939, later to be called Tropicana. The frequented establishment sat on 6 acres in the outskirts of Havana, centrally located for suburbanites as well as residents of the capital. A well-funded American entrepreneur purchased it in 1945 and transformed it into the Tropicana that rightfully earned its worldwide fame. People from all over, including many tourists and American celebrities, would go to enjoy an evening of fine dining and shows that never ceased to delight.

Known as "*Cuba's Garden of Glamour*", Tropicana recruited some of the finest Cuban talent including Celia Cruz, Beny Moré, and Olga Guillot. The guest list throughout the years included celebrities Marlon Brando, Ernest Hemingway, and Elizabeth Taylor to name a few.

A Tropicana brochure from 1953 read:

Good fortune may smile at Tropicana — in the glittering Club Room. When dice roll or the chuck-a-luck wheel spins, everyone wins at Tropicana. It's fun! It's exciting! It's at Tropicana!

Inaugurated in 1956, Cubana Airlines' Lockhead Constellation started a weekly Tropicana Special charter from Miami to Havana. Tropicana dancers would serve drinks and dance in the aisles to the delight of all onboard. Anaheim, CA had Disneyland for children and Havana, Cuba provided the adults with Tropicana. The well-to-do would take the shuttle on a regular basis, employees of Tropicana knew many by their first names.

Approaching the nightclub, the first things in view were the neon lights and ocean blue sign displaying "Tropicana". As the couple drove towards the main entrance in their convertible, they always noticed the yellow ceiling above them. The circular driveway would meander around the neon lights that decorated the structure, and because of the covered driveway it never mattered how stormy the weather was, nobody driving into Tropicana ever got wet.

This was a night of near perfection, the stars were aligned, and life was grand for the Buendias. As they neared the entrance, parking attendants eager to please, surrounded them. The minute they saw the blue Pontiac convertible, they knew gratuities for the evening would be generous. So as to not look unprofessional trying to beat each other to the car, the attendants had agreed to take turns parking this special automobile. After all, this couple frequented the club.

"Good evening, Doctor," stated Jose enthusiastically. "Until what time will you be staying with us tonight?"

Jose and the other parking attendants wore black pants with gray stripes. Their red hats matched the vests of the same color.

"Tonight we will be staying at least until two, Jose. It is a very special evening for Ana and me, we are celebrating our 20th wedding anniversary."

Earlier that day they had visited Adlai at Adlai Carrasco Photography to treat themselves to a photo-shoot with one of the best. Adlai, known to his clients by his first name only, put everyone at ease and worked magic with his camera, handling it as a sculptor uses his chisel to create a masterpiece. His family emigrated from the Canary Islands twenty years prior and made a name for themselves through Ariel Carrasco's hard work on the island. Many say that his carpentry skills rivaled those of any in the country; Adlai was always very proud of his father for this and many more reasons. His mother was a successful school teacher in Matanzas for many years. Rosa, a beloved aunt, also got her teaching degree at a young age. As fate would have it, she decided to pursue a different career altogether. They lost her to an illness too early in life, she was dearly missed by all in her family.

"Dr. Buendia, Mrs. Buendia, I wish you many congratulations. Time really flies by, I remember when you were both barely newlyweds. May you spend a special evening here at Tropicana."

"Thank you, Jose. I'm sure my husband and I will be treated as always, we never dreamt of going anywhere else to celebrate such a special occasion." Ana reached into her purse and pulled out a ten dollar bill to tip Jose.

"Thank you, Mrs. Buendia. You have always been generous, and I've appreciated that throughout the years."

"My pleasure, Jose. We shall see you later tonight."

They were led to their usual table near the stage. The stage was set up in the center, surrounded by a tropical rain forest theme. Many referred to the interior of Tropicana as *paradise under the stars*. The entire ceiling flickered with stars as if they were dining in the middle of a forest. The décor never ceased to amaze Ana, and the extravagant shows were known worldwide.

"Arsenio, I am thrilled to be celebrating our anniversary, but I can't believe it's been twenty years. Does it show?"

Ana was a very secure woman, but she was known by all to fetch for compliments.

Arsenio responded with a smirk, without skipping a beat, "My dear, I am now accompanying my young bride into Tropicana. You are a fine wine."

Henrique approached the table with a bottle of wine. After wishing them many congratulations, he opened the bottle, let it breathe, and poured. Ana noticed that it was a 1938 Chateaux Margaux.

"Arsenio, is this the bottle we purchased on our honeymoon?" asked Ana. She was obviously choked up.

"Of course, my dear. From the moment I acquired this wine in Paris, I've envisioned a special anniversary such as this. My life changed for the better on March 15, 1938, and I thank you for that. Cheers, my love. Here is to many more glorious years with our health and family. May we continue to prosper in our beloved country."

"Cheers to that, dear."

As they finished their toast, the curtain rose.

On the main stage, two vertical arches towering above the performers brightly displayed hundreds of bulbs. The third horizontal arch wrapped itself around the other two creating a dazzling three-dimensional display.

Trees throughout the nightclub, some going through the ceiling, added to the tropical atmosphere. On center stage there was a tree serving a dual purpose — it complemented the lush surroundings and served as a springboard for dancers hiding in the branches.

The showgirls started off the evening by dancing to a Mambo beat that got everyone in the audience involved. The men would discreetly enjoy the wonderfully choreographed dances trying their best to glance and not stare, lest their wives or girlfriends might take offense. Collectively known as the *Flesh Goddesses*, they were renowned the world over more for their voluptuousness than for their ability to dance - even though the latter was almost as impressive as the former. The dancers from Havana rivaled the Parisian Can Can Girls and the Rockettes from New York.

Their ability to involve the audience was second to none. The scantily clad dancers walked among the trees on a catwalk in order to give everyone a close-up of their "*dancing abilities*". A few years before the Buendias's celebration, a gentleman in his mid 60s suffered a mild heart attack on getting an up-close look of one of the sexy, half-dressed dancers as he dined with his wife. The man survived, but never outlived the ribbing from close friends and family. If his wife had not been so worried for his well-being, she probably would not have spoken to him for months.

As the dancers moved to the rhythm of the music, they disbanded and began their struts on the catwalk around the club. These gorgeous women, wearing revealing outfits and dancing provocatively to the music, would get within inches of the male guests as the men enjoyed the show. At this point in the evening, the wives and girlfriends would grab their partners' hands to serve as a not-too-subtle reminder — remember with whom you're going home tonight! And boy, did it work. Of course, all the gentlemen understood the importance of peripheral vision in order to enjoy the eye candy and to minimize the risk of having to sleep on the sofa for a few nights.

"Arsenio, holding your hand tonight feels like the very first time. We have accomplished the impossible, we've stopped time. May it always be like this." Ana shed a tear of joy, she was aware that not every couple could acquire the magic they had.

Arsenio was not the type to take interest in half-naked women. He was faithful and conservative, but even he fell under the dancers' spell as Odysseus had fallen for the siren's fatal song. Luckily, his trance was temporary. Once he left the club, he focused on one woman, his beloved Ana.

"Honey, if a genie would appear and ask me where I would rather be this very moment, I would send him on his way. I couldn't think of anyplace better than here with you," he told Ana.

Ana looked him in the eye and smiled.

"Honey, I am famished. Are we ready to order our meal?" asked Arsenio.

"Absolutely, I'm hungry as well. Let's see if you can remember what I ate the first time we came to Tropicana, impress me." Ana was putting Arsenio to the test, it had been over twenty years since their first date. It was small gestures such as these that really pleased her.

"You're on, my dear!", replied Arsenio with a smirk. His memory was good, especially vivid when it came to his wife.

"Henrique, we are ready to order."

"Dr. Buendia, I'm ready when you are."

"Doctor? Henrique, how long have you known me? I knew you when you were still in diapers, stop calling me Doctor. You know my first name, please use it."

Arsenio had known Henrique and his family for many years. Henrique's brother had taken a couple of courses with Dr. Buendia a few years back, he was currently attending Law School. The family emigrated from Spain to Cuba during the summer of 1898. Things got very difficult for many Spaniards during the Spanish American War and Henrique's family was no exception. The family arrived at the Havana Harbor only five months after the explosion of the USS Maine. The sinking of that ship will forever be surrounded by speculation, nobody was ever able to prove that it was Cuba's handiwork to lure the United States into the War in defense of Cuba.

For three generations, the family struggled to get ahead in Cuba. There were a couple of college graduates within the family, but most worked hard wherever they could find decent paying jobs. Henrique felt that his fate as a server was sealed, although serving at Tropicana was a fate many wish they could obtain. When Henrique was born, his mother deliberately spelled it with an H to honor her Portuguese ancestry from her father's side, while still giving her boy a very "*Cuban sounding*" name.

"All right, Arsenio," replied Henrique. "Let me know what you would like, my friend."

"The young lady will have the surf and turf, medium-well with garlic mashed potatoes. I will have the porterhouse, medium with asparagus. We are good with the bottle of wine, two glasses of water for now. Thank you."

"Very well, sir…I mean, Arsenio."

"I must say, tonight you have impressed me. Nicely done, you remembered your meal as well as mine."

Ana wanted for time to slow down, she wanted this evening to last forever.

Both Ana and Arsenio, along with the other 1,700 patrons, eagerly awaited the main event.

In 1950s Cuba, communist ideologies were securing a stronghold as more impoverished people wondered what had happened to their fair share of economic success. During his first term as president, the Communist Party of Cuba supported Fulgencio Batista. He became strongly anti-communist during his second term, maybe too little too late.

Among the communist organizations in the country, there were different variations depending on the financing capabilities available and the sector in which they operated. Some focused on media and spreading propaganda while others immersed themselves in operating across university campuses. They would infiltrate the universities and openly share their political beliefs as they recruited members and expressed their ideas in class. Dr. Buendia was all too familiar with this, having crossed paths with communists and communist sympathizers, especially in his political science classes.

Among the smaller organizations, one of the better known was Monetary Equality for All (MEFA). They were heavily involved in recruiting university students while obtaining college degrees themselves. The members understood that the path to revolution, should it get to that point, needed to involve the educated population. The efficacy with which they were achieving their goal was nothing short of impressive. As poverty spread, their membership increased. It was this direct correlation that helped them excel.

Tonight, at Tropicana, twenty members of MEFA dined among the elite and financially independent. They too, eagerly awaited the main event.

Ana and Arsenio had finished their dinner and were ready for their second bottle of wine.

"Arsenio, I can't wait to see the Garcia couple perform. They are always the smash of the evening, no easy feat having to follow that spectacular performance by those talented young ladies."

"My dear, the ladies entertained, of that there is no doubt. But when the Garcias perform, that is always the showstopper. All eyes will be on them from start to finish."

There was a 30-minute intermission. Stagehands made the appropriate changes in preparation for the next segment of the production, and patrons were encouraged to visit the bar for a drink or cross over to the adjacent casino, owned by Tropicana as well. Many did just that, ensuring the famed nightclub's continued success.

"Arsenio, would you like to gamble?"

"Ana, since when have you known me to give my money away except for a good cause? I will never be a gambler, other forms of entertainment interest me much more."

"All right then, there is something I would like to give you. I want you to remember this evening and our twentieth anniversary forever. I hope you like it."

Arsenio had given Ana her gift a couple of nights ago, as he was too eager to wait. Certain idiosyncrasies and childlike behaviors of his made him more appealing to Ana throughout the years.

Ana handed him a beautifully wrapped box. Arsenio accepted it and was dying to know its contents. He really had no clue as to what it could be.

"Ana, you know what they say about gifts in small boxes. Oh, I wonder what this is." Arsenio could not contain his excitement.

He felt like he did on Three Kings Day as a child, pulling his gift from under the family Christmas tree. Coming from a poor family, he always understood the monetary difficulties his parents endured. Somehow they ensured that the tree would be up every holiday season and that each of the brothers had a gift to open on Three Kings Day. Both Guillermo and he were forever grateful to their parents for their sacrifices.

He opened his gift with speed and precision, knowing exactly where to pull off the wrapping paper so as to not waste precious seconds. It was refreshing to see someone of his stature with such a simple and down to earth nature. His face said it all as he finished opening the gift.

"Ana, you didn't!"

"Arsenio, I did," responded Ana with a chuckle.

Arsenio excitedly analyzed the gift along with the instruction manual that accompanied it. It was a Rolex Oyster Perpetual stainless steel watch. With a 14K solid gold bezel ring, it was a beautiful thing to look at. The well-known crown logo sat atop the Rolex name inside the watch. The two tone gold and silver band added to its beauty.

"Anita, I can't begin to express how much I love my gift. I will forever treasure this, what a lovely gift. Thank you so much."

"I knew you wouldn't buy yourself such an extravagant gift. I also know your affinity for dress watches."

"How did you pull it off?"

"I called Aldo in New York, he did the leg work, and I wired him the money. He sent me the watch and I received it shortly thereafter. Of course, along with the watch he sent the latest recording of La Bohème, which I've listened to three times already."

"Aldo and his operas," Arsenio said with a smile. "I'm surprised he hasn't been evicted from that fancy apartment of his for blasting his music all the time. Let's make time tomorrow to listen to it together, you know that's my favorite Puccini opera. We must visit Aldo in New York next spring, I miss him dearly."

The curtain rose halfway, a sign that the show would begin in five minutes. Everyone who had left their seats shuffled back to their tables. Those already at their tables whispered final comments, their anticipation approached full capacity.

"Here we go Anita, sit back and enjoy."

As predicted by many, when the curtain rose and both dancers appeared, all eyes were on them. Something extraordinary was about to take place…

The impact of the following events were long lasting on all who were present. It's not that these activities were rare to Cubans in these volatile times, but something like this occurring in the prestigious Tropicana caused shock and anxiety.

MEFA members were scattered at different tables around the stage, four per table. They had dined and held conversations with the others at the table, blending in until now. As soon as the dancers took their positions on stage, all twenty members stood up and took off their loosely fitted clothes to reveal their militant uniforms underneath. That is when chaos paid Tropicana a visit.

"Enjoy your drinks in your fancy nightclub, get all you can now. Our time will come," declared a militant with piercing eyes and a dark beard as he marched around the nightclub floor.

"The common man has the same rights as the wealthy in this country and should be enjoying the fruits of his labor as well," shouted another as he picked up a bottle of wine from one of the tables and smashed it on the floor.

For the most part, people looked confused, but there was no mistaking the principal look they conveyed. It was that of fear, a particular type of fear that had been blending in with anger for the past few years like a poorly mixed martini. Too many of these demonstrations, too much talk of revolution and weakening on the part of their government, and now it was hitting closer to home than ever before.

Tropicana was their bubble, a place of temporary escape from certain realities. The breach of their safe haven could never be undone, nothing would be the same again.

The MEFA leader took the stage and spoke to the captive audience. Nobody dared move, the other 19 members served as guards ensuring that people would stay seated. Tropicana management let everything play out in order to keep the situation from escalating, there was no way of knowing whether or not they were armed. A MEFA member was keeping the nightclub manager "company" just in case he tried something.

"Ladies and gentlemen, we are here tonight to discuss the future of our country."

There was a collective gasp, some women sobbed and the men tried to conceal their fear. A couple sitting at the table a few feet from the exit attempted to escape, fearing for their lives.

"I wouldn't try that if I were you," stated the leader with an arrogant tone. "We have MEFA members outside to ensure that does not occur."

The couple rushed back to their table, feeling a shot of adrenaline that served as a reminder of how grave the situation at hand was.

"For many years too many of our people have lived in the streets, lacked basic necessities, and have been neglected by a corrupt government that caters to the wealthy. We need equality for all, not monetary advancement for few and poverty for many. Mr. Batista is padding his pockets at our expense and his loose change is donated to you. Where are our crumbs? Where is our loose change?"

"This is what our organization MEFA is all about, Monetary Equality for All."

At that point all MEFA members began to chant in unison:

"Monetary equality for all, monetary equality for all, monetary equality for all..."

They continued marching around the club. One of the members

retrieved signs connected to handles they had created a few days before and handed them out to the others. It spelled out their organization name in bright red letters. Underneath the organization name were three words that would stick in Arsenio's mind for the rest of his life:

Envision the Future

Envision the future, the Pontiac motto was now being used to destroy the country he loved so much.

As the parade ended, the leader once again took center stage.

"I do not wish to take up any more of your time. We will be passing baskets around and you will donate to this cause. Sharing of wealth is an integral part of making necessary changes beneficial to all."

As the baskets made their rounds, everyone dug deep into their pockets. Nobody dared give less than $50, fear served as a great motivator.

Just like that it was all over, twenty minutes from beginning to end. The members gathered their belongings, including the "donations", and quietly left.

Minimal physical damage was done, but the psyche of those 1,700 individuals changed forever that fateful evening.

Arsenio and Ana left without exchanging a word, she noticed a tear stream down his cheek.

Chapter Five
Guillermo's Café

T he sky was clearer than he had ever seen it, the water by El Malecón never calmer. Arsenio enjoyed evening walks, he could exercise and think. The walk served as therapy for him. It was 2 am and not a soul was out, Arsenio ambled down the street by the seawall with barely a thought in that overworked brain of his. This was just what he needed.

This is exactly what he loved about his city, the combination of beauty and safety. There was much happening in some parts of the city, they were not immune from the effects of gambling and pros- titution, but for the most part it was well contained. For a big city, Arsenio felt secure, it was a great place to raise his family.

He sat on a bench to admire the millions of twinkling lights that made their presence when most of the city was in a deep slumber. Arsenio had never studied astronomy, but was fascinated by concepts such as distances among the stars and the number of light years it takes to travel from one star to the next. After twenty minutes of resting, he headed back home.

As he turned towards Prado, he heard footsteps. The steps made a distinctive sound, that of heels belonging to boots. He quickly glanced back and saw two men, dressed in green fatigues with matching caps. They were holding rifles…their pace quickened. Arsenio sped up, quickening his pace with every step. His heart beat faster by the sec- ond, both from the brisk pace and his fear.

He could sense they were getting closer - they were. One of the soldiers reached out and grabbed his shoulder.

"Are you Arsenio Buendia?" asked the soldier, using a very firm voice.

"Why must you know?" inquired Arsenio, with obvious fear in his voice. His lip quivered, making it difficult to get any words out.

"We will do the questioning," exclaimed the other soldier.

Reluctantly, Arsenio responded, "Yes, I am Arsenio Buendia."

"Do you teach political science at the University of Havana?"

"Yes, I do. Why?" asked Arsenio, more curious than before. By now his shaking must have been apparent to the soldiers, the situation seemed to be getting out of control.

"Some students registered complaints about you. They said you are in favor of a democratic government in Cuba. Is that true?"

"I don't know wh..."

"Is that true???"

"I assure you, I've done nothing wro..."

As one soldier handcuffed Arsenio, the other continued...

"Arsenio Buendia, you are under arrest for your anti-revolutionary stance and your pro-democracy propaganda. Your offense is punishable by imprisonment of 25 years or death by firing squad, depending on the judge's disposition. Your sentencing will be set within the next week."

Both soldiers started to laugh as they mocked Arsenio for his predicament...

"Hahahaha...chalk up another one for us!!"

"NO, I DON'T DESERVE THIS! I JUST WANT WHAT'S BEST FOR MY COUNTRY!"

"Noooooooo! Who will take care of my family?"

"Arsenio, Arsenio, wake up honey," whispered Ana as she shook him and kissed him on the cheek.

"It was only a nightmare, my love," said Ana. She assured Arsenio that no matter how bad the nightmare was, it was only a dream. He was now back in reality, that was over.

"Oh my God, Ana. I just had the worst nightmare...I'll tell you later, I've got to dress and drive to Guillermo's. We have something important to discuss."

Arsenio dressed and drove to the café, trying to avoid the Pontiac billboard at all costs.

This was no ordinary Sunday, anyone at Tropicana the night before could sadly attest to that. It was painfully clear that skies were rumbling like never before and stormy weather was upon all of Cuba, few were immune. Those with proper planning might be able to weather the storm, but the others had no chance.

He pulled into the parking lot, treading over white pebbles that had given the café its unique look for years. Owners of other establishments would pave their lots as they became successful, Guillermo liked his just the way it was. A few Petticoat Palm trees in the parking lot added to a distinct appearance admired by its loyal customers. As a successful entrepreneur, he understood the importance of a term he coined – unique effectiveness. He took pleasure in creating terms, this was one of Arsenio's favorites.

The ocean blue lettering above the main entrance proudly displayed the proprietor's name. Although everyone referred to his restaurant as Guillermo's Café, he had decided to shorten it to Guillermo's. When building it fifteen years earlier, all went as planned except one thing - as the construction crew finalized everything, they noticed that little room had been left for the sign, the eleven characters currently occupying that space barely fit.

"Is anyone home?" Arsenio asked as he entered.

"Come here, brother."

His bear hug disclosed that Guillermo was privy to certain information Arsenio had not yet shared. Only hours after the Tropicana incident, news had scattered across Havana.

"Come, Arsenio, you need a strong cup of coffee today."

"Hermano, we need to talk. I am contemplating some drastic moves. As my older brother, you must be an integral part of my plans."

"It sounds serious, have your coffee and we'll talk."

Arsenio gulped down his coffee, he was anxious to discuss his plans with Guillermo.

"Would you like to have Nora join us?"

Arsenio's response was immediate, "No, I want this to stay between us for now. Discretion and secrecy are more important now than ever."

There weren't many diners yet, only a few regulars. An elderly couple that had been married for over fifty years would have breakfast there every morning. The only other patron was Eva, a single woman in her forties who bordered on eccentric. She lived in a creaky shack, not two miles from Guillermo's. Her taste in clothing was eclectic, with her wardrobe consisting of every color in the rainbow and styles ranging from the 1930s to the present. She usually attempted to wear all those colors and styles on the same day. Guillermo and Nora referred to her as *Rainbow Girl,* even though she appeared harmless, they couldn't take a chance.

"Arsenio, for complete privacy, let's go to the party room and close the doors."

"Don't ever take privacy for granted, especially in our current environment," replied Arsenio.

They walked through a pair of sliding glass doors that led to a room with a dozen tables that could accommodate at least sixty guests. Guillermo rented out this room for parties of all kinds, from children's birthday parties to religious events such as communions and confirmations. The room was too small for most wedding receptions, but some weddings had been celebrated there as well.

The rear patio adjacent to the party room had a partial view to the ocean and was included with package deals when renting the hall. Guillermo, splendid negotiator that he was, would omit this detail until the very end to make it seem like he was "throwing in" the patio for free.

"Here we go, it's a bit windy to sit outside but we have a nice view from this table. Now, what is so pressing?"

"Guillermo, what I am going to tell you may come as a shock to you. I have intentions of permanently moving to the United States."

"Brother, what happened last night affects nothing. It's been like this for almost a decade, there are minor communist uprisings, but at the end democracy wins out and squashes the bug. You have nothing to worry about."

"Do you consider what the Castro brothers and their fellow thugs are doing out in those mountains minor? They've been at it for years and our citizens continue sticking their heads in the sand. Just because we can't see it doesn't mean it's not happening," emphasized Arsenio.

"Remember what I do for a living, universities are the first to experience uprisings. Communist students infiltrate higher education first, next they go after the media and attempt to censor free speech. Before you know it, they will attempt a coup d'état."

"Slow down, slow down. You are getting way ahead of yourself. Most countries in the world have communist parties, few of those countries are taken over by communists."

"We are ripe for the picking, poverty is increasing, the pro-communist government from a few years ago has made a 180 degree turn, and they now strongly oppose communism. The signs are on the wall."

"Arsenio, I cannot deny that what I see scares me, just last week a couple of youngsters were executed by a group of militants for expressing anti-communist sentiments. I have hope that the howling gusts of democracy will overcome the diminishing winds of communism."

"That's just it, communism is not diminishing. Its winds are blowing stronger than ever. And a word on hope, my dear brother — hope is both our greatest virtue and a blinding flaw, depending on its use. When holding on to hope for a lost cause, you are bound to overlook opportunity when it knocks. It's knocking, brother. The door is ajar and closing fast, we must get out while there is still time."

"All right, I promise to be receptive, tell me your plan."

Arsenio began slowly, finding difficulty in verbalizing the thoughts that had haunted him for so many months, "Well, when a communist regime takes over, their modus operandi are as follows..."

"They begin by over-running universities with communist propaganda, media censorship eventually occurs, followed by a complete take-over of government buildings. Next, they focus on seizing properties and freezing bank accounts, with particular emphasis on the wealthy. They do not attempt to reinvent the wheel, since Marx created his system this has occurred countless times. Even before communism, tyrants would take control using similar methods. The efficacy with which this can be completed is scary, you can blink and not know what hit you."

"Yes, I can't disagree with your argument. Continue." Guillermo's eyebrows became one as he listened intently.

"Luckily it hasn't gotten to that point yet, you continue to have your assets intact as do I. My contention is this; we must sell our properties and liquidate investments within the next eight months. I have a very bad feeling about the next year or so. Aldo will be instrumental in helping us get established in New York. We must start all over again, we've been left with little choice."

"Arsenio, with news as important as this why didn't you want Nora to be part of this discussion?"

"Brother, not even Ana knows yet. Of course we will share with them and they will participate in the decision-making, but for everyone's safety few should be aware of our plans at this stage. One can never be too careful."

"I will consider what we have discussed, please understand I could not make any final decisions without consulting with Nora first."

"Understood, I feel the same. Think about it and we'll talk again soon."

With that, they stood and hugged. Arsenio exited the café and walked towards his car. He started the engine and closed the top, it looked like rain. Those ominous storm clouds were brewing.

A few hours after Arsenio's visit, a couple of men walked into the café to rent the party room for a bachelor party. Two men walked into the café, one dressed as a militant. Guillermo found himself in a difficult situation. Deny them the rental and anything could happen, accept them as paying customers and he would be accused of being communist by association.

"Gentlemen, how may I help you?" asked Guillermo.

"One of our close friends is getting married and we would like to rent the room in the back for a party," responded one of the friends.

"First, let me have your name."

"My name is Joseph, I'm the best man."

"Joseph, I'm Guillermo, the owner of the café. I will ask you a few questions, following that we can discuss certain details, then you can let me know whether you're interested in placing a deposit."

"Fair enough," responded Joseph.

"How many will there be in your party?"

"Thirty-five."

"The space will easily accommodate thirty-five. Please take a look at this brochure with your friend. The three food options appear on the menu along with the price per person. Just one more thing, no strippers or call girls are permitted at the party," specified Guillermo.

He believed in spelling everything out beforehand. On one occasion things had gotten out of control late into the evening, forcing Guillermo to call the police and file a complaint. There were $2,000 worth of damages to the café. Guillermo's insurance company covered the damages and sued the responsible members. Of course, Guillermo's insurance premium skyrocketed, the whole affair was a mess.

"Sir, we may be militants, but it will be a clean party, I promise."

The two men sat for a few minutes and considered their options. They must have heard of Guillermo's before because they didn't take long in deciding.

"Guillermo, please put us down for a party of thirty-five for Saturday, March 29th. We want option A from your menu. I see here that for an extra fee we can rent the adjacent patio, how much extra would that be?"

"Joseph, I don't usually do this, but I'm going to throw that in at no additional charge as a gift to the groom."

"Guillermo, I appreciate that. Here is a $50 down payment."

Guillermo gave Joseph his receipt and they left. All Guillermo could think about for the rest of the day was that loose fitting camouflage uniform with the black boots extending a quarter of the way up towards his knees. Those uniforms never ceased to turn his stomach.

March 29th came and went, the group had their party at the café without incident. That is, there weren't any fights or damage to the restaurant. Joseph was the only one to wear his uniform that night, anyone with a uniform under the current administration ran the risk of incarceration. As the best man, he was in charge of making the toast congratulating the groom on such a joyous occasion. This toast would cement itself in Guillermo's mind forever. Joseph waited for the end of the evening to give his speech, the open bar took precedence over the toast. Besides, with a few drinks under his belt, Joseph found it easier to openly express his feelings.

Clanking a spoon to his empty glass, Joseph commanded his comrades' attention.

"Gentlemen, we are celebrating something very special today — our comrade's lifelong commitment to the love of his life. Lucky are those with fates such as his. May he live a long and prosperous life alongside his lovely bride. When they bear children, may they live and enjoy in a country that offers them opportunities we have not been lucky enough to experience."

At this juncture in his speech everyone put down their glasses and boisterously applauded for a good two minutes.

Joseph continued:

"In our country, it is the few who succeed and the majority are jobless, homeless, hungry, and more often than not all of the above. This insanity ends now! The minority possessing such a large percentage of the country's assets is obscene, it is an affront to the ideals of our predecessors. Gentlemen, in less than two years we will reach our goal and the elite will topple like loose bricks."

"To the revolution, to our future!"

At the end of the night, when all were gone and he locked up, he knelt and thanked God that it was over. Guillermo was not a religious man. For years, nothing instilled more fear into people's hearts than men wearing camouflage and the zealousness that seemed to accompany their attire.

That night, before he fell asleep, he thought about that day's events. Guillermo came to the conclusion that what occurred that day was only the tip of the iceberg. The question was not *whether* communism would drastically alter their lives, but *when*.

Chapter Six
Debate Ablaze

On the way to work that morning, Arsenio couldn't help but think of the role destiny played in people's lives – that is, if it existed at all. He had always believed that people create their own destiny, through hard work and perseverance almost anything could be accomplished. Lately, this belief had waned. Despite these thoughts, he looked forward to that day's debates. He was sure these debates would reestablish his belief that future events were well within his control.

Arsenio drove into the parking lot looking forward to the day. Despite the clouds and upcoming storm, he was in high spirits. His pensive mood in the car had not affected that. Two of his classes were presenting midterm assignments, both were debates - one of them was of particular interest to him.

He carefully dodged the newly placed scaffold as he made his way across campus towards his Nature of Politics class. In the last few weeks the number of locations where the scaffolds appeared had multiplied, for some reason they had doubled their efforts within a short period of time. They were the experts, he would teach and they would repair whatever needed fixing.

He rarely gave conventional tests for midterms or finals, Arsenio believed in challenging his students. They had to write individual papers and debate on an assigned topic.

In Nature of Politics, after discussing numerous types of governments throughout the semester, two stood out above the rest in terms of popularity – democracy/capitalism and communism. On this day, the final debate would take place for a grade; the students' individual proposals would serve as the other part of their midterm grade.

Manny and Alyssa were debating the pros of capitalism and democracy, they were leading their team in the debate. Lily led the other team along with Rebecca, defending communism and its ideals. Dr. Buendia was shocked at the turnaround Lily had demonstrated since the beginning of the semester, within two months' time her political beliefs had done a 180.

"Class, get into your groups and finalize any thoughts before the debate, we will commence in less than ten minutes. May I please speak to the four debaters for a minute?" Dr. Buendia motioned to Manny, Alyssa, Lily, and Rebecca.

"We have debated a number of times before, you are all familiar with the process. Ricardo, my teaching assistant, will serve as moderator and judge. Any questions or concerns should be directed towards him. He is experienced and impartial, I leave you in good hands."

All the students took their seats, the four debaters in the front of the class near the podium. Ricardo sat directly in front of the podium behind a small table that looked a bit unstable, the weight of his briefcase and papers did not pose a problem, but should he lean too much on the table, the audience would get more than they had expected.

"Ladies and gentlemen, welcome to the *Spring Semester Debate for Nature of Politics at Havana University*," Ricardo said, displaying a professional demeanor. He dressed for the part with a dark blue suit, a dark gray shirt, and a striped tie. His shoes were mirrors.

Dr. Buendia's competent assistant only needed to review the basic guidelines of debating, as the students were already familiar with the appropriate policies and effective debating strategies. Ricardo could tell they were well trained in their craft.

"The resolution being considered in today's debate is the following,"

"*The form of government in Cuba that would best serve its people is Communism.*"

There were a number of sighs and much whispering at the utterance of those words.

The proposition side is the Affirmative and the opposition side is the Negative.

Affirmative Team: Lily (1A) and Rebecca (2A)
Negative Team: Manny (1N) and Alyssa (2N)

"This debate consists of eight speeches. The first four speeches are constructive speeches; the teams lay out their most important arguments during these speeches. The last four speeches are rebuttals; the teams will extend and apply arguments that have already been made. The constructive speeches are used to build up your arguments either in favor or against the resolution. During the rebuttals you only respond to material the other team has already presented."

Debate Format

Speech	1 AC	1 NC	2 AC	2 NC	1 NR	1 AR	2 NR	2 AR
Time	8 min.	8 min.	8 min.	8 min.	4 min.	4 min.	4 min.	4 min.

A (Affirmative Team) — N (Negative Team) — C (Constructive Speech)
R (Rebuttal)

"One from the Affirmative Team, you have eight minutes," said Ricardo, as Lily approached the podium.

<u>Lily</u>:

"The Industrial Revolution brought about many advances in technology, too many to name in the brief time I have. From electricity to the airplane, we can do things now that were not imagined 100 years ago. Capitalism has exploited workers realizing its goals for the true leaders of their countries – the wealthy elite. The true nature of the capitalistic beast is seen in its methods, the way in which wealth distribution is determined through laws and regulations encouraged by those governments."

"Few would dispute the great advancements that have taken place in the last century, many dispute methods used by democracies using their capitalistic systems as shields. They are attempting to shield the wealthy from contributing their fair share, robber barons are still with us. Capitalism's true nature made its appearance along with new industries and forms of manufacturing. This course is titled *Nature of Politics*, our textbook should include a chapter titled *Nature of Capitalism*. I volunteer to pen that chapter, I have opened my eyes to the effects it's having on the poor of our nation."

"In capitalistic societies around the world, the technologies created to manufacture new products affected working classes everywhere. During the first 60 years of the Industrial Revolution, working conditions were by far the worst for the poorest of the poor. Child labor was the norm, as were 15-hour workdays, and accidents on the job because of low lighting and hazardous conditions. Laws to protect those affected were slow in catching up with the ever-changing technology. Owners of large corporations got rich and continue to do so off the sweat and blood of the working class. The gap between the wealthiest and the poorest continues to expand. My description resembles that of our country's current day situation, change must take place."

"B.F. Skinner paid homage to Henry David Thoreau less than ten years ago by writing *Walden Two*. Paralleling Thoreau's *Walden* from a century earlier, Skinner emphasized the importance of putting aside material goods and replacing them with things that really count – their lives in the commune, sharing of all material things, and displaying selfless behavior. Through the main protagonist of the novel, Skinner proposes behavioral engineering - training Walden Two's citizens from birth to create a utopian society. In Skinner's utopian society, materialistic greed is non-existent. Everything in their engineered society is shared by all. His society analyzes people's strengths to carefully choose a profession for each citizen, it is precisely these well thought out scenarios that communism wishes to simulate, creating a better way of life for all."

Lily continued her speech for the allotted eight minutes, many in the audience shook their heads in disbelief.

Manny and Alyssa were diligent in their note taking, they waited their turns, ready to pounce when given their opportunity to speak.

"One from the Negative Team, you have eight minutes."

Manny:

"Democracy, created thousands of years ago by Athenians, has thrived because of its fairness to its citizens. In creating a governmental system that offers the average citizen a say in *who* governs and *how* they govern, it ensures that those citizens get what is in their best interest. The late 18th century, with the American and French Revolutions occurring within less than two decades of each other, exemplifies this point. People sacrificed everything to obtain democracy. It offers the most basic of needs – freedom. Freedom of expression and religion are two of many, extended to its people by this form of government."

"Checks and balances within the government, coupled with the media, are powerful instruments in minimizing corruption. It holds representatives accountable to the general public and to the laws of the country. Laws are created to protect people, not to create injustice based on political or religious ideologies."

"The competitive nature that encompasses democracies through capitalism is what helps it achieve its goals. It is this nature that motivates people to work hard, it gives them the drive to outdo each other. It is this nature within the system that helps stabilize prices and achieve the highest possible quality of products and services. I too would like to include a chapter titled *Nature of Capitalism*, but I would include facts about a system that offers something to its people which no other system in the world has been able to duplicate."

"Paine's *Common Sense* and Rousseau's *Social Contract* paved the way for a world free from tyranny, where the oppressed would gain victory over blood-thirsty despots, and now you are asking our people, a free people, to willingly subject themselvesh to the shackles of a communist society?"

"I say no, a thousand times no!"

"Lastly…"

Manny's introduction was cut short by a thundering applause.

The number of communists in Dr. Buendia's class this semester was unprecedented, but it was clear that those in favor of democracy still represented the majority.

Manny obviously possessed the gift, that which is needed to rouse up an audience, captivate their attention, and demand their respect using his words with precision. Alyssa needed to maintain that same passion and involvement with her audience during her constructive speech.

This classroom was a microcosm of what was currently taking place throughout the country, speeches in favor of democracy must resound throughout, crushing any possibility of communist advancement in people's hearts. After all, the public was being deceived. Communists used words like daggers, each deceitful idea plunging deeper into the hearts of those fighting for Cuba's survival, as they were fed nothing but lies.

"Ladies and gentlemen, let us remember that the competitors are timed. Your applause will decrease the amount of time they have left and may be detrimental to their final scores. Hold your applause to the end."

With that, Ricardo instructed Manny to continue. No time was added to the clock, Manny ended up losing approximately forty seconds.

After that introduction, the audience stayed erect in their seats and barely winked as they listened to Manny and absorbed everything he said. Heads were shaking, most in the affirmative. The communists in the class couldn't wait for Rebecca to step up to the podium, they were sure she would regain some lost ground.

Rebecca:

"Poverty is a multifaceted concept which includes social and political elements. Worldwide, it is a chronic problem that has gotten out of control. There are people struggling to eat in many parts of the world, surviving in cardboard boxes, and lacking medical supplies. In the capitalistic societies guilty for creating this monetary inequality, people live with obscene amounts of materialistic wealth."

"How much does each person need in order to live a satisfactory life? At what point do you stop the insanity of accumulating wealth in excess while your brothers and sisters around the globe struggle to get their daily morsels of food?"

"In 1776, Adam Smith in the *Wealth of Nations* argued that *poverty is the inability to afford, not only the commodities which are indispensably necessary for the support of life, but whatever the custom of the country renders it indecent for creditable people, even of the lowest order, to be without.*"

"Life expectancy in Developed countries from 1950-1955 was 66. In that same time span, life expectancy in Developing countries was 41.7 and the poorest 36.4. Through the studies and counts conducted it has been determined that the three main contributing factors to such short life expectancies in the 20th Century are lack of food, lack of proper shelter, and lack of medical supplies."

"As Adam Smith pointed out almost 200 yeas ago, even the poor are entitled to *commodities that are indispensably necessary for the support of life.*"

"It is time that we take from the obscenely rich and give to the poverty stricken. After all, Adam Smith titled his book *Wealth of Nations*, not *Wealth of Individuals*."

Rebecca ended up making an eloquent argument for communism, she definitely gained back some of the lost ground attributed to Manny's heartfelt speech earlier. She effectively spoke on behalf of struggling people everywhere, pulling at heartstrings in the audience. Her well organized speech and demeanor added to the efficiency with which she spoke, as she simultaneously conveyed her message through her words and stage presence.

Alyssa:

"Human beings have different tastes, some enjoy the beach and others team sports. There are wine connoisseurs, opera aficionados, and philatelists. Sometimes tastes overlap, you can enjoy listening to opera while savoring a glass of Chateau Margaux."

"There are, however, some things humans need for survival. We are geared for survival, humans can survive without food for seven days, and without water for three days. My question is this — is survival all we want?"

"It is indisputable that with few exceptions, we seek pleasure and economic well-being while attempting to avoid pain and suffering. Sharing these commonalities, we should all fight for the same things. Our ideals are similar, the desired outcome the same."

"John Stuart Mill once stated, *Pleasure and freedom from pain are the only things desirable as ends*."

"His argument for the principle of utility holds that *actions are right in proportion as they tend to promote happiness, wrong as they tend to produce the reverse of happiness*."

"Utilitarianism attempts to make a majority of the population happy."

"How better to accomplish that than to let people govern themselves through open elections, a constitution that provides ample opportunity for revision as the need arises, and a number of freedoms not sustained in many governments around the globe?"

"How better to accomplish that than by having a market that promotes competition and growth? It is through Laissez-faire that markets self-correct, ensuring long-term growth and success."

"How better to accomplish that than to resist the urge to intertwine government with religion?"

For the duration, Alyssa passionately articulated her speech, leaving everything she had at the podium. When her eight minutes expired, the temptation was to continue. As she sat, she felt a sense of accomplishment. This was a mature young lady, fully knowing what was at stake. Not just the debate in her class for a letter grade, her focus was on the overall picture – the survival of her country. The struggle, and hopeful victory over communism, is what she thought of on this sunny afternoon.

"Students, take a 15 minute break, we will reconvene at that time to conclude our debate with the rebuttals," stated Dr. Buendia, with mixed feelings about the progress thus far.

On one hand he took great pride in his star pupils, Manny and Alyssa. Their arguments were clear, concise, and to the point. These are necessary in a good debate, he knew from the start of the semester that they would make him proud.

What bewildered him was the change he noticed in Lily. It wasn't a minor tweak in her political ideology that could be attributed to sharing with other students throughout the semester, her conversion was surprising to all. There was a trigger, nobody changes like that without major causation. Dr. Buendia had pondered this for many weeks, he planned to discuss it with Lily in the near future.

After the break, students came back into the class and took their positions.

"The second half of the debate consists of rebuttals. During rebuttals each debater has four minutes to respond to either of the opponent's constructive speech."

"Manny, representing the Negative Team, goes first."

Manny:

"There was much irony in Rebecca's mention of Adam Smith during her constructive speech. She argued the merits of communism quoting an author whose life's work dealt with defending free markets. It is through free markets and competition that people strive to get ahead."

"I quote Adam Smith, *It is not from the benevolence of the butcher, the brewer, or the baker that we expect our dinner, but from their regard to their own interest.*"

"Should the day come when that butcher, brewer and baker are told they must complete their tasks with little compensation, monetary or otherwise, their interest in working to the best of their ability will decrease. Should we live to see the day when equal pay takes hold and workers involved in menial work get the same pay as doctors, professionals will become profoundly dissatisfied with their field. Satisfaction takes hold in many ways, but workers must know that the harder they work and the more they study, the greater their compensation. Motivation must be present in an effective society, communism does away with that. Rebecca, you must reevaluate *Wealth of Nations*, that is if you've read it."

Once again, the audience applauded. Manny had definitely done the job the professor was secretly hoping for. He tried his best to remain neutral, but one of Arsenio's traits was that he wore his heart on his sleeve. His family loved him for it, his students admired him for it, but that is a trait that at times can be detrimental. He wouldn't get within three blocks of an automobile dealer without taking Guillermo to help him seal the deal, he felt the dealer could see right through him.

The students knew he was pro-democracy, his expressions and comments conveyed it. His teaching style gave him away. But even the communist students were forgiving of the professor, he was entitled to his opinion, as they were of theirs. Besides, he was one of the greatest educators they had ever seen. His student evaluations were among the best at the university.

"Lily from the Affirmative Team is now at the podium with her rebuttal. Lily, you have four minutes," stated Ricardo as a reminder.

Lily:

"Alyssa's major point in her constructive speech dealt with Utilitarianism and its importance in ensuring happiness for most. She may as well be arguing for communism, not against it. It is this belief that we communists hold near and dear to our hearts. At this moment, a small percentage of the Cuban population is enjoying the good life. Unemployment is increasing along with poverty. Homeless people are everywhere in Cuba, people are struggling to meet basic necessities on an everyday basis."

"Is that Utilitarianism? Are the majority of Cubans enjoying the prosperity that many claim we have in this country? Or could there be a better solution, a different form of government that would enact laws to help change the way wealth is distributed in this country?"

"These are questions I pose, I leave it to you for consideration and hopefully an eventual solution can be found to these serious issues."

"I must admit, this has been one of the best debates I've been part of this semester. All arguments are convincing and thus far the rebuttals strong," said Ricardo.

"Alyssa will continue, giving her rebuttal for the Negative Team, followed by Rebecca for the Affirmative Team. By the end of the class, Dr. Buendia will have the results."

"Alyssa, you may step up to the podium."

Ricardo had been taking notes throughout the entire debate, he didn't want to leave anything to memory. He had participated in many debates in his undergraduate studies, he remembered well what winning meant to him. After the two following rebuttals, he would step out for at least half an hour, use the rubric that Dr. Buendia had provided, and determine the winners of the debate.

Like Dr. Buendia, he too needed objectivity when scoring. Ricardo reminded himself that the arguments are what counted, he needed to exclude his political beliefs when considering the participants' eloquent arguments. That was easier said than done.

Alyssa:

"Lily's reference to Skinner's _Walden Two_ does not help her team with their argument in defense of communism, it detracts from it. The conflict it brings forth is the following."

"Karl Marx, the father of communism, spent his life attempting to create a system where the proletariat would have a fighting chance to get ahead. With the advent of the Industrial Revolution, the bourgeois imposed much pressure on workers to perform. Laws were still not in place to protect workers from the technological advancements that helped create sweatshops, long workdays, and subpar working conditions."

"These abuses were offset in capitalistic societies in the early 20th century with the creation of unions, legislation that addressed the need for change, and media exposure."

"Here is where Lily's mention of *Walden Two* creates confusion: she argues for utopian socialism, a system which Karl Marx referred to as folly. Marx was in favor of scientific socialism, a system that could be proven to be effective. Utopia, according to Marx, could never be achieved."

"Furthermore, the system Marx created is obsolete because of the protective measures that have been taken in countries around the world. The standard of living in capitalistic countries such as the United States has increased exponentially since *Das Capital* was first published."

"Sharing of wealth through force will never work, proper steps must be taken to assist those who lack proper food and shelter. Rebecca touched upon that need by quoting Smith, but Smith's emphasis through his published work was not on creating a system that would redraw all wealth parameters. Smith's ideas were less radical and much more effective – through effective legislation the wealthy will contribute their fair share."

"Quoting Smith and Skinner to prove the feasibility of communism in our country is ludicrous. And using the words utopia and socialism in the same sentence is an insult to our audience's intelligence. They deserve more, stick to facts, and offer well thought out arguments."

Rebecca:

"I must thank Alyssa for her assistance in arguing for our side today, utilitarianism is the reason communism is needed. Mention of the French Revolution also helps accentuate certain points we emphasize in our debates for communism."

"First of all, the utility principle argued by Mill states that what is good for most is what should be applied. I am in agreement, especially when a minority of Cubans are well off and the others are either barely making it or living in poverty. Many in Havana live well, but drive outside the city limits and you see something very different. Communism takes hold only if the population feels the need for change. Hunger quickly spurs need for change."

"During the French Revolution, changes came about for similar reasons. People were suffering, people were hungry, and people were ready for change. One of the parties vying for position in France brought forth what we are suggesting - sharing of the wealth. How can we as a society accept a minority holding over 50% of the country's assets when so many go hungry?"

"My dream is that someday our children will have to go to a museum to see what abusive, manipulative, capitalistic societies looked like..."

The applause for Rebecca topped that of Manny's, rare for a rebuttal.

"Nicely done by both teams and by our four debaters. You may take a twenty-minute break as I tally up the points and analyze my notes. I will name the winner in a few minutes. Afterwards, Professor Buendia will take what I give him and assign a grade to each student," said Ricardo.

When the students walked back in twenty minutes later, they found Dr. Buendia already in the classroom. He too was curious to see who would be classified as the winner. As a microcosm of the Cuban society, the decision could be telling.

"Class, I have the results," remarked Ricardo. "It was a close, well articulated debate on both sides. After much consideration of the comments, along with the point system Dr. Buendia and I developed, I have decided that the Affirmative Team is the winner of today's debate. They have done an effective job in convincing me of the following resolution:

"The form of government in Cuba that would best serve its people is Communism."

Arsenio was shocked, he was sure Manny and Alyssa had stolen the show. Their arguments were concise, to the point, and they quoted framers of democratic societies throughout history. Their rebuttals effectively devalued the Affirmative Team's use of quotes from political philosophers.

Hearing Ricardo name the winners and restate the resolution stung Arsenio, it was a shock from which he wouldn't recover. At the time he could only hope for the best, but things didn't look good. He took a deep breath and let Ricardo finish.

"The Negative Team was not as effective in dissuading me from that belief. Congratulations to Lily and Rebecca, nicely done."

This was a sign of things to come when the stakes would be much bigger, when the prize would not come in the form of a letter grade.

Chapter Seven
Intimate Dinner Party

As Ofelia prepared the evening meal her mind was a whirlwind of thoughts.

I need to do something for myself, I must get out of this dead-end situation, thought Ofelia. Soon, very soon, I'll get out. I've never felt this trapped, like a lion in a cage. My appetite for life is increasing while my opportunities stagnate. I feel like doing something different, maybe a little wild.

Ofelia had kept these emotions bottled up for too long. She was a young lady full of vigor and to a lesser extent aspirations for...well, she aspired to bigger and better things than her present situation offered, she was still contemplating what she wanted. More importantly, she had to figure out how to go about acquiring what she was after. This all sounds very confusing, much like Ofelia's thinking of late...

"Ofelia, what are we having for dinner tonight," asked Angel, who's appetite was known around the neighborhood. He startled Ofelia, whose mind was elsewhere.

Luisa, Carlos's wife, would buy food for four. Mario did not have a huge appetite, but Angel more than made up for that with his frequent visits to his good friend's house.

"Angelito, tonight we are having Ropa Vieja (Shredded Beef), white rice, and plantains. A meal fit for a king."

"Wow, may I invite Mario? That's one of his favorites as well," said Angel.

"My dear, you know there's always enough for guests. Besides, Mario is like family," responded Ofelia with a smile.

"Thanks Tia Ofelia, you're the best!"

With that, Angel ran off to spend some time with Mario and invite him to dinner. Who knows, maybe Carlos and Luisa would surprise his parents and tag along.

For the last ten years, Ofelia had dedicated herself to the Buendia family. Often times her life was indistinguishable from theirs. Family vacations, birthday parties, and special occasions were all shared together. It was an ideal situation for all, but Ofelia ended up lacking an identity and a life of her own.

She was desperate for independence, all the while fearing the loss of those who had grown so close to her. She loved them dearly, confusion abounded at this stage in her life. Only time would tell what fate had in store for her.

Angel picked up his friend and they walked to Maceo Park. The two would often spend an afternoon walking around the Antonio Maceo Monument, discussing topics as they enjoyed the view and breathed in the ocean air. The park, with the ocean as its backdrop, was stunning. Elders would frequent it, sit on a bench, and feed the pigeons. Youngsters would visit the park, sometimes after sunset to share amorous moments.

Jose Antonio Maceo was a Lieutenant General during the Ten Years' War fought with Spain for Cuba's independence. This war was the precursor to the Spanish American War, eventually leading to full independence for Cuba.

The monument proudly displays Maceo on his horse, with the horse standing on its hind legs. The sculptor did a magnificent job of conveying that Maceo was in the midst of battle. Also known as the *Bronze Titan* because of his skin color, Maceo, along with Jose Marti, were two of Cuba's greatest leaders in the struggle for independence.

As sons of university professors, conversations about political events was something they had grown accustomed to and actually enjoyed as young men.

"Mario, are your parents dining with us tonight? Mami and Pops would love it."

"They were showering when I left, maybe there will be a party at your house tonight," said Mario with a smile on his face. Angel loved it when both families got together. The family feeling was no different than when Aunt Mercy or Uncle Guillermo would come to visit.

"That's great, hopefully they come and the party lasts late into the night."

"Good time at that party a few weeks back, huh?" Mario playfully elbowed Antonio.

"Always a great time with you, buddy."

They stopped to admire the ocean. In science classes throughout his academic career, teachers had explained to Angel why the ocean looks blue. Having a photogenic memory like his father, he knew the reason verbatim:

The ocean looks blue because red, orange, and yellow (long wavelength light) are absorbed more strongly by water than is blue (short wavelength light). So when white light from the sun enters the ocean, it is mostly the blue that gets returned. The sky is blue for the same reason.

He could appreciate the scientific explanation behind it, but the deep blue of the Caribbean waters and skies would amaze him for the rest of his life.

"Angel, where are you? Dude, you spaced out one me."

"Just thinking, Mario. We live in a glorious place, look at that ocean. Take a good look around you, we need to appreciate our surroundings, we might not always have it." Angel's smile dissipated. His pensive mood had brought on some melancholy, but with Mario at his side it wouldn't last.

"Buddy, you're thinking too much like your old man. Race you to the statue!"

Mario had the magic touch of helping Angel forget things that bothered him. Angel was sure it went both ways, that's why they enjoyed each other's company so much. Their compatibility cemented their friendship, from taste in sports to political views.

They were like brothers.

Carlos and Luisa showed up for dinner at the Buendia Residence, it was a complete surprise. Arsenio was thrilled to have his buddy over, Ana and Luisa got along well and always enjoyed each other's company.

"Ana, pull out the best bottle of wine we have, we've got very special guests," said Arsenio as he tapped Carlos on the back.

"I'm humbled, my brother," shot back Carlos with a smile.

"Carlos, what did you think of the article on the front page of El Pais this morning?"

"Luisita, let's get out of here. The men have started to talk politics," jested Ana as she blew her husband a kiss.

Luisa followed Ana to the wine cellar to choose a bottle. The wine room was Arsenio's pride and joy. After purchasing the house, they added a wing that included the cellar. Ana enjoyed wine with her dinner, but she wasn't familiar with the good years or any other details about wines. Red with meat and white with fish — she understood. But if she was having steak and was in the mood for white wine, she had no problem with that. Many considered this a faux pas, she was simple and didn't find the need to follow etiquette books to the letter.

"Luisita, you're more familiar with wines than I am, which of these two is better?"

"Let me take a close look." Luisa read both labels and closely analyzed the bottles.

"Definitely the one to the left, Ana. It's obvious why."

"You see, I told you that you knew more! Why is it?" asked Ana, eager to learn more about wines.

"The bottle in your left hand is bigger."

They both chuckled.

"Luisita, you've never been more correct," said Ana as she put her arm around her.

Luisa and Carlos were the perfect couple. He worked long hours and she would always have his meals ready for his arrival after a long day on the job. She was loving, understanding, and a wonderful mother to Mario. He had gotten more attention from mom in the last couple of years, it was nice to have her home full-time.

"Ok, gentlemen, here is your wine," yelled both ladies in tandem.

Being together always got them into a giddy mood.

"Are you sure you didn't already consume a bottle before bringing us ours?" asked Carlos, with a big smile on his face.

"We are drunk with joy, my dear," responded Luisa.

Ofelia called them into the dining room, dinner was ready. All were hungry.

The large, happy family sat down to enjoy Ofelia's wonderful meal.

After dinner, Carlos and Arsenio were off to the library for brandy and cigars. Was it a library or a home office? Arsenio jokingly corrected family members who called his favorite room of the house, with the wine cellar a close second, an office. He argued that with over 800 books, it must be called a library. He enjoyed collecting first editions, especially history books.

History was by far the genre best represented with over 80% of the books dealing with some form of history, from ancient Greeks and Romans to more contemporary history such as the French Revolution and the history of Cuba, he would spend hours reading. It wasn't rare for him to surf from one topic to the next from week to week, sometimes from one day to the next.

He was especially fascinated with United States history, appreciating the ideals drawn up by the American founders. That is what he wished for the future of his own country - a government that respects individualism and protects rights to free speech and uncensored media.

The United States was thriving because of these ideals, why do things have to be different for their neighbor in the Caribbean?

Bookcases lined the walls of the library with well-organized books on display, most books were in mint condition. Organized from shortest to tallest, they were also shelved by genre. To Arsenio this was what the kitchen pantry was to Ana – she would display the labels facing forward, his books needed to be in perfect order. From a very young age he taught his children how to handle and appreciate books.

There were two large leather chairs with matching ottomans and a table conveniently located between the chairs that made it the ideal place for these two friends to have drinks, smoke cigars, and discuss their favorite topic – politics.

"Arsenio, this is the life, my brother. Our bellies full, drinking and smoking in your office, and chatting with a dear friend."

"It is the life, my man. But please remember, this is a library," winked Arsenio.

"You're still with that? Yes, your library," responded Carlos with a smile.

"Good man."

"How is your semester so far, Arsenio. I can't believe it's over in a few weeks."

"The semester has gone well, there are two students in particular who have impressed me very much. They are both in my Nature of Politics class."

"Lucky you, freshmen and sophomores," joked Carlos.

"It has been interesting, we are now discussing pros and cons attached to different kinds of governments. As has been the case the last few years, there are many communists and communist sympathizers in my political science classes. This year, Manny and Alyssa are doing a great job defending democracy in our debates."

"That's always good," shot back Carlos, "as professors we must maintain neutrality, that gets more difficult every day."

"Absolutely."

"On a different note, what is the latest with Adolfo? I haven't heard from him in a couple of weeks," stated Arsenio.

"Well, he's back at it. The other day he was bragging about the student with whom he's having an affair. She's in her twenties! I think he's completely lost his mind," said Carlos.

"Wow, do you know the student?"

"No, he's keeping that under wraps. We both know him well, before long we'll know everything about her. I'm surprised his wife has never found out about his affairs," whispered Carlos, just in case the ladies were within range.

"Well, there's little we can do to rectify Adolfo's ways. He seems to be in a bad place right now and I no longer know how to reach him."

"On a different note," Arsenio continued, "what is the latest you have heard about the communists' efforts? What happened at Tropicana is serious, Carlos. We are at a precipice, many of us do not realize the abyss that awaits. False hope betrays, we must prepare ourselves for the worst as we hope for the best."

"I've experienced it with my students as well. Teaching at a university, we have a good pulse of what ails society. How are you going to prepare?" asked Carlos.

"Carlos, what I'm about to share with you no one else can know, including Luisa. I haven't shared it with Ana yet."

"I understand."

"With the grace of God, we will be out of Cuba within a year. Permanently. The government will topple, it's just a matter of time. If we wait too long, we will lose it all and find ourselves trapped in Cuba under a regime that is sure to strip us of all our rights. The time to make a move is now."

"That's a lot to take in, Arsenio. How do you give up your life's accomplishments and material wealth to move to a foreign country?" asked Carlos, incredulously.

"At this point, how can you not?" responded Arsenio.

"I need to chew on this a bit, Arsenio. I agree that the time for a decision is now. I understand your views, but there are so many other things to consider."

"Well, my brother, you have a lot of work ahead of you. The sooner you decide, the better. At my end, the wheels are already turning."

Carlos and Arsenio nursed their drinks, little more was said the rest of the evening.

Chapter Eight
Girls' Night Out

The morning after the dinner party Ofelia dragged herself out of bed, dressed, and went downstairs to make Sunday breakfast for the family.

"Good morning, Ofelia. How did you sleep?" asked Ana.

"I slept well, Ana. It was difficult waking up, I'm a bit tired."

"You worked hard last night. Thank you, we all had a great time."

"Always my pleasure, Ana. What do you want for breakfast?"

"Let me make breakfast, sit and enjoy," insisted Ana.

"No, I couldn't. Please tell me what you want this morning."

"It's a done deal, Ofelia, I'll make banana pancakes, I know they're your favorite."

Ofelia knew she wouldn't win. She couldn't think of a better family to have as an employer, caring and unpretentious.

"Thank you Ana, what are your plans for today?"

"Our customary drive by El Malecón, followed by lunch, and maybe a walk with the kids later on. Nothing extraordinary, just enjoying the simple things in life," responded Ana with a smile.

"It may not be extraordinary but it sounds really nice." Ofelia would give anything to have a family of her own and a structured life like Ana's. She lived vicariously through them, that had to end.

"Ofelia, I don't know what time we'll be returning. Why don't you take the evening off, maybe call up a couple of friends and treat yourself to an outing?"

"That would be nice," admitted Ofelia. "I could call Jenny and Celia, it's always a lot of fun with them."

Ana pulled out $60 and handed it to Ofelia. She hesitated at first but ended up taking the money. Her friends were better off financially than she was, Ofelia could go to a really nice place with this money and have some to spare.

"Ana, thank you so much, this means a lot to me."

This is just what Ofelia needed, an outing with her close friends. She intended on forgetting everything that night, all bets were off. Ofelia was focused on one thing for the evening – enjoying herself.

"Have fun with your friends, Ofelia," responded Ana.

Ofelia called Jenny and Celia around 4 pm with the good news, she was hoping they would be available that evening. Both were available and ecstatic, they decided to pick up Ofelia at the Buendia residence at nine o'clock and leave from there. Jenny was the only one of the three who owned a car, she picked up Celia first and made her way to pick up Ofelia. They still didn't know where they were going that evening.

As they arrived at the residence, Jenny started honking the horn.

"Jenny, stop honking the horn. Take a look around you, this is a fancy neighborhood where people don't honk their horns," said Celia with concern.

"Then tell me what the horn is for! It's for honking," replied Jenny as she honked a few more times.

"Stop honking," said Ofelia as she locked the door.

As Ofelia neared the car, she whispered to Celia in the passenger's seat, "I really don't know where we picked this one up, we can't take her anywhere."

Ofelia was wearing a smile, but she would frequently get upset at Jenny for doing things like this. Jenny would frequently embarrass Celia and Ofelia. However, all three enjoyed each other's company and got along very well.

"All right, now that we're all here, where are we going? Ofelia doesn't get out much, let's make it a special night," said Jenny.

"Money is no object," added Celia, jokingly.

"Well, if you girls are up to it, we can go somewhere fancy to-night," said Ofelia with a huge grin.

"Ofi, did you win big at the casino? You want to go somewhere fancy and your sundress is beautiful. Is it new?" inquired her close friend, Celia.

"The dress is new, but I have not won any money. Ana generously gave me sixty dollars for this outing and I intend to spend every penny partying tonight!"

"Me too," cried Jenny.

"Let's decide on a place, I'm in," said Celia.

"Dr. and Mrs. Buendia go quite a bit to a place called La Floridita. It's upscale enough for them, but I've heard them say it's not even close to being as upscale as Tropicana. That could be the place for us. We might even hook up," suggested Ofelia.

"What has happened to our Ofelia? Jenny, have you seen her? !Esta es una loca! It's scary how she's starting to remind me of you, Jenny," laughed Celia.

"Let's go girls, promise we won't hold back tonight. Put that short dress to work tonight, Ofi," winked Jenny as she pulled away from the house.

La Floridita was an upscale restaurant known as the *cradle of the daiquiri*. Founded in the 1930s, it was known for its fine cuisine and luxurious ambience. The circular dining area had a mural at the opposite end of the bar with doorways leading to nowhere a few feet apart from each other. The doorways were draped in decorative damask fabric, matching that of the chairs. The circular bar could seat forty. This particular upscale restaurant was famous for serving the best daiquiri in all of Cuba. For many years it was one of Ernest Hemingway's favorite haunts.

"Ladies, we are here, let's do some damage," declared Jenny.

"Jenny, start off slowly. We both know what you're capable of," warned Celia.

Celia was always the voice of reason, she would frequently keep her friends out of trouble and at times she needed to play the role of pacifier when things got ugly. Jenny could bend the elbow when out with friends and Ofelia wasn't too far behind. It was understood by all three that Celia would drive home that night and they would sleep at her place if need be.

"Ofelia, scan the area for good-looking men, I don't want to pay for drinks all night," blurted out Jenny.

"We'll be fine paying for a few, then we can sit down to dine. The night is young, let's order a drink at the bar," replied Ofelia.

"Ladies, my name is Moses. Everyone calls me Mo, what can I get you?"

"Mo, what do you recommend?" asked Ofelia.

"Is it your first time here, ladies?"

"Yes, replied all three."

"Well, this bar serves an amazing daiquiri, I highly recommend it."

Ofelia took the initiative, "Three daiquiris, Mo. Sounds great!"

"Coming right up. Would you like anything to eat?"

"Not right now. We should savor these world famous daiquiris first. Maybe later, thank you," said Ofelia.

As Mo prepared their drinks, the ladies told him their names and exchanged niceties.

When the drinks were ready, he handed them each a beautifully prepared drink in a 12-ounce daiquiri glass. With the right mix of white rum, lime juice, sugar syrup and liqueur, it tasted divine. The crushed ice that was mixed into the drink made it very refreshing.

Celia nursed her drink, Ofelia and Jenny were drinking them like they were lemonades. Before they knew it, they were ordering their fourth drink. That's when *he* walked in.

He went straight to the bar, ordered a whiskey, and avoided look-ing anyone in the eye. The bartender did not refer to him by name so it seemed to be his first time there, at the very least he did not frequent La Floridita.

He was of average height, dressed casually, and was attractive. Light green eyes, a good head of hair, and a confident walk caught Ofelia's eye. The way he ordered his drink is what immediately attracted him to Jenny — with authority, there was no hesitation in this man's speech or demeanor. His tone conveyed that he knew exactly what he wanted.

"Girls, get ready to go fishing, look what just walked in," men-tioned Jenny as she looked in the direction of the recently arrived patron who sat only two bar stools down from Ofelia.

"Jenny, get a hold of yourself. If you walk up to him he's going to think you're a lady of the night, or at the very least that you're too assertive for a woman. Remember what happened last time you tried something like that. Let's just sit, drink, and have a good time," ad-vised Celia.

"That brawl wasn't my fault, how was I supposed to know he was married?" shot back Jenny.

"That's just it, we must stay put and play it by ear. He seems nice enough, but give it time, don't scare him off," added Celia.

Ofelia discreetly observed the man. She was already under the influence but well aware of her surroundings. She liked what she saw in this man, something about him had struck her since he walked up to the bar. She continued drinking and having a good time with her friends.

Like a shark circling its prey, he observed Ofelia sitting at the bar for almost one hour, downing daiquiris at a rate of one every 15 minutes. If nothing else, she was well on her way to getting drunk, assuming she wasn't there yet.

The stranger ordered a second whiskey and moved down one stool, inching closer towards Ofelia.

"Good evening, Miss. May I be bold enough to ask you what your name is?"

"My name is Ofelia, what's yours?"

"I'm Antonio. I must say, I couldn't help but notice you. May I buy you another daiquiri, you need a refill."

"I've already had a few, I need to slow down," said Ofelia.

"Then drink the next one very slowly. Barkeep, another daiquiri for the lovely lady," Antonio ordered without considering Ofelia's wishes.

"I don't join just anybody for drinks, Antonio. You seem like a nice guy. Let me introduce you to my friends. This is Celia, and sitting to her right is Jenny."

"Nice to meet you, ladies. Is there a special occasion you're celebrating tonight?"

"We are celebrating life, Antonio. Is there anything greater?" asked Ofelia.

"Life is a great thing to celebrate, lovely lady. Here's to life and everything that comes with it," replied Antonio as he lifted his glass.

The ladies responded likewise, they lifted their glasses and toasted to life.

By this point Ofelia had outdone even Jenny with five drinks, Celia was on her second drink and did not have intentions on ordering any more. Weighing no more than 54 kg (120 pounds) and lacking experience with heavy drinking, Ofelia was drunk. For a novice she held her liquor well, but she was drunk nonetheless.

Celia and Jenny moved down a few barstools to give Antonio and Ofelia some privacy, it was obvious they were interested in each other and that their conversation tonight might lead to something else.

"Ofelia, what are some of your interests?" asked Antonio.

"When I was a girl I took ballet lessons, always wanted to be a ballerina," said Ofelia. She wasn't slurring words yet, but her speech was a bit off.

"What do you do for a living now?" he asked.

She responded after hesitating, "An elementary school teacher. I've taught 3rd grade for four years."

Ofelia was embarrassed to admit that she was just a house servant. Even though she loved working for the Buendia family, she could feel that she was quickly outgrowing that role. Maybe she wanted to do something else with her life, she aspired to something more. Should she find the right man, she might be ready for marriage. Here she was, decked out and giving it her best shot.

He sensed she was lying, maybe it was the hesitation, her facial expression or something else. He didn't care, she was beautiful and he wanted her.

"Interesting, my mother is a teacher. Where do you teach?"

"Well, it's a school on the other side of Havana. The commute is bad at times with so much traffic. It's a private school, St. Joseph's School. Did I tell you there's a lot of traffic?"

"Lots of traffic, yes. My mom works for the public school system, she loves it too." Antonio had her exactly where he wanted her. He loved fishing, there was nothing as satisfying as setting up the bait and reeling in the prize.

"Do you like boating?" asked Antonio.

"I've only been on boats a few times, but I love it," fibbed Ofelia.

"Great, if you're not busy I'll pick you up in my yacht by the marina closest to the International Hotel next Saturday. We can have lots of fun together, Ofelia," said Antonio.

"A yacht? I'd love to, Antonio. I've never been on a yacht," gleamed Ofelia.

"It's only a forty-footer but I'm proud of it, it looks great and rides even better."

"Bartender, two more drinks, please," demanded Antonio.

"Ofelia, I like you," said Antonio.

With that, Antonio stood up, took her by the shoulders, and kissed her long and passionately, as she sat in full view of her friends and the other patrons.

"I'm starting to like you too," replied Ofelia.

She thoroughly enjoyed the kiss, the taste of liquor they shared added to the sensuality of the moment. It suggested the beginning of something more than just a kiss, that feeling thrilled Ofelia. She hadn't felt this tingle in a very long time.

"Let's dance Ofelia."

"But there's no music," she replied.

"We will make some beautiful music together, my dear," responded Antonio, with sexual undertones.

They danced for at least ten minutes before Antonio pulled her away to a corner behind the bar, by the entrance to the restrooms.

"Ofelia, I've known you an hour and it feels like it's been forever."

"Like I said, I like you too, Antonio."

"We should go somewhere private."

"I'm here with my friends, maybe we could go out alone some other time," reasoned Ofelia.

Antonio's hesitation let on that whatever plans he had were for tonight. Pressing like a good car salesman, he continued.

"Maybe after your friends leave we could go somewhere together," he said.

"That's not a good idea, Antonio. We came together and we will leave together."

"Fine, you win. But you can count on going out again with me in the future," Antonio whispered in her ear.

"That's a deal," replied Ofelia, smiling as she looked him in the eye.

They went back to the bar. Ofelia felt guilty having left her friends to be with Antonio, but she was sure they would understand.

"Did you know that Cuba is not only famous for sugar cane and cigars? Cuba has the best rum in the world – Bacardi," stated Antonio.

"I've never had any," responded Ofelia, demonstrating her naïveté.

"Well, we must do something about that," replied Antonio with a wink. "Barten…"

"No, I've had too much to drink already," insisted Ofelia.

"If you can't drive, I can take you home later."

"Antonio, I came with my friends. I'm not driving, but I've had my limit."

"Trust me Ofelia, just have one drink so you can experience the best rum in the world."

She couldn't resist, there was something about him that had won her over from the start, "Just one, Antonio."

Antonio grinned from ear to ear, they enjoyed their drink.

Three drinks later, Antonio grabbed Ofelia by the hand and left the bar area.

There were two sets of bathrooms, one by the bar and a set by the dining area. There were no more meals served in the dining area past 11 pm, only the bar remained open. It was almost 12:30, Celia and Jenny were ready to go home, but they couldn't find Ofelia. Not thinking much of it because they knew she was accompanied, they went back to the bar and had some buttered bread and Coca Cola as they got ready to leave after finding Ofelia.

"Come this way, my dear," whispered Antonio to Ofelia. I have a surprise for you.

Though drunk, Ofelia knew exactly what was happening. Her decision would have probably differed should she have been sober, but even inebriated as she was she was loving every minute.

"Really, I love surprises. Give me a hint, how big is it?" flirted Ofelia.

She could hear her own heartbeat, fully knowing what her surprise was. Ofelia felt alive.

"Close your eyes and follow me," demanded Antonio.

He held her hand and led her into the men's room in the desolate dining area, locked the door, and put both hands underneath her arms. He kissed her passionately as he lifted her onto the sink.

Antonio slid his hand under her dress, enjoying the moment and the look of ecstasy on Ofelia's face.

"Antonio, take me! Do anything you want with me!"

She enjoyed him, showed him how drunk she really was, doing things she had never done before. A memorable moment of bliss, never to be forgotten.

She was so happy, her wish was for that feeling to last forever.

They both dressed and discreetly left the men's room.

"Antonio, I'm liking you more by the minute," said Ofelia with a smile.

"You're growing on me as well, kid," responded Antonio.

Ofelia detected sincerity in Antonio's tone and words.

She gave him her telephone number, knowing he would call her again. When they found her friends, Antonio and Ofelia kissed and parted ways.

She never saw him again.

Chapter Nine
Varadero Getaway

Towards the end of spring semester, Arsenio planned a weekend getaway for his family. Ana considered his spontaneity a virtue, always following his lead. Ofelia usually accompanied the family on these outings, but she decided to stay home this time. Ofelia hadn't been feeling well and she wanted to recover.

Angel, at nineteen, did a great job looking over his sisters when they travelled. Maria was fifteen and well behaved, Barbara was the baby of the family. At six years of age all she wanted to do was eat and play.

Arsenio realized how blessed they were. It wasn't about their wealth, it was all about his family, without them he would be lost.

They were packed and ready to go by 6 am, there were few things Arsenio enjoyed more than road trips with his family. Neither Angel nor Maria had a problem waking up, Barbara had some difficulty until she found out her mom had plans to stop at her favorite bakery for breakfast. From that point on her eyes gleamed with anticipation.

"Daddy, can I buy anything I want at the bakery? I'm really hungry," she stated emphatically.

"Within reason, Barbarita. You don't want to get a tummy ache."

"Ok, Daddy. I love you!"

The magic behind those three words always did something to Arsenio. Should Barbara decide to place a bid on the bakery and all its contents, he would buy it for her. That adorable little girl had him wrapped around her little finger, and they all knew it.

Before leaving, Ana checked the locks six times. This was a habit that was as much a part of her as organizing the cans in the pantry, making sure they were facing forward. She was also a big fan of "consolidating" food to save space - two cereal bags become one, and like magic Ana has created space in her kitchen.

Lucerna was a pastry shop owned by two brothers who acquired their culinary talents in their native country. After moving from Switzerland to Cuba, they opened their shop and before long they were well known, especially for their éclairs and cappuccino. Barbara and Ana were huge fans of the éclairs and Arsenio of the cappuccino. It was located two shops down from the beauty salon Ana went to every week. Barbara always begged to go with mom when she would get her hair done so that she could eat an éclair afterwards.

After having breakfast at Lucerna, the family got into their convertible and started their journey. It was time to bond and forget about their worries, leave behind the mundane, and step into a world with no politics. The political environment was the only part of Arsenio's life from which he needed escape, every other aspect was perfect.

"Ladies and Angel, in a little over two hours we will be in paradise. You will set foot on the most beautiful beach known to man, Varadero. We haven't been there since Angel was four, so it will be a new experience for all of you."

"Arsenio, maybe he remembers," said Ana.

"No mom, I remember our trips to Miami Beach, but not Varadero. Mario goes there all the time, he's showed me photos. I've never seen sand that color," added Angel.

"Angel, Varadero beach will knock your socks off. It sets the standard for all beaches worldwide. This will be a glorious weekend."

"Absolutely!" replied the three children in unison.

"Is Varadero the beach that Marjorie went to with her mom a couple of years ago?" asked Maria.

"Yes, that's the beach, Maria."

"I was invited to go and you said no, remember?"

"I also remember that you had just met Marjorie and you were only thirteen. I was not going to let you drive two and a half hours with people I had just met."

"Good point mom. I still love you," said Maria, with a playful tone.

As they approached Varadero, Barbara insisted on changing into her bathing suit in the car. She refused to waste one minute of daylight. It wasn't rare for her to go into the pool after breakfast, remain up to lunchtime, only to return after the obligatory one-hour wait to properly digest her food.

That was the l-o-n-g-e-s-t hour known to mankind. If it were up to the children, they would consume all their meals on floating trays instead of adhering to a rule that had never made its way into any medical journal. How could one hour guarantee that the children would not get cramps? It was an old wives' tale. Nonetheless, Ana and Arsenio were ruthless when counting down. Their watches always had a second hand, especially useful on vacation.

"Daddy, how long ago did we eat?" asked Barbara, fearing her father's response.

Arsenio replied with a grin from ear to ear, "It's been over one hour, Babita. Unless you eat again, you can go swimming after we check in at the hotel."

"Daddy, what if I eat something small? Will I still have to wait an hour?" inquired Barbara.

"Honey, your mom can go with the three of you to eat something while I check in. By the time we're all done, it will almost be time to go swimming. Deal?"

"Deal, Daddy!"

Arsenio made his way across the checkered lobby floor towards the semi-circular check-in counter. The contemporary furniture, upholstered in vibrant colors with flower pots at each end, provided guests an opportunity to sit and chat at their leisure. Spaced out columns and cathedral ceilings added to the palatial look of the hotel.

"My name is Gregorio, welcome to the International Hotel at Varadero, are you checking in?"

"Yes, Gregorio. I have reservations for a party of five for two evenings. Kindly hurry, my six year old will have my head if I take too long. She can't wait to get into the pool."

"I understand, sir," responded Gregorio as he chuckled, "I have two of my own."

Within minutes, Gregorio had completed the check-in process in an efficient manner. Now Arsenio could focus on what was truly important - his family.

Minutes after entering the room, the bellhop followed with the luggage. Arsenio thanked him and tipped him five dollars. Not long after that, Ana returned with the children and Arsenio's lunch.

"Me first!" yelled Barbara as she ran to the bathroom to change.

"Why does she always get her way, mom?" asked Maria with a resigned tone.

Sibling rivalry sometimes paid a visit, but these siblings adored each other and would look out for each other at all times.

"I don't know what she's going to do in there without her bathing suit," said Ana with a smile.

"Here honey, take this to your sister so we can all change and enjoy the rest of the afternoon poolside. Tomorrow we'll start off the day by going to the beach."

"All right, mom."

The Buendia family took the elevator and exited to the pool area. Arsenio already felt his load quickly lifting. This is the effect his family had on his state of mind, it counteracted that of the tumultuous political times they were currently experiencing. He was looking forward to replenishing the tank, both body and soul must be at full strength, the fight ahead would not be easy.

The rectangular, Olympic sized pool offered a white canopy at one end for those who desired protection from the Varadero sun. There were blue and yellow chaises to spare that could easily be moved from one section of the pool to the other. Sun worshippers followed the powerful rays, others avoided it.

Extending from the hotel roof was a red tiled awning that added shaded seating. This area offered easy access to the restrooms, restaurant, and the bar.

Barbara started playing in the pool with her goggles as Angel and Maria hit a beach ball back and forth. They were all lathered in protective lotion, this powerful sun was no joke. Arsenio and Ana made themselves comfortable in two lounge chairs in the shade. They would join the children later, after a three-hour drive they wanted to relax by reading a while.

"Arsenio, what are you reading?"

"One of my favorite novels, can you guess which? You'll win a piña colada if you guess correctly."

"Are you reading *From Here to Eternity* again?"

Arsenio's belly laugh could be heard across the pool, "Is there any other novel?"

"Pay up, I'm thirsty," Ana said emphatically, with a huge grin.

"You got it, kiddo!"

Arsenio motioned to one of the poolside attendants and ordered the drinks.

"Ana, remember five years ago when that movie came out?"

"Yes, you went with your father to the premiere."

"What amazes me is how an ordinary event such as going to a movie with your father can end up becoming unforgettable," Arsenio stated solemnly.

"You were both very close, that made everything you did together special. Even though he passed away at an early age, always remember those special moments. They will get you through rough patches."

"I married you for your brains as well as your beauty."

Arsenio stood up and began to tickle Ana. This was one of the many ways he had of expressing his love for her, but he needed to be careful, she would always pay him back.

"Truce Ana, truce," he said as he backed away.

"This was sorely needed, my dear. There is no greater pleasure than having you by my side as our children enjoy themselves in the pool."

Ana quietly reached out, grabbed his hand, and smiled. Her gesture communicated everything he needed to know.

"Daddy, Daddy, I'm hurt!" exclaimed Barbara, limping out of the pool.

As she made it to her dad, she pointed to her foot. She had unknowingly stepped on a pebble in the pool and experienced some pain.

Arsenio immediately wrapped a towel around her, gave her a big hug, and uttered a phrase that requires some translation:

"Chata, mi niña."

This frequently used phrase in the Buendia household is used by Arsenio when something unpleasant happens to the baby. It is a combination of Baby Talk with Castilian. The etymology of "chata" is as follows:

Chata (adjective)
stems from the word "pobrecita", meaning "poor little girl" in Spanish. It originated in the mid-twentieth century, most likely in the Buendia household. Its pronunciation mimics the way a baby would say "pobrecita".

The humor in this anecdote is that nobody ever heard Barbara utter that word as a baby, it was all Arsenio's doing.

"There you go, honey. Does it feel better?"

"Yes, Daddy. Thank you."

With that, Barbara returned to the pool and continued swimming.

Arsenio looked up and admired the deep blue sky. He loved his sky. Yes, it was his. His sky, his country, his freedom, his peace. This, and so much more, is what he and his compatriots were fighting to uphold.

The deeper the blue, the whiter and puffier the clouds.

There was no chance of stormy weather here, everything was perfect.

The following morning the family attempted to sleep in late... well, most of the family, anyway.

"Mommy, wake up Daddy! It's time to eat. We have to go to the beach!"

"Barbarita, it's not even seven yet. The beach is closed."

"Mommy, I'm six...I know they can't close the beach."

"Read your book and we'll go in a while."

Barbara reluctantly grabbed her book and read while waiting for everyone to wake up. Angel and Dad could sleep through a hurricane, Maria was starting to toss and turn.

Exactly one hour after breakfast, the family set foot on Varadero sand — white, powdery, and enticing. People walking the streets with no intention of going onto the beach could not resist. Many would remove their shoes, roll up their pants, and continue their journey on this glorious beach — a beach with few equals.

They all agreed the day was young, they would enter the ocean later. Mom and Dad began to read as Barbara built her sand castle. Maria and Angel walked by the shore.

"Angel, did you know it's Dad's birthday in a few weeks? I overheard them making plans for the big day."

"I am aware, let's shop around for a nice gift when we get back."

"All right," responded Maria with enthusiasm. She loved to shop.

"Princess, have you noticed Pop's behavior lately? He seems to have a lot on his mind, I'm afraid he's bottling it up. It's what psychiatrists call *repression*, it could have long term physical and emotional effects if not treated."

Angel was a sophomore at his father's university. His vocabulary was excellent for someone his age, and he enjoyed showing off what he learned in school.

"Angel, I have noticed that Dad hasn't been himself lately. Much of it may have to do with his job as a political science professor. With all the talk of communists taking over, I'm sure any defense of communism greatly affects him. He must have a number of communist students who register for his classes."

"That is amazing insight, my lovely sister. You are sharp as a whip, kiddo," replied Angel, expressing great pride in his sister.

"I'm going to have a chat with him. Now, let's enjoy our walk," said Angel, sporting a smile.

They walked, splashed about, and joked around as good siblings do. Angel wet his sister's hair and tossed sand at her as brothers do. They were having fun, just like the good times they shared when younger. When Angel was ten and Maria six they would play their dad's records and sing along using invisible microphones. Amazing memories, unforgettable times.

"Let's turn around, we've been walking for...Mario?"

"Mario, what a surprise, brother! What are you doing here?"

"Didn't Maria give you the message?"

"Ouch, I forgot. Sorry," said Maria apologetically.

"Oh, what are we going to do with that lovely sister of yours?" Mario smirked. His crush for Maria went back to when he was younger.

"I'm here with Juan and Rene, we wanted you to round out the foursome, but Maria told us you would be down here with your family. Neither Alex nor Joey could make it, they're taking extra courses this semester and need the extra time to catch up. Let's get together tonight, we'll pass by your hotel to pick you up."

"For sure, we'll get together later," declared Angel. He was delighted to find his three good friends in Varadero.

Angel noticed what Juan was holding and laughed, ever since they had known each other he would bring, if nothing else, this one item to the beach.

"Buddy, are they predicting rain?" mocked Angel, pointing to the umbrella in Juan's hand.

"It just so happens, my soon-to-be soaked friends, that they are. And there's only room for one," replied Juan, with his distinctive smug look when saying anything remotely funny.

Later that afternoon it rained a great deal, there was only one person on the beach who wasn't getting soaked.

That evening at dinner, the family enjoyed their meal while casually discussing school.

"Angel, how are your courses at the university this semester?"

"Mami, I am doing well in all but one class. The biology course my dean recommended is very difficult. I will pass it with a C, should I work diligently for the rest of the semester."

"There will always be some courses more difficult than others. How are your psychology classes?"

"Those are my favorite classes, in almost two full years I've aced them all."

"Excellent, son."

"Maria, your turn," said Dad as he chewed on a piece of his filet mignon.

"Dad, everything is going well. The other day I got an A on my narrative writing piece. They asked me to describe my hero."

"Really, what does he look like?" asked Arsenio, anticipating her response.

"He looks just like you, Dad."

"Well then, I will need to read that when I get home." His heart melted.

"Pops, guess who I saw today?" asked Angel.

"Hey," interrupted Barbara, "aren't you going to ask me about my school?"

"In just a minute, Babita. Who did you see, Angel?"

"I saw Mario, Juan, and Rene at the beach today."

"That's great son, are Carlos and Luisa here with Mario?"

"No, they came alone. I was invited to come with them but they knew I was coming with you guys."

"Well, you can go out with them in the evenings if you'd like."

"Absolutely, Pops. Sounds great!"

"Very well, Babita, I can't wait to hear all about your school."

"I drew a picture for you and Mami last week, the teacher liked it a lot."

"That's our girl," said Mami. She always loved the relationship Barbara had with her father, not all dads were like Arsenio.

"What else, mi niña?" asked Arsenio.

"Every morning we play a game called "*Tell me about Dinner*", it's a lot of fun."

"What is that all about?" inquired Arsenio, his heart beating faster.

"We sit in a circle and the teacher asks us to tell her about our discussions with our dads and moms at the dinner table the night before."

"Oh, and sometimes our teacher calls the principal and asks us to repeat what we said," added Barbara.

Arsenio was taken aback, things were moving much quicker than he thought. He would have to pay Guillermo another visit. There was no time to waste, much needed to be done.

His response to Barbara was brief and nonchalant, he didn't want to upset anyone on their weekend getaway.

Chapter Ten

Twenty-Four Hours

April 15th - 16th
7 pm – 7 am

A rsenio's pain from the waist up was intense, especially around his shoulders. He was barely conscious, having no idea where he was. As he tried to move his arms, he realized that something prevented him from doing so. He heard voices, but could not see. Within the next few minutes he would become very drowsy and go to sleep, a deep sleep, a slumber like no other.

This twilight zone, neither here nor there, was becoming an annoyance. He needed some clarity as to what was taking place, fear was setting in. Could this be another one of those nightmares he had been experiencing for the last few months? If it was, this was one of the strangest yet. Strange, surreal, lonely. He felt lonely, where was everyone? More importantly, where was *he*?

Ana and the children had stepped out for a bite to eat, they had been by Arsenio's side for over ten hours without a morsel of food. People had mentioned great things about the food in this place, not that quality was what they were looking for at a time like this. Anything to sustain them through such a difficult time was all they needed, they must rush back to Arsenio.

"Mom, will Pops ever walk again?" asked Angel with tears in his eyes.

"Angel, you can ask such stupid questions!" exclaimed Maria as she broke down and cried.

"It will be difficult, but your father will walk again. We all need to have faith and stay strong for him, like all the times he's hidden his fears to help us through tumultuous times," responded Ana in a somber tone.

"Let's postpone this conversation. We need to eat something in order to be with your dad, he has never needed us as much as he does now," said Ana, gaining her composure.

The three purchased some sandwiches and drinks, the quickest option available. They ate their food like a bird swooping its prey.

They rushed to the elevator and pressed two, the hospital met or exceeded its reputation thus far. They had been here since early morning, rushing to the hospital the minute they got the call.

As they entered room 223, their heartbeats increased. They couldn't believe their eyes, he was moving his head. They promised themselves they would think of his ambulatory progress at some other time. For now, the man they knew and loved was conscious.

Awakening from his deep sleep, Arsenio was sure he heard Ana sobbing. Angel and Maria whispered something out of earshot to each other. Not sure what was happening, he tried to speak, unsuccessfully.

"Children, he's waking up! Arsenio, honey can you hear me?" Ana asked with a tremendous amount of grief in her voice.

"Pops, try not to move. It is very important that you stay still. Maria, go get the doctor right away," implored Angel.

"Arsenio, give me your hand. My love, you're in the hospital. You have experienced a bad accident, but you're going to be just fine," said Ana.

"Can you speak, Pops?" asked Angel.

Arsenio was barely able to move his mouth, partially due to the anesthesia and a bit to the shock of the recent events. His day had started early, here he was almost twelve hours later in a predicament that few would have survived. Arsenio was physically strong, but it was his disposition that would get him through this. His family would do everything in their power to assist Arsenio in winning this battle.

"My love, squeeze once for yes and twice for no," said Ana.

"Can you do that for us?"

Arsenio squeezed once.

"Are you in great pain right now?"

Two squeezes

"Are you in some pain?"

One squeeze

"The doctor will be speaking to us soon, I'll let him know. Maybe they can do something for the pain."

"Do you remember everything that happened?"

Two squeezes

"Do you remember anything?"

Two squeezes

"My love, you're in the hospital, as you've probably surmised by now. Give me a few minutes and I will explain why you're here. First, I want to let you know that you're getting the best care available, everything will be fine. What the doctor has told us so far is that you need a lot of time to recover, with time all will be well," Ana told her husband.

Ana kissed Arsenio on the forehead and told him how much she loved him. She and the children left the room and looked for the doctor, they couldn't wait to hear specific details from him.

"Mom, why did you lie to him? The doctor did not say everything would turn out just fine, the outcome depends on a lot," said Maria, incredulously.

"Maria, he has been through so much. He woke up not long ago, having no idea where he was and lacking knowledge of what events have transpired within the last twelve hours. The last thing we want to do is add more fear into the equation. Let's talk to the doctor first and play it by ear. One thing they told me is that the first twenty-four hours are critical, let's survive those and work on the rest later," said Ana.

"Mom, you are wise beyond your years," said Maria, with the shadow of a smile.

They saw Arsenio's doctor in the hallway, Ana tracked him down.

"Doctor, my husband has been back in his room for hours. We need details, we must know if he will ever walk again," implored Ana.

"Mrs. Buendia, let's step into this room. If you'd like, bring Angel and Maria."

They walked into a dimly lit, private room. Four windows were adorned with dusty, worn out draperies. The room's dilapidated look matched the gloom they felt that day. Ana and the children were scared to death. Few doctors were better than Dr. Carreras, there was never any doubt about his abilities.

"I am not going to sugarcoat anything, it is important that we all stay on the same page and understand the situation at hand. Ana, your husband has suffered serious physical trauma and we are not sure he will ever walk again. There is some spinal cord injury, the full extent is not yet known. There is more than a fifty percent chance there will be some loss of mobility."

When Dr. Carreras ended the last statement, everyone in the room took a deep breath in disbelief. They were living a nightmare, any minute they would awaken from it and continue with their everyday lives.

Dr. Carreras continued, "The spinal cord is a bundle of nerves and other tissues contained and protected by the vertebrae of the spine, which are the bones stacked on top of each other that make up the spine. It is composed of many nerves, and extends from the brain's base down the back, ending close to the buttocks. The closer the nerve damage to the neck, the more paralysis to the body."

"Doctor, we see the condition he's in, please explain the procedure being utilized to minimize the damage done by the impact he sustained. We are all praying for a full recovery, which is still possible. Is that correct?" asked Ana, awaiting the response she wanted.

"As far as the possibility of full recovery, I've already expressed my concerns. We will do everything we possibly can, he is in good hands. I know his family will support him every step of the way, and if you folks are religious, pray for his recovery," suggested Dr. Carreras.

"As discussed before his surgery, your husband will be in traction for an extended period of time, let me describe it to you. Traction is the use of a pulling force to treat muscle and skeleton disorders. We have estimated that your husband will be in traction for approximately one month. Keys to success are the positioning of his extremities and minimal movement. Skeletal traction uses weights, counter-weights, and pulleys as an exacting technique, aligning the damaged area. Through this pulling force, the affected area will hopefully heal with minimal permanent damage. Of course, the goal is complete recovery."

"His bed has the capability of doing a 360 for an important reason. Since he can't move for the next month, he will be facing the floor almost half the time to avoid bedsores. The nurses attending him have been well trained, they will turn his bed every few hours."

"Do you have any questions?"

"Just one question, when will the bandages come off his eyes?"

"They should come off in less than a week, since the impact was to the upper part of his body his left eye was severely swollen. As I said earlier, it's more for precaution than anything else," said the doctor with a smile.

"Don't hesitate in asking questions, there are never too many," he added.

"Not at this time, Doctor. Thank you," said Ana.

"Ana, just one more thing."

"Yes, Dr. Carreras."

"While in traction, your husband cannot move – at all. For the next month someone else must satisfy every need Arsenio has, from feeding him to scratching his nose; if he moves, he risks damaging that spinal area more and his chances of ever walking again will be slim to none. Is that understood?" emphasized Dr. Carreras.

Ana bowed her head, she knew what they were up against. This would be the greatest struggle of their lives.

"Yes, Doctor."

The fear Dr. Carreras had just instilled in Ana was not unfounded, everything he had told her was accurate. He needed to be stern to emphasize the gravity of the situation. He knew this wouldn't be easy for them, but if he were to heal, they must be perfect for the next month.

Ana and the children returned to the room. They talked to Arsenio, but he was too weak and groggy from all the medication to respond. He would constantly doze off.

Ana walked out of the room to find a pay phone, she needed to contact Ofelia. She found one and inserted her coin.

"Hello, Ofelia. This is Ana, I'm at the hospital with Angel and Maria."

"Ana, how is Arsenio?" asked Ofelia with a concerned tone.

"Ofelia, he is in traction. The accident was bad, much praying must be done. I'll explain everything whenever I get home, I know how much you love him. How is Barbara?"

"She's fine, she fell asleep a little while after having her supper. Don't worry, Ana. I've got everything under control. Stay there as long as you need, Barbara will be fine," assured Ofelia.

"I know she's in good hands, thank you."

Ana and the children gathered three chairs and sat in a semicircle by Arsenio's bed, few words were exchanged.

Before they realized it, the sun crawling in through the blinds woke them up. It was seven in the morning.

<u>April 15th</u>
<u>7 am – 7 pm</u>
(24 hours prior)

Dr. Buendia set his alarm clock for seven that morning, half an hour earlier than usual. He needed to make a stop before going to his office, after that he would teach his first class of the day.

Arsenio showered and dressed, he felt energized for the day ahead. The weatherman predicted sunny, cloudless skies with a temperature of 29 degrees Celsius (84 Fahrenheit). It was a perfect morning to take the top down, that always put a smile on Arsenio's face.

Within the past few weeks he had succeeded in putting to rest any thoughts about the political tumult taking place in Cuba. He focused on his family and on teaching his classes, this immersion provided him with renewed strength and improved his overall long-term outlook.

Dr. Buendia drove down El Malecón hoping to feel a mist off the crashing waves, but there was no wind, and the ocean was calm. He was born and raised in Havana, but he couldn't get enough of his city and these wonderful views. Teaching at such a prestigious university exhilarated him, breathing in the ocean air soothed him, and experiencing the sites and sounds of the city moved him.

He rounded the statue of Alma Mater and entered the university parking lot. Arsenio put the top up, took the keys out of the ignition, and pocketed them. The professor walked towards the campus with a display of vitality. He entered Dr. Martin's office to discuss Adolfo - Arsenio had dashed off a note to him the previous week promising a visit.

"Arsenio, how are you? It's been a few weeks since we've seen each other. Did you enjoy you trip to Varadero?" asked Alejandro.

"What a question that is, Alejandro. Is there a more beautiful beach? We had an amazing time," responded Arsenio.

"Sit, please. How much time do you have before your first class?"

"Well, I have almost two hours, but I need to stop by the office to complete some paperwork. Sometimes I think there's as much clerical work involved as teaching."

"Arsenio, you don't have to sell me on that. As director I still teach a few courses, but my clerical obligations outweigh my teaching duties."

"Tell me, what's on your mind about Adolfo? Is it that new student he's playing around with?" Alejandro winked and smiled.

"Do you know about the new one? I wasn't going to blurt out what I know, maybe I would have worked it into the conversation," said Arsenio.

"Well, according to him this is the one, his soulmate. He can't stop talking about her, I'm surprised he's kept it from you," said Alejandro.

"Let's just say he and I are not as close as we once were. Our political views are clashing more than ever, he even assaulted me a few months ago before winter break," responded Arsenio.

"Yes, I heard about that. How's that nose, slugger?" Alejandro asked with a smirk.

"Don't start, Carlos ridiculed me enough for the two of you," replied Arsenio.

"Back to the girl, he says she's in one of your classes. Maybe that's why he hasn't approached you. Can you imagine, a married man in his forties falling in love with a girl in her twenties?" asked Alejandro as he shook his head in disbelief.

"He is getting nuttier by the day," shot back Arsenio. "Who's the girl?"

"Even if he would have told me, I wouldn't be able to share that with you. Lucky for the two of us, he didn't say. That takes the decision out of my hands."

"Oh well, even after what happened I will always wish him well. He needs to stop acting impulsively with these girls and needs to think about his family," shared Arsenio.

"Agreed," is all Alejandro needed to reply.

"Alejandro, thanks for meeting up with me. It was good seeing you, have a great day."

"You too, slugger!"

"I'm going to stroll to my office, it's a gorgeous day," remarked Arsenio.

"Enjoy your walk."

He exited Alejandro's building and started to walk towards his office. As he had promised himself, he paced himself to enjoy the gorgeous weather. Today he was in no hurry to reach his final destination. Arsenio had walked only a few yards before bumping into Carlos.

"Arsenio, what's up brother? I see you're enjoying the day," mentioned Carlos.

"Hey, Carlos. Absolutely, I've never felt so alive. The weekend trip with my family rejuvenated me, and this wonderful weather does something to me," responded Arsenio with a smile.

"In that case, let's sit and chat for a bit if you have time," suggested Carlos.

"I came early to catch up on paperwork, but considering the weather and the company, I guess the work can wait," said Arsenio.

They grabbed the nearest bench and began to talk. There was a light breeze and very low humidity, a delight to the senses. Arsenio's first class consisted of only fourteen students, many had dropped the course a couple of weeks into the semester. He was tempted to teach outdoors today.

"Were you in to see the old man?" asked Carlos.

"The old man? If you're referring to Dr. Martin, he's only a few years older than we are," said Arsenio.

"So, what was the topic of conversation today?"

"Adolfo and his newest fling, this could be the one, according to Alejandro," snickered Arsenio.

"Alejandro? It must be nice to be a first name basis with Dr. Martin, I didn't know you two were close."

Carlos was obviously ribbing Arsenio, he knew the type of relationship Alejandro and Arsenio had. They both started together as Associate Professors the same year and worked their way up.

"Anyway, he told me it was one of my students from this semester. As I put the pieces together, I'm deducing who it might be," stated Arsenio.

"Spill the beans, Sherlock. Who do you think it is?"

"Let me provide you with the evidence first. We always share stories about our students with each other, so I want you to tell me who you think it might be."

"Fair enough," said Carlos.

"Aldo's political beliefs are now at the other end of the spectrum, he is a communist with blinders on. He will not even consider any other form of government," stated Arsenio.

"Agreed."

"I have mentioned Lily to you, please restate some things I've said about her behavior this semester," requested Arsenio.

"She and Manny are two students you've spoken highly of this entire semester. You predicted they would be the two top debaters defending democracy towards the end of the semester," said Carlos.

"You also mentioned that Lily had done a 180 regarding her political beliefs. She and another student won the debate defending Communism," continued Carlos.

"That is all accurate, Carlos," replied Arsenio.

"So, you've deduced that Adolfo's new love is Lily, and he is the one who influenced her political beliefs."

"Correct again, Carlos."

"I must say, Arsenio, you have rock solid evidence. Courts have convicted with less circumstantial evidence than that," said Carlos as he laughed.

"Case closed, my friend," emphasized Arsenio, imitating a judge to the best of his ability.

"All right pal, see you soon." Arsenio waved as he slowly walked away.

Carlos waved and started walking in the opposite direction.

As Arsenio approached his building he looked at his watch, that lovely timepiece Ana had given him on their anniversary. He remembered the magic from that night and mentally discarded the bitter ending to the evening. It was 9:15, he had enough time to stop by his office for half an hour and still make it on time to his ten-o'clock class.

He looked up for a moment and noticed additional scaffold, Arsenio could not wait for this work to be completed. The university looked awful with so much scaffold up, dodging it as he walked by was getting on his nerves. As he was about to look down, something occurred that changed his life forever.

The professor heard the crack, but there was no time to react. In the blink of an eye the concrete façade that tore off the building was on him. Everyone on campus within earshot immediately looked in his direction, Arsenio was buried under the rubble, only his lower extremeties were left exposed to the light of day. From his knees up, Arsenio was completely covered by concrete. Within a matter of seconds, well over fifty people surrounded him, all wanting to help.

It didn't take long for the ambulance to arrive, a professor looking out the window from his office called right away. Campus Security arrived within minutes to cordon off the area in order to provide safety for those near the building. Everyone in the building was asked to remain in their offices while the proper authorities investigated and approved an evacuation.

The Fire Department was notified, they were needed to remove the rubble with great care as quickly as possible. Five firemen rushed to the area that covered Arsenio's head, with the proper equipment they removed the debris in under two minutes. He was breathing with great difficulty.

The medical team gave Arsenio oxygen as the firemen worked on the rest of the concrete covering his body. What both teams pulled off that day was nothing short of miraculous. As soon as the firemen finished, the medical team carefully placed him on a stretcher and drove him to the hospital. From the time Arsenio heard the crack of the concrete to the time the ambulance drove off to the hospital a total of 16 minutes elapsed, the efficiency displayed by the men and women who saved his life that day is the reason he is still alive.

The ambulance arrived at the hospital and the team rushed Arsenio to the emergency room with as much care as possible. They understood the importance of maintaining physical stability with minimal movement of the patient, his future depended on it. Should he ever walk again, a special thanks could be given to all those who handled him like a porcelain doll.

The chief surgeon took control of the situation at the entrance as the Ambulance team was rolling in Arsenio. He started updating his intern on Arsenio's situation, time was of the essence. Dr. Carreras, Dr. Gomez and two nurses walked alongside the patient towards the emergency room.

"His left eye is extremely swollen, not knowing the extent of the injury, we must sterilize the area and bandage both eyes," said Dr. Carreras.

"Yes, Doctor," replied Dr. Gomez. Dr. Gomez would assist tonight, but the bulk of what needed to be done was the responsibility of Dr. Carreras.

"We must get him into the operating room, run X-rays, and determine what to do next. Surgery will be needed, what kind is yet to be determined. His upper torso is badly injured, the physical trauma from the accident may have caused some damage to the spinal cord.

Again, the X-rays will determine the steps to follow, but chances are some form of traction will be required," concluded Dr. Carreras.

Dr. Gomez listened intently to everything Dr. Carreras said, not only was this a critical injury, but Dr. Gomez must learn from his mentor. Not all interns were lucky enough to be taught by one of the best in the country, he was conscious of how much he could gain from Dr. Carreras's expertise.

Dr. Carreras was the first of his family born in Cuba, his parents emigrated from Spain around the turn of the century. The turmoil taking place in Spain during the Spanish-American War triggered the move, as was the case with so many other first generation Cubans. When they had their only son, they promised themselves their only child would get everything necessary to become a success - private schools, tutoring, whatever it took. He had been practicing medicine for over thirty years, knowing that he owed his parents the world.

Arsenio was resting comfortably only forty minutes after entering the emergency room. He was administered painkillers intravenously and his oxygen helped him breathe. The experts on the medical team were analyzing the X-rays to determine the next step.

Ana and the two children arrived with Carlos, they were asked to sit in the waiting room as one of the nurses went to retrieve Dr. Carreras.

"Nurse, I must see my husband now. Waiting is not an option!" demanded Ana.

"Mrs. Buendia, I assure you, Dr. Carreras will be with you as soon as is physically possible, he is with your husband now. Your husband is in excellent hands," assured the nurse.

"Ana, everything will turn out fine. Arsenio is one of the strongest men I know, both physically and mentally. If anyone can pull out of this, he can," Carlos consoled her as best as he knew, meanwhile harboring so much fear in his heart for his dear friend. Arsenio was a brother to him, but he must remain strong for Ana's sake.

Minutes later the doctor walked into the room to address the family.

"Mrs. Buendia, I presume?"

"Yes, Doctor," said Ana.

"I'm Dr. Carreras, your husband is now resting with minimal pain. He is receiving pain medication intravenously and is currently sleeping. Oxygen and his medications have put him at ease. We will soon learn the results of the X-rays so that we can determine what the next step is," explained Dr. Carreras.

"Doctor, my name is Carlos and I'm a close family friend. Will he need surgery?"

"Carlos, your friend has been through a lot of physical trauma, chances are good some form of surgery will be needed. I need to wait for the X-rays to say with certainty," responded the surgeon.

"Should it be needed, can we see him before the surgery?" asked Ana.

"I will check up on him once more, if all his vitals are good I'll let you visit him for a few minutes. I must warn you, he has been through a lot. His eyes are completely bandaged as a precaution, his left eye took quite a hit. Your husband is sleeping and will not hear anything you say. Bringing in your two children is up to you," warned Dr. Carreras.

"Thank you, Doctor," replied Ana and Carlos, almost in tandem.

Carlos and Ana pulled the two children aside and warned them of the situation. If they were to see their father now, it would cause too much of an impression, considering the accident had happened only hours before.

"Mom, we can both handle it. We need to see Pops," insisted Angel.

"There is no way anybody will keep me from seeing Daddy today," emphasized Maria with tears streaming down both cheeks.

"Honey, he's going to be fine," Angel assured Maria as he put his arm around her. He was scared to death of never seeing his father again, like Carlos, he kept those emotions to himself. He needed to be strong for his mom and sisters, they needed him now more than ever.

As tears flowed and fear amassed, the concerned family members sat patiently in the waiting room. They had to combat certain thoughts they were having, thoughts of Arsenio never walking again, losing his eyesight, and even thoughts of death. It took someone very strong to win this battle, the mind is a powerful thing. Positivity must dominate, especially considering the dire circumstances.

Alejandro did not immediately hear about the accident, his office was a bit of a walk from the site of the accident. Carlos, as he left the university, instructed a student to get the news to Dr. Martin as soon as possible. Here he was less than an hour after the ambulance, extremely concerned about his friend's well-being.

"Ana, what is the latest news?" asked Dr. Martin as he peeked in the door.

"Alejandro, it's good to have you here. He's resting, they have given him oxygen and intravenous painkillers. His eyes are bandaged as a precaution, his left eye took a bad hit," responded Ana.

Alejandro gave her and both kids a strong hug, he slapped Carlos on the back. They noticed he was on the verge of tears, fighting the urge to cry.

"Dr. Carreras will be his surgeon, should it get to that. Chances are good he needs some form of surgery, the accident was bad," added Carlos.

"Either way, he will be fine," confirmed Ana. "I am sure of that." Her will was strong and her positive nature even stronger.

"Carlos, do me a big favor. Please call Ofelia to update her and make sure Barbara is all right. Ask her to update family members, she'll know what to do," requested Ana as she kissed him on the cheek.

For twenty years she had considered Carlos family, like a second brother in-law. Guillermo and Carlos were both amazing, she knew they would see Guillermo and Nora as soon as they could get to the hospital.

Carlos left the room searching for a payphone, he wished to make this call brief so that he could return to be with the family. He also wanted to be there for any more information the doctor might have on Arsenio. A nurse offered him the phone at the nurse's station.

The phone rang once before Ofelia picked up at the other end.

"Hello, Ana? Is everything all right?" asked Ofelia, lacking breath. She was obviously sitting by the phone, very worried.

"Ofelia, it's Carlos, everything is as good as can be considering the circumstances. Arsenio is resting comfortably right now, he is heavily medicated and in stable condition."

"Oh, thank God. How are Ana and the kids?"

"They are fine, Dr. Martin is here accompanying us. Ana wants you to please call the rest of the family to let them know what has happened," said Carlos.

"I have already called Guillermo and Nora, they just closed the café and are on their way to the hospital. Mercy will also stop by soon," replied Ofelia.

"Perfect, if you can think of anyone else, please call them," requested Carlos.

"Carlos, I don't mind watching over Barbara, but I really want to see him as well," expressed Ofelia.

"Give me a few hours more, I'll leave in the early evening to be with Barbara so that you can visit Arsenio."

"Thank you, Carlos."

By the time Carlos returned to the waiting room, Dr. Carreras was starting his explanation of the necessary surgery. He quietly walked in, stood by Maria's side, and listened.

"Skeletal traction is needed, your husband broke three bones and we will place pins so that those areas heal. It is considered minor surgery. As a doctor I can tell you there is no such thing as "minor surgery". With that said, the risks are few. Once the pins have been placed, he will be in traction for at least one month. I will describe that process and what the next month entails after the surgery," explained Dr. Carreras.

"Are there any questions?"

"Doctor, will he walk normally after rehabilitation?" asked Dr. Martin.

"It is too early to speculate, but he has sensation in his lower extremities. That's a good sign."

"Thank you, Doctor," said Alejandro.

"When can we see him?" asked Ana.

"I promise that as soon as he is stable after surgery, I will let you in. The surgery is scheduled for two o'clock, we should be out by four-thirty. I estimate that by seven o'clock you'll see Arsenio. Fair enough?"

"Yes, Doctor. Thank you so much for everything," Ana said in a whisper. So much had happened in such little time that she felt the life had been sucked out of her.

They sat down, no words spoken, for at least an hour. All of them were mentally exhausted, completely drained of energy.

The human spirit is well equipped to deal with many adverse conditions, uncertainty is not one of these.

Guillermo and Nora arrived when the surgery was halfway through, they entered the waiting room and greeted all who were still there. Dr. Martin had already left, Ana promised to call him as soon as Arsenio came out of surgery.

"We are so sorry about this, Ana. When something like this comes out of nowhere, it makes it more difficult. We spoke to Ofelia, she said that considering how bad it could have been, we should be thankful. Is that true?" asked Guillermo as he said a little prayer.

"The doctor told us he is stable, the surgery is only part of the story. He needs to be in traction for at least one month, I'm in agony thinking about it," expressed Ana.

"One day at a time, Anita. We will all get through this together, I promise. Luisa and I will be with you and help you out anyway possible," said Carlos.

"I know that, Carlos. Believe me, without my family by my side I would not survive this," said Ana, as she fell back onto the couch weeping uncontrollably.

"Uncle Carlos, what should we do?" whispered Maria, teary eyed.

"Honey, sit by her side, hug her, and whisper nice things into her ear. All will be well, I promise."

Nora approached Ana, she sat on the other side of the couch. She had a heart of gold and loved Ana dearly, the thing with Nora was that she wasn't very expressive. Her heart went out to people, her actions rarely expressed her true emotions.

"Anita, say the word and Guillermo and I will do anything. If you want us to take Barbara until the situation improves, say the word. I know you have Ofelia, but we can handle the food for you indefinitely, and if you ever need money to cover hospital expenses that's what we're here for," offered Nora as she smiled and kissed Ana's cheek.

"Nora, I am grateful every day for those surrounding me, you know if I need anything I'll go to you, thank you," responded Ana.

"Ana, who's the doctor? I don't want just anybody treating my baby brother, he's the only one I've got," said Guillermo.

"Nothing to worry about, Guillermo, Dr. Carreras is one of the best. Spinal and skeletal injuries are his specialties, our boy is in good hands," said Ana with a genuine smile.

The mental anguish she felt was immeasurable, she endured the pain as best as she could, mostly for the children's sake.

Ana and Maria fell asleep resting up against each other, the only one still awake in the room was Guillermo. He took the opportunity to take a walk and check up on Arsenio's progress, it was past five o'clock with no word yet. The family had been through so much, he didn't want to wake them.

Minutes after Carlos left the room, Mercy entered. She tiptoed to Ana, they were all asleep. She gently tapped her on the shoulder and they embraced. At this, the others woke up as well.

"Mercy, so good to see you," said Ana.

"I'm sorry it took me so long, I was in an emergency session with a patient. I called the nurse's station a number of times, they've done a wonderful job of keeping me up to date on Arsenio's condition. Is he still in the operating room?"

"Yes, since two o'clock."

"I'm sure they'll finish soon and everything will be fine," said Mercy with an air of confidence.

Guillermo found Dr. Carreras, they both entered the room minutes after Mercy's arrival.

"Doctor, how is Arsenio?" asked Ana as she jumped off the couch.

"The surgery went well, he is in stable condition, you will all see him within the next few hours. As discussed earlier, Arsenio needs traction for at least one month. The bandages are still on, he will regain sight in both eyes. I will return with more details, rest assured we will continue to do all we can. The success we had in the surgery room is only the tip of the iceberg, much more needs to be done, we need to run more tests to determine what permanent damage he sustained, if any. Please be patient, as we get information you'll be the first to know. I'm not going home tonight in order to stay with Arsenio, he needs all my attention at this stage," said Dr. Carreras.

"Thank you, Doctor," said Ana.

They went back to their chairs in the waiting room. Again, few words were spoken. Those holding magazines were going through the motions, flipping the pages served as a relaxer, it gave them something to do with their hands. Two hours of flipping progressed quickly, morning had turned to evening in what seemed like an eternity.

The last twelve hours took on a life of its own, it was a world within a world, on the time continuum it flew by...or did time stand still for the last twelve hours? Ana couldn't decide...maybe it was a little of both.

The clock continued to tick, it was seven o'clock in the evening.

Chapter Eleven
Thirty Days

T he first few days were the most difficult for Arsenio and the family, it was a period of adjustment. Arsenio's mental anguish, however, would worsen as his hospital stay prolonged. The family needed to accept that recovery would be slow, and the efforts needed were immense. Arsenio's task was tremendous, he couldn't move. Everything was done for him, his job was to do *nothing*. Someone as active and self-sufficient as he was would find this the most difficult challenge of all.

Ana stayed with him for days, sleeping in a chair by his side, never thinking of herself. She would talk to him about everything from current events to the children, and read some of his favorite works of fiction. She was saving his history books for a later time.

"Good morning, my love. How are you feeling?" Ana asked, not expecting a response.

"Good morning," responded Arsenio in a painful whisper, to the best of his ability.

The impact had not broken his jaw but caused enough injury to prevent Arsenio from speaking with his usual eloquence, he could barely get the words out.

"Mom, he's obviously in pain. I don't think we should ask him questions, he might cause more damage if he forces his speech," suggested Maria.

"Mouthing short responses at this stage is good for him, I checked with the doctor and he agrees," replied Ana.

"I guess so, Mami."

When lunch came, Ana prepared to feed her husband. Most of his nutrients were provided intravenously, he was fed only liquids and puréed foods. His meals for the next thirty days consisted of only this and no solid foods in order to minimize the risk of movement on Arsenio's part. Digestion was also a problem, being in bed for a month would cause digestive problems were he fed solid foods.

Fear lingered in Ana's heart, understanding that if Arsenio were to move too much, he would end up in a wheelchair for the rest of his life. She and his loved ones would do everything in their power to ensure that doctor's orders were strictly followed.

"Here we go, my love. It's lunch time," said Ana enthusiastically.

She carefully spoon fed him the purée and gave him his drink through a straw. The nurses made sure he was facing up during meal times, turning him upside down to prevent bedsores mostly during the times his family wasn't there or at night.

"How does it taste, Pops?" asked Angel.

"Now you know what foods you'll be eating forty years from now when you have no teeth."

Arsenio smiled for the first time in days. Ana had instructed the children to keep conversation as light as possible, knowing the importance of bringing up Arsenio's spirits.

Nearing the end of the first week, Arsenio realized the difficulty of staying still for long periods of time. The ability to move around, the freedom to do as you please without anything or anyone restraining you can be taken for granted. Sometimes you realize what you have when it's too late, hopefully it is not too late for him. Arsenio prayed every night for his mobility to return.

As Arsenio was finishing lunch, Guillermo walked in.

"This is what I call the good life, my brother! You're in bed and your lovely wife is feeding you," joked Guillermo. He had always been a kidder.

Arsenio looked his brother in the eye and smiled, it still hurts too much to speak.

"Brother, you are looking much better. In no time you'll be passing by the café for your bread and coffee."

"He has improved a lot these past ten days, look at those rosy cheeks ," said Ana, smiling.

"He just has to put in his time and let the healing take place, thank goodness for modern medicine. I love you, brother," said Guillermo, without losing eye contact with Arsenio.

Angel and Maria inched closer to the bed, they wanted to spend some quality time with their father before leaving the hospital. It was late Sunday and they had school the next day. Ana and Guillermo stepped out of the room to leave Arsenio with his children.

Outside the room, Guillermo began to inquire about Arsenio's condition.

"Anita, what is the latest update from the doctor?"

"He's not out of the woods yet, Guillermo. As painful as this is, there is still the chance that he will either walk with great difficulty or never walk again. Traction is a step in the right direction, but no guarantee," explained Ana.

She continued, "We are preparing for the worst and praying for the best."

"I can't argue with that strategy, Ana. I have a good feeling about the outcome, though. If intuition counts for anything, I know all will turn out well," said Guillermo.

"I can't help but feel the same, Guillermo. I just need to prepare my children for the worst, should it come to that."

It was late, all were exhausted. It had been a long, arduous day for the family. Ana promised Arsenio she would go home with the children tonight - the first time she would sleep in her bed in ten days. Eight hours of sleep would do her a world of good, it would allow her to reenergize for the next day.

"Arsenio, are you sure you don't want me to stay?" asked Ana, knowing she needed some rest, but experiencing a sense of guilt by leaving.

"Ana, please go. See you in the morning," responded Arsenio in his laborious whisper.

"All right, my love. I will return first thing in the morning to feed you breakfast. I love you."

"Love you more," responded Arsenio.

"Love you more" was a term all five family members had used as long as they could remember. Its origin was unknown, but it didn't really matter. Arsenio started using it when Angel and Maria were very young, it belonged to them. He probably borrowed the line from a movie, the same way Angel borrowed "Pops" from the Spencer Tracy classic *Father of the Bride*. Elizabeth Taylor, beautiful and talented, called her father "Pops" throughout the entire movie. From that day forth, Angel's dad was "Pops" to him.

The family said their goodbyes and left the hospital, feeling much better than they had only a few days before.

Nightmares don't only happen in your sleep, they can just as easily occur in broad daylight. Arsenio was living a nightmare, strapped to his 7 x 3 device that everyone called a bed. Confinement was the source of his mental anguish, lack of freedom coupled with uncertainty can torment as much as any torture apparatus. He tried under all circumstances to keep these negative thoughts from his family, they had already been through enough. He had survived through almost three weeks, yet he wasn't sure everything would turn out fine.

When given too much time, his mind found ways of occupying itself. Even though his family had been with him, Arsenio felt lonely. His lips didn't have to move, he started talking to himself about his fears and concerns, disliking some of his conclusions.

Prisoners in solitary confinement go through similar experiences, resulting in a number of psychological illnesses such as depression, anxiety, psychosis, and paranoia. The latter two are extreme examples that are exacerbated when the individual is in isolation for long periods of time. Arsenio was experiencing the former two to a great extent.

This was the last of many conversations Arsenio had with himself:

Arsenio:
"Why did I have to walk under that scaffold? Why tempt fate?"

Self:
"Don't blame yourself, there was no way of knowing. Fate cannot be programmed, this will make you a stronger man."

Arsenio:
"Stronger? I'm probably never going to walk again, burdening my family for the rest of my days!"

Self:
"Your family would never consider you a burden. The doctor has said there's a good chance of regaining some form of mobility."

Arsenio:
"*Some form*, that's the key phrase. If I end up with the ability to twitch my nose, his prediction has been validated."

Self:
"The mind will get you through this, approach this as you've approached everything else in your life and you will be fine. Know from the start that you will succeed, know that nothing can prevent you from achieving your goal, whatever it takes. Visualize the end result and do what must be done to get there. *Always remember the power of positive thinking.*"

He was a key player in determining his own future, it wasn't just up to his doctors and family members. They were members of the team, each offering Arsenio whatever they could depending on their expertise, but he needed to contribute.

Without his own full effort, he would never regain the ability to walk. More importantly, he needed to regain the will to live.

This epiphany was instrumental in guiding Arsenio along the way, everything else he did with his life hinged on it. His family was grateful for the insight he experienced that day, a change in his life also reflected on their own lives, their dependence on him was great.

The final week of his stay, Dr. Carreras called all the family members together for a very important meeting, everyone involved understood the importance of this gathering.

"Ofelia, did you call Guillermo and Dora?" asked Ana.

"Yes, they will be here at nine o'clock to pick you up," responded Ofelia.

"Ofelia, as long as Barbara is asleep, stay in bed. I know you haven't been feeling well lately."

"I appreciate that, Mrs. Buendia. I've already made an appointment to see the doctor."

"It's half past eight, I will wait for them outside," said Ana. Her nerves were getting the better of her. She had survived a full month, but this was the moment they had all waited for. She tried to stay positive, telling herself it was good news. That wasn't helping her nerves much.

It was a weekday, Ana insisted that Angel and Maria go to school, she didn't tell them about the meeting. She was really hoping she could surprise them with good news after school.

Guillermo and Dora arrived fifteen minutes early, they too were anxious. They drove to the hospital to find that the others were already present. Carlos, Mercy, Dr. Martin and Dr. Carrasco were all there. It was really sweet of Dr. Carrasco to take time from her busy schedule to be there, it showed what she thought of Arsenio.

Dr. Carrasco had been instrumental in reassigning Arsenio's classes for the rest of the semester when the accident occurred. She had a lot of pull at the university along with a heart of gold. Her son Adlai was the accomplished photographer who had taken Arsenio's anniversary portraits just weeks before, it was great having her there.

"Good morning, Dr. Carreras," Ana said as he entered the room.

Arsenio's family and dearest friends had all gathered to listen to Dr. Carreras. They didn't take their eyes off him, like a felon on trial ready to hear his verdict.

"Folks, you know that Arsenio is nearing the end of his stay here with us. It has been very difficult on him and grueling on you as well," stated Dr. Carreras.

"Yes, doctor," they replied.

He interpreted their brief response, they were beseeching him to explain as quickly as possible.

"Through a process of physical therapy lasting a few months, Arsenio will fully recover," said Dr. Carreras with a big smile on his face.

Everyone hugged everybody else, there were kisses to spare. The warm feeling they experienced was indescribable, for the time being no other worries existed.

"Manolo, thank you for everything," expressed Ana with a huge hug and a kiss on the cheek.

Dr. Manolo Carreras remained a close friend, a member of the family, for the rest of their lives.

Chapter Twelve
An Announcement

Ofelia was getting up to make breakfast for the family. The children were getting ready for school. Arsenio, back to 100%, dressed for work - he was teaching the second summer session. Ana had errands to run and an early lunch date with Nora.

Conversation during breakfast was usually light; the children were still waking up, Ana needed for her coffee to kick in, and Arsenio was mentally preparing for his classes.

"Arsenio, what time do you get home today? I thought it would be nice to go for a drive when the children get home," suggested Ana at the breakfast table.

"I can be home as early as three. Where do you want to go, my queen?" asked Arsenio with a grin.

"I'd love to park near El Malecón and walk towards the ice cream place, you know I'm predictable," responded Ana.

"You just want to walk there and then head back, or are you walking there with a purpose?" jested Arsenio.

"Daddy, we want to eat ice cream first," interjected Barbara.

"He knows, sweetie. One of these days you'll understand his dry sense of humor," said Ana as she jokingly smacked her husband on the back.

They finished breakfast and went their separate ways. Ana took Barbara to school, Maria walked to the high school, and the two men drove in separate cars to the university. Only Ofelia remained, doing the dishes, wishing she could stay in bed all day doing nothing. She continued feeling sluggish. Ofelia made another appointment, this time with a different doctor. She needed to understand why she was feeling this way.

The doctor's office was full, luckily she had an appointment. Ofelia checked in and sat down, there were magazines to entertain her while she waited. Celia's sister recommended this doctor, she said he would answer all her questions and put her mind at ease.

When it was her turn, Ofelia walked in and introduced herself, fearing the diagnosis from the start.

"Hello Ofelia, my name is Dr. Lopez. Please come in and have a seat. I've read the forms you filled out, it's good to see that you are a young, healthy patient. Everything will be all right," said Dr. Lopez, sensing fear in Ofelia's look.

"Thank you for your assurance, Doctor," responded Ofelia. "You are highly recommended."

"That's always good to know," responded Dr. Lopez.

The doctor conducted his examination of Ofelia, making her feel comfortable by talking of things such as her job, family, and interests. He was very good at what he did, Ofelia liked him a lot.

When the examination was over, Dr. Lopez told Ofelia that she would get a call when the results were in.

Ofelia went home and started making an early dinner for the family. They would be home by three and probably wanted to eat before heading out for their drive.

Everyone was home by a little past three, they all appreciated the lunch Ofelia cooked for them. They ate and were on their way, excited about this midweek outing.

After a ride by the ocean they parked near the ice cream parlor, entered the chocolate scented establishment, and sat at the table by the window.

"May I help you?" asked their server.

"Jose, please give us a few minutes," requested Arsenio.

Their server wore a white uniform with red overalls that matched the décor of the ice cream parlor, his plastic tag clearly displayed his name in red lettering with a white background.

"You know what I want," said Ana.

"A chocolate sundae," they all yelled in unison as they laughed hysterically. The few customers in the place must have thought they were nuts.

"Angel, chocolate or strawberry?" asked Pops.

"Strawberry, please."

"I'll take chocolate, Daddy," said Barbara.

"Me too," added Maria.

"Angel, I'll join you with strawberry," said Arsenio.

When Jose returned, Arsenio placed the order. They spent a magnificent afternoon together. After the scare with Arsenio's accident, life took on a whole new meaning for them.

When they got home early that evening, they found Ofelia asleep. They were concerned about her. Ana promised herself she would inquire about Ofelia's visit to the doctor the next morning, for now she let her rest.

Ofelia had visited Dr. Lopez, a gynecologist, thinking that she might be pregnant. She prayed this wasn't the case, being that she had that sexual encounter with Antonio just once and never saw him again. Havana was known for its night life, from nightclubs and shows to couples getting together for one evening, never to see each other again.

Dr. Lopez collected a sample of Ofelia's urine to perform the pregnancy test. A female frog was injected with Ofelia's urine to see if it produced eggs within the next twenty-four hours, this particular frog produced eggs. This confirmed that Ofelia was pregnant, the accuracy of this test was fairly high.

The doctor called the receptionist into his office and asked her to set up a follow-up appointment with Ofelia. He needed to tell her that the test was positive.

The phone rang once, Ofelia picked up before the second ring.

"Hello," said Ofelia as she answered the phone.

"May I speak to Ms. Cruz?" asked the receptionist.

"This is the office of Dr. Lopez," she added.

"Ofelia Cruz, speaking."

"Ms. Cruz, your results are in. You may come in as early as today if you would care to make an appointment."

It was currently eleven in the morning, Ofelia would need at least two hours to prepare and get there.

"May I go at one?" she asked.

"We have that slot available, see you then."

Ofelia left the house at 12:15, giving herself enough time to make it to the doctor's office by 12:50. Ana was still home, she would make up a little white lie if asked where she was going.

As she was out the door Ana caught up to her.

"Ofelia, are you by any chance going to the grocery store?" asked Ana.

"Yes, I'm going to pick up some bread and milk." Ofelia always knew what they needed, this lie was a breeze.

She was feeling quite guilty lying to Ana, but if the test came back negative, why bother telling them about a non-existent pregnancy?

"Please pick up some eggs, I made Arsenio a four egg omelet last night and we're short of eggs," requested Ana.

"No problem, I'll add that to my list," replied Ofelia as she hustled out the door.

The doctor's office was a direct route taking the bus. On the way back she would stop a few blocks short of the house to buy the needed groceries.

Ofelia got to the bus stop and sat down to wait, her mind wouldn't stop. She was very confused, Ofelia always knew she would eventually want a baby. These, however, were not ideal circumstances. The bus arrived, she paid and boarded.

She made it to the doctor's office in twenty minutes. Ofelia walked up to the second floor and checked in at the reception area. Now all she had to do was wait, and think. If she was pregnant, that explained her fatigue and stomach problems. What if she wasn't pregnant? What then? Her physical ailments would be attributed to something else, and that would cause other concerns.

"Ms. Cruz, please step this way," called out the assistant.

Ofelia followed her into the doctor's office and sat by his desk. Minutes later, Dr. Lopez entered the office and sat at his desk. He informed her of the results, not knowing what her reaction would be. After all, Ofelia was a single woman in a predicament most young ladies would not want any part of.

"Doctor, that's what I expected. Please let me know what comes next in terms of follow-up visits, I want this baby to be healthy," responded Ofelia calmly. She surprised herself with her composure, she had predicted quite the opposite in reacting to this news.

"That's great to hear, Ofelia. After every visit, you will go and make an appointment with my receptionist. I will keep her abreast of your progress and she will pencil you in accordingly," said Dr. Lopez.

"Meanwhile, remember that you're now eating and drinking for two. You must consume nutritional foods such as fruits, vegetables, and lots of protein. On your way out you will get a packet with informative material," continued Dr. Lopez.

"Many congratulations and the best of luck, I'll see you soon," ended Dr. Lopez.

"Thank you, Doctor," replied Ofelia, sheepishly.

She was quite ashamed of her pregnancy under these circumstances, the father would probably never meet the baby. All because she had too many drinks and agreed to a one night fling, in a public restroom nonetheless.

Ofelia knew she would have a very difficult time breaking the news to the family, her embarrassment weighed heavily on her.

She got home to find the family there, Ana was the first to approach her.

"Honey, where have you been? We were worried," she stated.

Ofelia had completely forgotten to stop by the grocery store, she was thrown for a loop with the news of her pregnancy.

"And where are the groceries? Is everything all right, Ofelia?" added Ana.

"Mrs. Buendia, we need to talk," whispered Ofelia, forcing out the words.

"Of course, you know we're always here for you. Let's step into the library. Do you want Arsenio to be part of it?" offered Ana.

"Not right now, let me tell you in private first. Only a woman can really understand my predicament," said Ofelia.

Ana knew. That last phrase told her everything she needed to know, Ofelia was going to share something with her that only a woman could understand. Coupled with the fatigue and stomach ailments, Ana deduced that Ofelia was pregnant.

They sat in the leather chairs that were angled, almost facing each other. This was Arsenio's favorite room of the house, he referred to it as his library. Here he would work and read for leisure, losing himself in his library for hours.

"Mrs. Buendia, I'm not proud of what I'm about to tell you. It shames me to be in this predicament."

Ana knew what was coming, she also knew Ofelia took it very seriously and understood her concerns. She only refers to her as Mrs. Buendia at times like these.

"I am pregnant," admitted Ofelia, bowing her head in humiliation.

"Who is the father? I didn't know you were dating," said Ana, trying to hide her disbelief. It affected her that much more having two daughters of her own.

"I'm not dating anyone." Ofelia gulped and took a deep breath before continuing.

"Do you remember the evening you gave me money to go out with my friends a couple of months ago? I met someone that night and had sex with him," added Ofelia. She held back from telling Ana *where* the encounter had taken place, that was too embarrassing for her to admit.

"I never heard from him again," she mentioned, anticipating Ana's next question.

"Well, that's a lot to take in at once. When do you intend to share this with Arsenio and the children, they need to know," explained Ana.

"Ofelia, you intend to keep the baby, right?" she asked, fearing the young girl's response.

"Of course, Ana. I would never consider the alternative."

"Then you should share this news with Arsenio as soon as possible," suggested Ana.

"I'll tell him sometime this week. Thank you for listening and understanding."

"I understand, and we will back you up all the way. I can't say I'm not disappointed in you, Ofelia. I'm as disappointed as if you were one of our children, but all will be well," exclaimed Ana. She wasn't able to look Ofelia in the eye for the duration of this statement, Ana was clearly affected by the news.

Mrs. Buendia's statement and demeanor stung Ofelia like darts being flung at her, she was always trying to impress the family, hungrily striving for their approval. Disappointing them affected her as much as the letdown she felt regarding her own actions.

Ana left the room, contemplating how this would change their lives. As disappointed as she was, she knew this announcement wouldn't change how they felt about Ofelia. The family would help bring up the new addition as if it were one of their own. Ana needed to ensure Ofelia of this.

Ofelia had the conversation with Arsenio the following morning, it was Saturday and the family was home. Ana had not shared it with him out of respect to Ofelia, she felt the future mom should be the one to break the news.

"Dr. Buendia, may I speak to you in private?" asked Ofelia.

"Absolutely," responded Arsenio. "Let's step into my library."

Arsenio was not as shocked as Ana. He knew what it was like to be in your twenties, alert to the dangers of going out in a big city where liquor and sex conjoin in an explosive manner. Ofelia was not immune to that.

He immediately assured Ofelia that keeping the baby would not pose a problem. She could count on medical expenses being covered and assistance from them in bringing up this new family member. He called this a blessing, Ofelia was grateful for those words.

Having left his library after their conversation, Ofelia felt better than ever. Her sense of self and empowerment over the situation had increased exponentially. She was very grateful to Dr. Buendia for that, they truly were family.

Should the anticipated date of birth for her baby be accurate, Ofelia would give birth January 1st, 1959. A New Year's baby, what a glorious day that would be.

Chapter Thirteen
Power of the Press

N ot once, in all the years he had received his daily newspaper, had Arsenio read such a disheartening article, an article that instilled fear in people's hearts and could incite revolution, not that the Castro regime needed any prodding.

The article included facts, as every informational piece has. What upset him about this particular bit of journalistic leniency was the writer's effort to inform the public of future events, lacking basis and using a speculative tone, fully knowing that speculation could cause what most wanted to prevent — revolution. It seemed to Arsenio as if the journalist were attempting to manipulate a situation, one where the volatility of the Cuban government helped magnify the power of the press. Revolutions are fought and won in academia and through the media, Arsenio was experiencing this from both ends. Regardless, the editor was remiss in allowing the publishing of that piece.

Since his accident, he had attempted to stay away from political contemplation, but he saw no harm in inviting Carlos over for some lunch and political debate on this gorgeous Saturday afternoon; he felt good as new. Ofelia would serve them a well-cooked meal and both would later partake of brandy and cigars in his library as they tried to change the world through discourse.

His routine remained the same for many years; Arsenio stepped out to retrieve his newspaper every morning, and returned to his library to read for twenty minutes after breakfast. After skimming through the major articles of the day, he would head off to work. He was not satisfied until he read it cover to cover - on weekends he would read his paper nonstop after breakfast until noon. Arsenio owned a pair of pajamas with little horses on it that he would always wear, his family loved seeing him relax in those pajamas as he read his paper.

Lately, it seemed that political discourse was dominating the contents of the paper like never before. There were political crosswinds, with the anti-Batista communists gaining people's trust through deception. The Fidelistas never claimed the moniker of communists, and they fooled many up to the end.

Arsenio felt a bond with his newspaper, always trusting the print contained within. He had subscribed to El Pais (The Country) for over twenty years. The professor was as conservative as they came, El Pais was the most conservative newspaper in the country. He would pay for his subscription in person with the main headquarters being only a few blocks away.

Most people paid in person hoping to someday win the house the paper gave away monthly. When paying in person, you were given a numbered receipt. Every month, a subscriber walked out of the El Pais headquarters owning a new house. This, along with its journalistic integrity, made it the top Cuban periodical. Arsenio knew what he would do with his prize should he ever be lucky enough to win it, he would transfer the deed to the first of his children to marry.

On this Saturday morning, El Pais gravely disappointed him with that article, a sure sign of things to come. Journalists were no longer referring to the revolution as a possibility, most of the articles referred to it as a certainty.

In 1958, Cuba had four major newspapers. Each paper met the needs for certain niches depending on political beliefs. The following were the major newspapers at the time:

1. Diario La Marina — known for backing up Batista's regime
2. Prensa Libre — objectivity was their main goal

3. Avance – covered many perspectives
4. El Pais – most conservative newspaper

Diario La Marina had bashed Castro and his regime for years, also warning of the possibility of revolution sooner than later. Few took these warnings seriously, they knew the paper was pro-Batista and considered many of those articles hyperbole.

Prensa Libre and Avance had smaller circulations and did a good job of sticking to facts, even though many considered them liberal newspapers, especially when compared to El Pais.

Arsenio continued reading in disbelief.

"My love, are you going to stay in all day? It is lovely out," commented Ana.

"Carlos is dropping by later this afternoon, it's still noon. What would you like to do, my queen?"

"Let's visit Guillermo and Nora, it's been a while. We can sit and chat on their balcony as we enjoy the ocean breeze," suggested Ana.

"Sounds like a plan, give me twenty minutes to get ready," responded Arsenio.

They left the house twenty-five minutes later, driving with the top down. It was a splendid afternoon, offering the right amount of sunlight and an ideal temperature. Ana and Arsenio knew what they had, especially after the ordeal they had experienced. From their family to their socioeconomic status, they appreciated every minute of their lives together. That's what made this morning's article that much more difficult for Arsenio to accept.

"Honey, park by El Malecón for a few minutes, I'd like to get down and enjoy the view with you," suggested Ana. She looked at her husband adoringly, as if they were still newlyweds.

"Si mi niña, cualquier cosa para ti," responded Arsenio, teary eyed. These were tears of bliss and fear, the future frightened him.

His life was so perfect that any threat to its stability or possible

collapse was enough to bring him to this simultaneous state of remi-
nisce and melancholy. He needed to master the skill that so many
seemed to possess, that of brushing things off and letting little bother
them. It was one skill he would never acquire.

They parked the car and started walking along the famed seawall.

"Honey, hold my hand like it's the first time. Do you remember
what you bought me on our first date at El Malecón?" asked Ana.

"I haven't the slightest idea!" joked Arsenio.

"Stop it!" responded Ana, gently punching his chest.

"Guarapo…Guarapo fifty cents…Guarapo fifty cents…" yelled
out Arsenio in a deep voice, attempting to imitate the Guarapo ven-
dors who sold the sugar cane drinks for fifty cents a cup.

"Let's look for the vendor, you're going to buy me one just like you
did on that date."

"I wouldn't have it any other way, my love," whispered Arsenio
lovingly.

They came across the vendor and bought their treats, enjoying
their sweet drinks as they continued their walk down the coast. It
wasn't a very humid day considering it was already August. Arsenio
would soon start the Fall semester at the university. With the election approaching, the upcoming semester was sure to be a hotbed of
stimulating conversations and intriguing debates.

After enjoying their Guarapos, they sat on a bench facing the
ocean. Arsenio couldn't help but share his concerns with Ana.

"Ana, I read a newspaper article this morning that will stay with
me for a long time," stated Arsenio.

"Honey, don't start upsetting yourself over political articles again.
Is that why Carlos is visiting later, to discuss politics? Remember what
the doctor said, the least amount of stress possible," Ana reminded
her husband.

"Anita, I promise I will retrain my nervous system to react differently when encountering differing political views, but I can't cover

the sun with my thumb and pretend something is not there when our government's issues are glaringly obvious."

"I don't want to change you, Arsenio. I only want you to take things less seriously, we want you with us for a long time," said Ana as she stroked Arsenio's hair.

She knew how much he enjoyed that, it had a soothing effect on him like nothing else she could think of. When Arsenio worked long hours, he would consume extra coffee to stay awake. He always paid the price at bedtime, not being able to go to sleep until late into the evening. Sometimes Ana's fingers through his hair was the difference between getting some sleep and no sleep at all.

"Thanks, honey, you're the best. I want you to sit with Carlos and me tonight, we *are* going to discuss politics, as you predicted. I know you're not blind, Ana, it's just that you deal with adversity differently than I do. The current political situation calls for serious decision making. Anyway, we'll talk more tonight. For now, let's enjoy the walk and each other's company. Te amo, Anita," said Arsenio as he stopped to give her a big hug, followed by a kiss that reminded her how much he still adored her.

They continued walking down El Malecón, each one trying to stay in the moment. The contour of their faces suggested a lack of success, both seemed to be in deep thought and very far off.

Carlos arrived at three o'clock, a little before Ofelia was expecting him. But he's family, members of the Diaz Family could show up anytime without invitation. Luisa and Mario each had something to do that evening, so Carlos made a solo appearance.

"Carlitos, we just returned from a wonderful walk," said Arsenio with excitement.

"El Malecón?" asked Carlos.

"Where else, my friend? We each had a Guarapo, I must skip dessert tonight," added Arsenio as he rubbed his belly.

"You're in good shape compared to Adolfo," stated Carlos with a smile.

"I guess I am. Say hello to the family and let's go into the library, I'd like to discuss something with you. I've asked Ana to join us."

"Oh boy, one of those," remarked Carlos with a grin.

"Are you ready for a brandy?" asked Arsenio as they entered the library.

"Maybe later," responded Carlos with a look of confusion. He wasn't sure why Arsenio had requested this meeting.

Ana peaked in and asked, "Honey, do you want to discuss that topic you had previously mentioned now or after dinner?"

"Now is better, Anita. That way we can relax and enjoy the rest of the evening," responded Arsenio. He felt tense.

They all entered, sat down, and made themselves comfortable. Ana was as puzzled as Carlos, wondering what news could be so important that Arsenio decided to close the door. He used to close the door to his library when the children were little, ever since Barbara started going to school he no longer found the need.

"Carlos, what newspaper have I devoted myself to for the last twenty years?" began Arsenio.

"Is that a trick question? El Pais, of course," responded Carlos as he shrugged his shoulders and looked at Ana. They still didn't know what this was all about.

"Correct! Anita, why do I read that paper and no other?"

"Because El Pais is so conservative it makes you look like a liberal."

"You know I don't like the L word in our house, but correct again," emphasized Arsenio.

"Buddy, get to the bottom of it, you're killing us here," pleaded Carlos.

"This morning I read an article in the aforementioned periodical that stated the following, I'll paraphrase:"

"Fidel and his followers could be running the country by Three Kings Day .

If that's the case, many would not need any other holiday gifts because a higher standard of living is gift enough. May we be lucky enough to celebrate the holidays with such splendid news."

"If this appears in the most conservative newspaper, what garbage are they printing in the others? An even scarier question is, how accurate are those statements?" asked Arsenio, trying to stay composed.

"Let me see the article," requested Carlos.

"I burned it!"

"You burned it? Where?" asked Ana.

"Right here!" Arsenio pointed to the small trashcan in his library, the ashes still in the receptacle.

"Arsenio, you're scaring me!" exclaimed Ana with incredulity.

"My love, I'm frightened enough for the two of us," responded Arsenio, trembling at the thought of Castro entering his beloved city.

Chapter Fourteen
Fall Semester

I t's possible to attribute what transpired that semester to the glaring similarities between the boys and their dads or it could be blamed on the political storms that had been brewing for years - its skies promising an inevitable thunderous climax. In any case, nobody in Havana anticipated or was ready for the events that took place that Fall, 1958.

Angel and Mario were really looking forward to the upcoming semester, they had enrolled together in a course on politics. They signed up with a professor other than Dr. Buendia or Dr. Diaz, it was university policy to have family members who attended the university choose non-family faculty as their professors. Like their dads, they were very much into politics and fighting the good fight against communism. It was not in their personalities to sit back and let things happen to them, they were go-getters who believed that through collaborative efforts, positive changes could occur in society.

It wasn't until the third day back that they took their class together, Professor Muñoz had a reputation for being tough but fair. A few students had recommended him to both Angel and Mario, stating that what they liked best was his method of teaching. He wouldn't just stand and lecture for hours, he believed in having students work collaboratively in class and on assignments. Their friends promised them that class with Professor Muñoz would never be dull.

Professor Muñoz resembled their dads in many ways, his political views mirrored theirs, leaving one to wonder whether that benefitted or hindered these young men during such turbulent times. Expressing their beliefs could lead to trouble, especially this close to the election.

This professor, similar to Arsenio in many ways, would have tremendous influence on Angel and Mario — a force that would help shape their destinies.

Angel and Mario met in the cafeteria before Dr. Muñoz's class to have lunch and discuss their expectations for the semester. Angel arrived first and secured a table, Mario came ten minutes later, quickly spotting his buddy.

"Angel, what's up, man?" asked Mario.

"All is well, my friend. I'm looking forward to this class. My dad teaches it all the time," said Angel. He knew that Mario's dad probably taught it as well. Angel felt great pride in knowing his father was one of the top professors at such an esteemed university.

"I registered so long ago I forget the title. What is the name of the course?" asked Mario.

"Nature of Politics. They say Dr. Muñoz teaches with great passion, things must get interesting in there," added Angel as he tapped Mario on the shoulder.

"Are you up to it, buddy boy? My dad says there are heated debates, democracy vs. communism, that sort of thing," said Angel as he playfully winked at Mario. He knew his friend despised public speaking. Mario could write papers endlessly, until his hand started to cramp, but giving a presentation or participating in a debate was not his forte.

"I'll be fine," said Mario. "Stop being a pain, let's get our food. We don't want to be late the first day of class."

"Let's go, pal." Angel put his arm around his best friend as they walked up to get their food. They had two different sets of parents, seeing how they behaved towards each other, one would not have known.

Carlos Márquez-Sterling was a presidential candidate in those upcoming elections of November, 1958. Through speeches and well thought out plans for economic reform, Márquez-Sterling intended to win the hearts and votes of his constituents. He had the experience needed to bring about necessary change, roles that included Speaker of the House and Secretary of Education and Labor. In 1940, he was President of the Constitutional Convention serving as the architect of Cuba's Constitution, drawn up that year.

In stark contrast, Fidel Castro's methods were intertwined with fear and intimidation, illegal actions and deceitful promises were the core of his modus operandi. How could illegal activities give birth to a non-tyrannical leader who would abide by constitutional law? This was the question many posed, clearly seeing the inevitable outcome, one that scared many. Knowing that fear would prevent a large number from casting their ballots that November, the future of the country seemed bleak.

Professor Muñoz would not disappoint, his courses were hands-on, closely tied to current events.

"Angel, over here! We only have ten minutes to cross over to the other side of campus and get to class on time," said Mario, short of breath as he pointed in the direction of their destination.

"Let's go then, buddy boy," responded Angel, as he took off running like lightning. The boys had not changed in ten years, they could still find time for games and playfulness. If only that could last.

As they entered the class, Mario whispered, "Let's sit in the back. That way we can scan all the good looking girls the first few classes and work our way from there."

"All right, Casanova," responded Angel with a wink.

The students' conversations ceased when they noticed the professor enter the class. Without hesitation, he took attendance and gave them their first assignment. Angel guessed that he would share the syllabus and other details with the class at a future date. It was an interesting way of doing things.

"Good morning, students, and welcome to Nature of Politics.

My name is Professor Muñoz, I will teach this class for the next four months. On your way out I will hand you the syllabus for the class, any questions will be addressed at the beginning of next class. Now, let us begin..."

"You have decided to take this course at a pivotal time in our county's history, thus making it imperative to go beyond textbook learning this semester. We will roll up our sleeves and attempt to regain control of our country. Anybody who's afraid of getting their hands a little dirty can drop the course now and save us all some time," continued Professor Muñoz, as he bit his tongue. He wanted to add that all communists or communist sympathizers should also drop the class, but that would have been extreme. He wasn't willing to jeopardize his position at the university - yet.

Francisco, a student with an oversized forehead and a baggy shirt, sitting in the back not far from where Angel and Mario were, courageously asked the first question, "Professor, what exactly do you mean by *getting our hands dirty?*"

"Young man, I'm glad you asked that question. There are those who think that university studies prepare you *for* life, university studies *are* life. Your training this semester will be hands-on, learn while you earn, as I like to say."

"I understand," uttered Francisco, almost under his breath.

It seems this professor needs little input from his students, he's got a course of instruction plotted for this semester and any deviation from it would not be acceptable. I'm able to read into his message, but I'm not sure I like it, thought Angel, sitting pensively at his desk while thinking of the many political conversations he had shared with his dad over the course of the past few months.

Angel had frequently attended his father's courses throughout the years, experiencing presentations and debates. It seemed to him that the professor's comments about this semester's expectations went above and beyond that. Being savvy about the overall political environment, he wasn't sure he felt comfortable with what Professor Muñoz was suggesting they do. If nothing else, his father had warned him to stay away from demonstrating and openly expressing his political beliefs.

Another side of him told him otherwise, preventing drastic changes from occurring in the current government was going to take a herculean collaborative effort costing much sacrifice and incalculable man-hours. Every individual was important in this battle, this struggle would determine the future of the country.

"What do you think of our first assignment?" asked Mario in disbelief, as he and Angel walked down the stairs.

"It's a little more than I expected, but I'm up to the task. We must get involved, Mario. If Márquez-Sterling doesn't win the election, the whole future of our country is up for grabs," emphasized Angel, sounding more like his father every day.

"With the elections two months away, all groups are attempting to sway voters utilizing strategies available to them. According to some articles, the rebels must keep Márquez-Sterling from winning the election in order to have a chance at toppling the current government. We must do everything within our power to procure his victory, continued democracy for us is contingent on that," convincingly argued Mario, taking hold of his briefcase with his left hand and laying it on a bench. It was only the first week of school, but already he noticed a fairly large gathering at the other end of campus with protestors wielding signs the two young men could not decipher from this distance. Mario's respite was brief, Angel suggested their first move.

"It seems to me like those students got a similar assignment to ours, we should take a closer look." As Angel stated this, he felt an adrenaline rush like never before. His sensory nerves perceived an environmental threat, thus sending a warning. *Fight or flight* is the common

term used to describe this defense mechanism available to our ances-
tors many years ago to warn of imminent danger. Millenniums ago
the dangers consisted of animals such as lions and wolves, currently
the danger is a pack of wolves dressed in sheep's clothing.

As they approached, they noticed the group was smaller than
originally perceived. All students held signs, each stated something
different, but the message was clearly the same. Their aim was chill-
ingly clear, their unity frightening – this was the communist party
demanding change.

Among the signs proudly displayed by the protestors were the
following:

Monetary excess for few, poverty for most, costs lives
Capitalism leads to obscene wealth for few, poverty for most
Communism leads to equality

The demonstrators' chanting could be heard half way across the
campus:

Share the wealth!
Share the wealth!
Share the wealth!

Suddenly, it started raining tomatoes on the demonstrators. Their
trajectory indicated they were coming from behind the bushes, raining in like bright red grenades that exploded with a "whoosh" on the
communist protestors. What started out as a peaceful protest was
likely to turn violent. Angel and Mario escaped, just before the police
swooped in.

Batista's regime implemented a zero tolerance policy, he needed to appear impartial, pro-communists and anti-communists alike
were prosecuted to the full extent of the law. His argument was that

demonstrations were likely to get physical, thus endangering the welfare of innocent people. He needed to create a strong front, one that would get the communists to back off. To most, this strategy seemed to be of little consequence to what would play out in the following months.

It was as clear as daylight to both boys that the tide had turned, communism had grasped a hold on the population. For years the communist party had attempted to successfully infiltrate everyday society, and it seemed to be well on its way.

"How many times have our dads gotten together to discuss politics, predicting this outcome? This is scary, Angel. Something must be done to counter these lies. Now I see why Professor Muñoz gave us this first assignment," stated Mario solemnly. His tone indicated a defeat of sorts, his body language quite the opposite.

"Let's set a date, draw up pamphlets, and begin promoting our demonstration. Both sides must be heard. Let's go to my house tonight to discuss strategies, our parents must know nothing of what we are doing," demanded Angel in a firm tone, preaching to the choir. Angel's determination was clear, he seemed to be less intimidated by this project than Mario. His friend's heart was in the right place, but fear prevented him from fully giving himself to the cause.

"Students, we find ourselves two weeks into the semester and a few of you are missing assignments. I must remind you of the importance of handing in work on time, deadlines must be met to get full credit. For today's assignment, you may hand in your papers after the group exercise. If those assignments are still missing by Friday, you will get zeroes. It is on you to remember, constant prodding to work should not be necessary at the collegiate level," said Dr. Buendia, who's frustration level was at an all-time high. He had grown accustomed to the fact that there would always be students who slacked, lacking drive and the innate ability to excel at higher education, but this semester it was about something else. Something bigger than the good professor and education itself was on the line, he wasn't accustomed to feeling out of control.

Arsenio, Carlos, and Adolfo met at their usual spot in the café. They had all been so busy the first couple of weeks, this was their first get-together this semester.

"Gentlemen, what's the good word?" asked Arsenio, attempting to disguise his discontent with the way the semester had started off.

"What's wrong, Arsenio?" inquired Carlos, already knowing the response.

"Nothing, why do you ask?"

Carlos responded with laughter. "We have known each other for over twenty years, and you've always worn your heart on your sleeve, my friend. Mario says Angel is an exact replica of you, we talk about it all the time."

"Talking behind your friend's back, are you?" Arsenio jokingly winked at Carlos, feeling better already. There was nothing like talking to his *brother* to relieve stress. He didn't want to discuss the source of his concerns in front of Adolfo, Carlos sensed this and changed the topic of conversation.

"Adolfo, how's your love life?" asked Carlos, dropping the ball on Adolfo's lap.

"Would you like the short version or a detailed response?"

Arsenio and Carlos looked at each other and smiled, "The short version," they responded in unison.

"Gentlemen, if all goes as planned, you and your lovely families will attend a wedding late spring, 1959. There will be much to celebrate, I'm getting married," stated Adolfo, wondering how his friends would respond.

"I will ask the obvious, aren't you already married?" asked Arsenio.

"That's temporary, my friend. I'm working on it, the divorce should be finalized by February. Then I will be free to marry the love of my life."

"What is the young lady's name?" asked Arsenio.

"Who said she was a young lady? Has someone told you something?"

"Have you ever been attracted to any type of women other than young ladies?"

Adolfo laughed, he seemed thrilled, maybe this woman really was the one.

"Her name is Lily, I think she had you for a course, Arsenio. As a matter of fact, I know she did. During dates she would brag about how well she was doing in your class." At this point, Adolfo was purposely antagonizing Arsenio. They were bound to get into an argument, he wanted to be on the offensive.

Arsenio took a deep breath before his next question, his face was red and the wrinkles on his forehead multiplied, "When did you start dating her?" he asked.

"March 2nd I took her out for dinner and we fell in love within a week."

"That explains the debate last semester," whispered Arsenio to himself, louder than he had intended.

"She was so proud of her work, winning that debate with Rebecca meant the world to her," said Adolfo.

Infuriated, Arsenio raised his voice as he posed his next question, "Was it her work or yours that helped her win that debate?"

Smugly, Adolfo answered honestly. He was blunt in his response, no longer caring about his "friend's" feelings. His earlier invitation to the wedding was only for effect, Adolfo wanted neither one of his colleagues at his wedding, a joyous event that would hopefully take place under a new, better regime.

"She did the work, I provided the inspiration."

"Brother, take it easy. Don't let this bastard affect you this way, you look like a volcano about to erupt. Let's get out of here." Carlos guided Arsenio out of the café, he was clearly affected by Adolfo's words. It wasn't losing the friendship that affected him, that had been a two-legged stool for months. The thought of Adolfo brainwashing a young, innocent student is what drove him mad.

"It seems this whole world is going to hell," shouted Carlos as they exited the building. That sentiment said a lot, Carlos was usually the more positive of the two.

Ten days of recruiting paid off, Angel and Mario now had a small army of over 100 students ready to defend democracy on a campus that seemed to be split on which type of government reigned supreme in people's hearts. Angel could never back down from a good political battle. His mom referred to him as Arsenio's clone, if not physically, most definitely every other way.

"Angel, we have scheduled our demonstration for next week. Believe me, I understand the importance. However, I don't want to get arrested like those demonstrators from almost two weeks ago. Teresa told me that those students have permanent records, that follows you around forever," concluded Mario, almost hanging his head in shame. He wished he would have it in him like Angel, fear was still creating a barrier preventing him from acting as his heart told him he should.

"Mario, I understand how you feel. I'm not immune to fear, brother. If you feel you need to back out, I would understand and would never hold that against you. Think it over, it needs to be your decision." Angel responded instinctively and from the heart. He too was afraid of consequences, but this was an opportunity he couldn't pass up, doing *nothing* was not an option. He needed to voice his opinion and represent those who thought as he did.

"I would never let you put your life at risk alone. You know you can count on me, we will go through this together. I'm certain, just needed to voice some concerns." Mario's tone was convincing. Angel felt satisfied that Mario had decided on his own, he didn't want to push his buddy into doing something against his will.

"We've been through a lot together, my friend. Do you remember the time we decided to skip school and go to the Havana-Almendares game instead? We got into so much trouble for that, but we got through it together. That will always be the case," said Angel with a smile and some perspiration appearing on his cheek.

"Can't we just skip school and catch a game instead of going ahead with the demonstration?" joked Mario, winking at his mate.

"I'm not letting you off that easily, buddy boy."

"We have sixty signs, approximately one per couple. Everyone has been notified of the time and place, they've also been advised to keep this under wraps. We wouldn't want anything interfering with such an important demonstration. Remember, we're less than two months away from the elections," reminded Angel, as if someone as conscientious as Mario needed reminding. Carlos was as involved in politics as Arsenio, conversations in his house were as frequent as those in the Buendia household.

"What else needs to be done?" asked Mario.

"We wait. Wait and pray. Next week, on the day of the demonstration, we will meet in the parking lot by Fernando's van where the signs will be. The plan is to demonstrate by Alma Mater in front of the university, exposure to pedestrians and those driving by is crucial. Our message must be universal," emphasized Angel.

"How much have we raised for bailouts?" Mario's question came with a tremor in his voice, he seemed to understand the danger of having a permanent record more than Angel.

"We've reached almost $800, that's a decent amount of money for now. If there are any arrests, it's doubtful the amount needed will be more than that." Angel noticed the look in Mario's eyes, he would talk to him later to reassure him about what was going to take place.

The outcome was very much in doubt, the strenuous effort against the opposition might just be too little, too late.

That morning, Angel awoke at a quarter past five. His adrenaline pumping, he showered and dressed within forty-five minutes. The note he left his parents on the coffee table said he was inundated with school work and was going to meet Mario to get an early start on their assignment, phrased this way it was more fact than fiction.

They met in the parking lot at seven and waited for Fernando; without him this would be a fiasco. All the signs were stored in his van, if they were to do it over again they would choose a neutral location for storing the signs. What if Fernando gets cold feet or gets sick?

He pulled into the lot minutes after Mario and Angel met. This was the moment of truth, the demonstration *would* take place. The consequences were unknown.

"Everything is going as planned, the rest know the meeting place is by the van no later than nine o'clock. We will instruct them to sit on benches or on the grass with open books until it's time. For all anyone knows, we are a group of students studying for an exam. We must not attract attention, nobody can know we are all together. The three of us will stand at three different locations within a fifty-foot radius of the van to welcome the others and guide them. Understood?" asked Angel in a friendly yet serious tone.

Angel continued, "By nine o'clock we must all have our signs and begin marching as we chant our slogan. We should start by Alma Mater and go down the steps leading to the street, exposure to rush hour traffic is important. Hopefully the media will hear of this early on and appear no later than ten o'clock. Cameras must be here when arrests are made."

"Let's grab something to eat at the café down the block, by the time we get back to the van I'm sure some of our comrades will start showing up," suggested Mario.

"Sounds good, but we can't take too long," added Francisco. He was quickly becoming an integral part of the team. They met him last semester and he had thus far proven his dedication towards their cause.

By a quarter past eight they had returned to campus, feeling like baseball players before a playoff game. They knew they would be fine once the big event commenced, but the anticipation was great and their adrenaline was flowing.

As the demonstrators arrived, they received their instructions from one of the three leaders along with a sign. They had been warned it was first come first serve for the signs.

These students were dedicated, there were over eighty present by 8:30. They were expecting approximately 120, that was 40 more than those who had demonstrated for the communists a few weeks before.

If only my parents would know what I'm up to, thought Angel. He didn't know whether his father would be upset or proud, maybe a little of both.

Before they knew it nine o'clock was upon them and it was time to march. All 123 present decided to march together for impact, going against the recommendation of some to split up in order to cover more ground. They started along the front of the campus as planned:

Democracy and freedom for all! Márquez-Sterling is our man.
Democracy and freedom for all! Márquez -Sterling is our man.
Democracy and freedom for all! Márquez -Sterling is our man.

People driving by spotted the protestors immediately, it was a sunny day with little humidity, many convertible tops were down and windows open. Along the street, cars honked their horns relentlessly. Most of Havana from the very start of the march was electric with honking and chanting.

They continued walking in double file, meandering around the campus like a snake after its prey. Their force and determination impressed, creating an impact on all who witnessed the march. Those watching and listening appreciated the efficiency with which they progressed and conveyed their message, their chant clinging to the hearts of most who heard.

They continued with the resoluteness of a heavy weight boxer who knows this is his last chance at the championship.

Democracy and freedom for all! Márquez -Sterling is our man.
Democracy and freedom for all! Márquez -Sterling is our man.
Democracy and freedom for all! Márquez -Sterling is our man.

As they rounded the corner their chant was muffled by what they saw and heard, a group of at least sixty students walking towards them chanting as well.

Communism and equality for all!
Communism and equality for all!
Communism and equality for all!

"Angel, how did they find out about our demonstration? This can't be a coincidence," yelled Mario, trying to get Angel's attention over all the noise.

"It isn't a coincidence, one of ours must have leaked it to them," responded Angel, using the sixth sense he possessed. He was astute in many ways, especially when it came to quickly piecing things together.

"What do we do?" asked Mario and a few others, looking to Angel for leadership.

"Continue to march, chanting louder than ever!" responded Angel like a general leading his men into battle.

Democracy and freedom for all! Márquez -Sterling is our man.
Democracy and freedom for all! Márquez -Sterling is our man.
Communism and equality for all!
Communism and equality for all!

Louder and louder, closer and closer.

Democracy and freedom for all! Márquez -Sterling is our man.
Communism and equality for all!
Democracy and freedom for all! Márquez -Sterling is our man.
Communism and equality for all!

All the nerves settled, they were focused on the task at hand. Not one backed down.

Proximity to their foe served as a reminder of the importance of their mission. The closer and louder, the clearer they saw. It became a frenzy where thinking was no longer needed, both groups clashed with brute force, hatred for each other's ideologies guided their actions. Only natural weapons were needed, fists flew wildly and bodies fell. Sirens were heard in the distance, police came down on them within minutes.

Students from both sides began running from the police, with so many students and so few law enforcement officials, getting away was easy.

Mario yelled to Angel, "What do we do?"

Angel responded, "Don't run, stay firm in the face of danger. We are leading this cause, we must not run."

Someone who witnessed it from an airplane as it approached for landing was quoted as saying:

"It was surreal, there were people running in every direction. Without sound it felt like I was watching a scene from a silent film where the world was coming to an end."

In total there were 29 arrests, 19 demonstrators from Angel's group and 10 communist protestors. Angel and Mario were arrested, Francisco got away.

Those arrested were taken to the station, most of them in a police van that held almost twenty demonstrators. There was a large holding area where the students were placed as they booked each one individually, a number of officers were working on this to expedite the process. Angel could sense that Mario was starting to panic, he would have to be the rock for his friend.

"Angel, do you know what a permanent record means? We are adults, not children!"

"Mario, you must stay calm. This is part of what it takes to demonstrate effectively. This will make the news and the public will understand the importance of voting for the right candidate next month. All will be well, my friend. I guarantee it." Angel's reassurance soothed Mario a bit, his belief in Angel was such that he looked up to him like an older brother, though they were the same age.

They had processed most of the students before getting to Angel and Mario. Angel had done his best to keep Mario distracted by discussing happier times, there were many from which to choose, being blessed with a friendship known to few.

"Next," called the officer in charge of booking, pointing to Mario. "Please step over to desk #4, the officer will book you. Once the paperwork is complete, you may call someone to bail you out."

Bail me out?...thought Mario. That phrase disgusted and frightened him tremendously.

"I'm Officer Gonzalez, I will ask you some questions. Let's start with your name."

"Yes sir, I'm Mario." His attempt at hiding the fear and intimidation he was currently experiencing failed miserably, his lip quivered and he shook uncontrollably.

"Do you have a last name, Mario?" asked Officer Gonzalez, expressing some empathy as he concealed his annoyance, these demonstrators had brought on a lot of extra paperwork within the last few weeks.

"Mario Diaz, sir."

Officer Gonzalez asked everything that was required. When he finished with Mario, another official took him to the holding cell. The next group of students came to be processed. The officer at desk #4 recognized Angel immediately.

"Angel, why are you involved in these demonstrations?" he asked in a discreet whisper.

"Don't you know the dangers involved?" continued Officer Gonzalez, shaking his head.

"Yes sir, I do. But at the time I felt the risk was worth the potential reward, saving our country from communism and possible tyranny. It will take much concerted effort on the part of many," stated Angel as humbly as possible, not able to contain the pride he felt in defending his political beliefs.

Officer Gonzalez shook his head again, this time with more emphasis than before, "Angel, you are identical to your old man!" stated the officer, cracking a smile.

"That's what my mom says." He responded with the shadow of a smile.

Ruben Gonzalez and Arsenio had known each other for over thirty years, they were friends in high school. Both grew close through playing baseball in school. Arsenio pitched and Ruben made most calls as his battery mate. Ruben was known as one of the best catchers in Havana, a bad back prevented him from continuing. They lost touch after choosing different careers, though they would periodically mail each other family photos.

"Angel, I'm calling your dad so he can pick you up. This never happened. Don't let me catch you back here again! Understand?"

"Yes sir. Is there anything you can do for my good friend?"

"Has he been booked?"

"Yes, Mario Diaz came just before me," responded Angel with a hopeful tone.

"I'm sorry, I can't undo paperwork. If you would have come before him then I could have helped you both," whispered Officer Gonzalez. He was breaking protocol by dismissing someone without completing the appropriate paperwork, that was grounds for termination.

"I understand," said Angel, hanging his head. He got off without a record and he wasn't able to do anything for his friend. It was his idea to hold firm and get arrested for the cause, now it was Mario paying the price. It didn't seem fair. That feeling of helplessness would follow him around for many years.

That day was engraved in Angel's memory, a snapshot in time that never ceased to haunt him.

The week before the elections, news spread around the country of Castro's plans to sabotage them through any means possible, among them threatening voters with physical harm and bombing chosen locations to show he meant business. This was terrorism of the worst kind, for there were many in the Cuban community who believed in him, at least for the time being. The lines were drawn and those voting for Márquez -Sterling risked their lives, terrorism at the polls was fully expected. The battle weary went to vote, nonetheless, understanding all that was at stake. Márquez -Sterling had won the hearts, trust, and votes of the Cuban people.

Most voted with their hearts, even though the rebel intimidation was great. The Cuban public had done what was asked of them. Fraud, however, made its appearance and overtook their efforts. The candidate who had rightfully won the elections never took control, his was a fate that affected millions. This seemed to be the beginning of the end. All anyone could do after those fraudulent elections was sit and wait, the religious prayed more than usual.

Chapter Fifteen
December, 1958

O ver two months elapsed since the demonstrations had taken place, the semester was almost over, and the holiday season was upon them. Ofelia was bigger than ever, very excited that her baby would soon make an appearance, forever grateful that she worked for a family willing to back her up in such a difficult, yet joyous time. She had approached this well, with the understanding that the father would most likely be out of the picture, Ofelia was ready and willing to play the dual role of mother and father, doing everything in her power to bring up a healthy, happy child. Arsenio had put her mind at ease, ensuring that all would be well. December was sure to be a busy month, all were hoping for the best.

Angel enjoyed sleeping late on weekends, this Saturday was one no different than any other; he slept until ten o'clock with intentions of going to a movie with Beatrice Rosario later that day. Beatrice was better known as Chary, many women with Rosario as their name, first or middle name, were usually called Chary; this had been the case with Beatrice Rosario since birth. She didn't enjoy going to the movies as much as Angel did, but she enjoyed pleasing him and he enjoyed the popcorn, *sometimes he would even share*. It had taken some convincing on his part, they were going to see *The Young Lions*. Ever since he had gone with his Pops to watch *From Here to Eternity* a few years before, Montgomery Clift had become one of his favorite actors.

They first met during the demonstrations and were drawn to each other from the start. His self-assuredness drew him to her, his green eyes helped the cause, and his personality sealed the deal. She had hazel eyes, an amazing smile, and a heart of gold. From the start, they felt as if they had known each other for much longer than was the case, their similarities were uncanny, and conversation flowed with ease.

Chary's impact on Angel was noticeable to all at home, especially mom — a mother always knows. He helped more around the house and complained a lot less. Love was in the air. In the short period they had been dating, every time they got together presented another opportunity to put aside their cares and focus on the one thing that mattered most - enjoying each other's company and strengthening a newly formed relationship that showed much promise.

His mom was the one to retrieve the mail that morning, their house was the first on the post carrier's route. Usually by no later than ten-thirty they would have their mail. She called Angel to give him the envelope that had arrived for him.

He immediately noticed two things: the sloppily printed handwriting and lack of return address. There was his sixth sense acting up again, something seemed off. He opened the envelope, his curiosity piqued as he ironed out the paper. Again, the message was printed out with the same sloppy handwriting that appeared on the envelope, he got the feeling it was purposely done to remain anonymous. The message was as brief as it was disturbing:

There was a leak in our group

The communist demonstrators were tipped off by Francisco

"What? It can't be, this must be a mistake," spoke Angel in a loud, bewildered voice.

"Angel, is everything alright?" asked mom.

"Yes mother, everything is fine." He needed to share this with Mario as soon as possible, he knew his friend would be as surprised as he was, they had taken in Francisco as one of their own.

Angel arrived at Mario's house in record time. The latest news about Francisco's actions put a new spin on things.

"Mario, I received an anonymous message in the mail stating that

Francisco was the one who leaked the news of our demonstration to the communists," said Angel, as calmly as he could.

"That's unbelievable! We knew there was someone who had betrayed us, I would have never guessed it was Francisco. Angel, he possesses a lot of information that could be damaging to us and our families." Mario paced back and forth, attempting to breathe rhythmically as he pondered potential repercussions for the blind faith they had placed in someone they barely knew.

"This act on his part might have severe consequences, but we must stay calm. Maybe it will all pass, even if the communists take over," argued Angel.

"From your mouth to God's ears, my brother."

"I have a feeling we will never see him again. After that day he has been nowhere to be found on campus. It is likely he registered for a few courses the last couple of semesters to gain access to university events such as political demonstrations. My dad has warned me of communist infiltrators and their ways." Angel was looking for an explanation, he was getting close to Fernando, his new friend's actions surprised him.

This was too much for Mario to take in all at once, he was still trying to wrap his mind around the idea that these demonstrations had cost him a couple of nights in jail and possibly a record for life, so he attempted to change the topic.

"How is Chary?" asked Mario, trying to provide a genuine smile. His grin lost the battle, the bitter information Angel had just shared crushed what little attempt he made at bringing himself back from his feeling of despair.

"She's doing well, tonight we have a movie date, *The Young Lions*."

"The new Montgomery Clift flick? Nice, I'm a Bogart fan myself." Even though it was before his time, *Casablanca* was one of Mario's favorite movies. The ending to that movie was like no other.

"She graduates in the spring, Chary can't wait to start teaching.

With the patience of a saint and her love for children, she will be an amazing teacher," said Angel. The love-struck teenager enjoyed boasting about his girl, he had experienced infatuation before, but nothing like what he had with Chary.

"I'm so happy for you, buddy. Hopefully someday soon I will find someone who does for me what she does for you."

"You will, my friend. I guarantee it," responded Angel with a sense of pride. He knew how extraordinary Mario was, any girl would be very lucky to have him.

Anxiously approaching the driveway, Arsenio dreaded what was to take place in his home that evening. It was Saturday night, he was returning from Guillermo's, and all family members had agreed to break their plans for the evening. This family gathering was sure to be etched in their memories for the rest of their lives.

It took him almost a minute to get in, the key shook in his hand making it difficult to open the door. His mind was running wild, not knowing which end was up. These were uncharted waters for Arsenio, the focus with which he completed tasks, minor and complex in nature, had earned him a reputation as someone who could be approached in times of need. His advice was always sound.

Upon entering his library he poured himself a brandy and settled in for the task at hand, one that sickened him. His family's safety was primary, that alone prevented him from second guessing his decision. His family entered his library, all except Barbara, who was sound asleep upstairs.

"Pops, I was going out to eat with Chary tonight, how long will this take?" asked Angel, who had a good idea what this meeting entailed.

"You'll survive, Angel. How was the movie last week?"

"Amazing, Brando actually convinced me he was German and Clift gave an amazing performance, as expected. We should go see it together," suggested Angel, noticing the gloomy look on his father's usual cheery face.

"That sounds nice, son. I'd like that." Arsenio's melancholic tone could not be disguised.

"What's up, Pops?"

"Go get Maria and you mother, son."

It's funny how your choice of words reveals inner feelings. Arsenio had referred to Angel as "son" twice within seconds, this indicated there was something very wrong. It was his way of reaching out to Angel, letting him know how much he loved him. Arsenio's heart was breaking, this was obvious to anyone who knew him well.

Arsenio and Ana sat in the two leather chairs, and the siblings on the sofa. He began his speech, trying to maintain his composure.

"I've spoken to your mother about the topic we will discuss tonight and..."

"Daddy, what is it? Please cut to the chase," interjected Maria.

He approached using a different strategy.

"There is a battle currently taking place in Santa Clara where the rebels are doing exceptionally well. Their ultimate goal is to control the capital, once they take over Havana, the government will topple and they will seize control of the country. If things go well for us, we could hold them off until late spring. That is a best case scenario. Cuba will fall to the communists, sooner than some think."

"What does that mean for us?" Maria asked, rattled by this news. She was not fond of politics, this news scared her.

"Aldo has set up an apartment for us in New York, your mother will leave with the three of you while I stay behind and get our finances in order. The house is already up for sale, hopefully it sells soon." Tears streamed down Arsenio's cheeks, the last time this occurred had been nine months earlier at Tropicana.

"I will not leave Chary behind!" blurted out Angel.

"Angel, I know how fond you are of her. She is a wonderful young lady, hopefully we will be back someday. Please focus on your father's plan, it might be the only way to stay together and maintain our freedom," said his mom.

"I'll stay with Dad, I'm sure he could use my help," suggested Angel.

"That is out of the question, I'll stay alone. It is too dangerous," shot back Arsenio.

Angel left the library, heartbroken.

"Mom, isn't there the chance that the rebels will lose?" asked Maria.

"Sweetheart, there are rumors that Batista is gathering his assets in preparation for the eventual downfall. Once Márquez -Sterling lost, all hopes were lost for maintaining a democratic government. I'm sure the rebels celebrated that day, his loss was their gain, a gain obtained through intimidation and fraud." Her father was so affected by this he could hardly end his statement, he was really shook up.

"Oh my God!" exclaimed Maria.

Angel stepped back in.

"How about Mario and his family, are they leaving too?" he asked.

"They are making similar plans to go to New York," ensured Arsenio.

"Son, I will talk to Chary's parents. They must understand the urgency of the situation. Considering the circumstances, I predict a major exodus within the next few years," remarked Arsenio.

"Carlos has the means to financially support his family during these difficult times, I will help Chary's family as much as possible," he added, knowing that in only a couple of months Angel and Chary had grown very close.

"When are we leaving, Dad?" asked Maria, convinced this was a drastic yet necessary move.

"Right after Three Kings Day. Travel during the holidays would not cause suspicion should anyone be on the lookout by that time."

Has it been a year since the altercation with Adolfo? Time really flies by, I wonder what he's up to, thought Arsenio.

The screams woke everyone up, it was a little past three in the morning and all was still. Arsenio picked up the Yankees baseball bat Aldo had sent him for Christmas, since moving to New York he had celebrated both Christmas and Three Kings Day. He ran downstairs hoping that he wouldn't have to use his new Mickey Mantle bat.

"Honey, be careful," shrieked Ana, not sure whether to call the police or wait.

He noticed the screams were coming from Ofelia's room. As he readied himself for combat, he heard her say:

"The baby is coming, please help. I need to get to the hospital, I'm ready to explode!"

Arsenio is not accustomed to cursing, but at that moment he yelled out a few choice words.

"Ana, come down quickly, Ofelia is going into labor. We must take her to the hospital!"

Ana ran downstairs and checked on Ofelia. It could very well be a New Year's baby after all, here they were on December 30th and she was ready to give birth.

"Arsenio, get dressed and I'll help you take her to the car. I'll contact Luisa so she can come and stay with the children, as soon as she gets here I'll take Angel's car and meet you at the hospital."

Between Arsenio and Ana they walked Ofelia to the passenger seat of Arsenio's car, each holding one arm in case Ofelia were to slip. They made it to the car just fine, the contractions seemed to subside, Ofelia was breathing easier and seemed to relax a little.

"I'm feeling better, but I'd still like to head out to the hospital now just in case," she suggested.

"Of course, honey. We wouldn't have it any other way. You're at ease now because your contractions seem to be spaced apart. When I gave birth to Angel it took two days, he didn't want to come out. He's still lazy, just take a look at his room," said Ana, introducing levity to the situation.

"Two days?" This shocked Ofelia.

"Honey, I wasn't pushing and in pain for two days. It just means that from the first contraction to the time of birth it took two days. Don't worry, you'll be fine," explained Ana in a soothing voice.

"All right."

"Ana, we must go. I love you, see you later." Arsenio entered the car, started the engine, and drove off. He was very excited, in a way he considered this his first grandchild.

What seemed like hours later, it actually took less than 20 minutes from door to door, Arsenio drove up to the emergency room entrance and explained the situation. An assistant rolled out a wheelchair for Ofelia, she was at ease now. They rolled her in as Arsenio parked the car.

After a brief registration, the doctor stepped into the emergency room and began asking questions.

"Hello Ofelia, I am Dr. Sanchez, I heard you went through a bit of pain this morning."

"Doctor, I have never experienced that much pain, it felt like I was going to explode."

"When is your due date?"

"January 1st," responded Ofelia with a smile. She couldn't wait to hold her baby.

"Very good, a nurse will come by to set you up with an intravenous drip," said Dr. Sanchez.

"Doctor, what's that? Is everything all right with my baby?" Ofelia sounded concerned, she had never heard of this before.

"I assure you, everything is fine. We are going to connect a needle to your vein and provide you with medicine and nutrients through it, it's not as bad as it sounds."

"All right, Doctor. Thank you."

Later that afternoon, Arsenio and Ana got an update on Ofelia's condition. All was going very well. Considering the due date, they were going to keep her in the hospital until she gave birth. Nobody wanted to risk sending her home only to have a repeat performance from earlier that day. Everyone agreed it was safer this way.

When they got home that evening, the children were very disappointed. They had expected the baby, but they would have to wait. Hopefully Ofelia would give birth the 1st of January and the New Year's baby would bring with it much luck for 1959.

Chapter Sixteen
Explosive New Year

Their custom was to celebrate New Year's Eve at home with the children and close friends - always with Carlos, Luisa, and Mario. They had gone to Tropicana a few times with Carlos and Luisa, this year they would definitely stay home awaiting the call from the hospital. The family got permission to visit Ofelia past midnight, Carlos and his family were going to surprise her as well.

Ofelia did most of the cooking, but everyone appreciated Ana's culinary skills, she too possessed the talent to delight the palate. Her specialty was Arroz con Pollo (Chicken with Rice), she would purchase only breasts and drum sticks. Her recipe included all the usual condiments with a little extra beer to add flavor. Arsenio was fond of the cheapest beers available, he always argued that the cheaper the beer, the better the taste.

Arroz con Pollo was on tonight's menu, with the cheap beer and undercooked just enough so that it would resemble a combination stew with rice. If the rice dried up too much the dish would lose much of its flavor.

"Mom, it smells great! May I have some? I'm really hungry."

"Angel, it's only four o'clock, I'm sure you can wait for Mario and his family to eat. Grab a snack for now."

"You are an amazing chef, you should cook more often."

"I'm a culinary goddess, the Athena of the kitchen, cooking and baking with my supernatural powers," said Ana, holding a cooking spoon high in the air as if it were about to discharge a thunderbolt.

"I love you, mom."

"I love you more, kiddo."

Just then the doorbell rang. Angel knew it was Mario and his parents, they always arrived early. After all, family was welcomed at all times.

"I'll get it, mom."

"Mario, I'm glad it's you," exclaimed Angel with as much excitement as if they were still ten year olds getting together for the afternoon.

"Let's go play catch in the backyard."

He immediately realized how rude he had been, so he hugged Carlos and kissed Luisa on the cheek.

"Get out of here," said Carlos, with a huge smile as he tapped Angel on the head.

They all took their usual positions. Luisa paired up with Ana in the kitchen, the boys took off to the backyard, and Carlos searched for Arsenio. He found him on the balcony contemplating too much at once, his brain was on overload.

As Carlos approached him, he realized his friend was in a pensive state of mind. It's almost as if he could read his mind.

"Don't blow a fuse, sport."

"Carlos, how are you old buddy? You're here early, good to see you. Let me go say hello to the family."

Arsenio greeted Luisa and Mario. After chatting with Luisa, he and Carlos grabbed a drink in the library and returned to the balcony. There was little Arsenio enjoyed more than spending time with a loved one on his balcony, breathing in the pure air, and enjoying the ocean view.

"I smelled Ana's Arroz con Pollo as I walked in," said Carlos, placing his drink on the circular table next to the cushioned chaise that would be his for the next hour or so. He settled in and faced Arsenio, delighted to be celebrating another New Year's Eve with his dear friend.

"We are in for a treat, my friend. My Anita is a great cook."

"Arsenio, have you received an offer?"

Carlos wasn't always this blunt, he usually encouraged small talk during their first drink. The second and third drinks were later needed for more serious conversation, whether it was politics or personal issues. Under the circumstances, he felt pressed for time and couldn't risk another sunset without asking his friend certain questions.

"We received an offer and accepted it. We are selling our house for fifteen thousand below market value, we can't get greedy."

"Ours is also up for sale, hopefully we get as lucky as you. Arsenio, much needs to be done."

"You're preaching to the choir, my friend. Carlos, are you moving with us to New York?"

"Absolutely."

"Angel will be thrilled, those two are inseparable."

"I agree," said Carlos with a smile. His eyes conveyed the pain he felt discussing what may end up being a permanent move from his native land. It was tearing him up inside.

"Our current situation is one nobody could have predicted a couple of years ago. The communists started years ago, slowly inching their way towards their goal, like a venomous snake hiding in the underbrush, striking at its prey at an opportune time," preached Arsenio, as if he were giving one of his classes.

"What is our antidote?" asked Carlos, amused by Arsenio's analogy.

"That has not yet been discovered, my friend. Hopefully our move to New York is temporary," replied Arsenio. He was starting to think that "*temporary*" could easily turn into ten or more years. He didn't feel the need to share this with Carlos.

"When is the closing on the house?"

"If all goes well, we will close late February. As soon as I close I will meet Ana and the children in New York, they leave right after Three Kings Day."

"Buddy, I'm going to lower the price of my house so that we could meet up with you soon after you leave," declared Carlos.

"These are difficult times, it's great to know we have each other. Both families will relocate to New York, and hopefully we'll be back on our island in a few years."

"Arsenio, I'll drink to that."

They lifted their glasses, finished their drinks, and enjoyed each other's company on the balcony until dinnertime.

The phone rang at 11:05 pm, Ofelia was in labor. They all got into Arsenio's car and drove to the hospital, a drive that took no longer than ten minutes, especially this time of night.

"Miss, we are here to see Ofelia Cruz, she's in labor. We got the call twenty minutes ago," said Arsenio, nervously tapping his fingers on the receptionist's desk.

Arsenio couldn't keep still, he was a sight to see when nervous. Once, when Maria was out past midnight with some friends, his nerves affected him so much that he actually pounded his head against the refrigerator a few times.

"Are you family, sir?"

"Yes, we're the grandparents and these are the aunt and uncle," he said impatiently, pointing to Carlos and Luisa.

"Only one person is allowed in the delivery room with the patient, since her mother isn't here, my suggestion is that the grandmother go up to be with her."

"Good idea. Ana, take good care of our girl. Please let us know anything as soon as you can, we will be down here waiting," said Arsenio.

"Honey, I'll go up. I know how much you love Ofelia, but please get a grip on your nerves. Everything is going to be just fine, a new addition to the family is a good thing. Ofelia is healthy and all will be well," ensured Ana.

"All right, see you soon. And honey, Happy New Year." Arsenio kissed Ana and hugged her, not wanting to let go.

Angel stayed home with Mario, Maria, and Barbara - this year they would not ring in the new year together. Arsenio sat with Carlos and Luisa in the hospital lobby, eagerly awaiting the new arrival. It was 11:52 pm, the new year was upon them. Along with Ofelia's baby, the arrival of 1959 had been eagerly anticipated by many who were awaiting changes.

"Familia, the countdown is on, in less than ten minutes we enter 1959."

"Imagine that, Arsenio, starting all over again in a new country. As positive as I try to be about this, it is so difficult to wrap my arms around this whole concept," Carlos said, tears streaming down his cheeks. Entering a new year under regular circumstances normally creates melancholy, add everything that was taking place and the feeling was indescribable.

"Carlos, one day at a time. Think of how lucky we are compared to most. Our wealth grants us the opportunity to leave this country before things get really bad, it is also instrumental in helping us get our new starts in the States. Focus has always been one of your key strengths, you will need it now more than ever," argued Arsenio.

Arsenio was always accomodating, many people appreciated his helpful advice. He would travel to his new home with that lucidity, a virtue that would surely help newly arrived Cuban immigrants who would approach him for guidance.

"Besides, keeping the family together is what matters the most. As long as the three of us are together with our extended Buendia Family, we can overcome obstacles," added Luisa. It destroyed her to see Carlos as distraught as he was.

"You're right, Luisita."

"Hey, look at the time," said Arsenio.

All three hugged and Carlos kissed Luisa. They walked to the payphone to call the children.

The three sat for a while reading magazines and thinking. Arsenio and his partner had exhausted all political conversation for the time being. They were cognizant of the current situation in Cuba, hopelessness started to set in. They knew their next move, there was no sense in further discussing it for now.

"It's almost one o'clock, I wonder if everything is well with Ofelia and the baby?"

"Buddy, calm down. I'm sure everything is fine. Besides, I don't see a refrigerator around here," said Carlos with a chuckle.

Luisa laughed the loudest, Carlos had recently shared that story with her.

A few minutes past one, Ana ran into the lobby, crying hysterically and sweating profusely. All three stood, expecting the worst.

"Ana, speak quickly," implored Arsenio.

"I'm not sure what's happening, I've given birth four times and I've never seen so much blood. Even the first time with Teresita, God rest her soul," said Ana.

"Did she give birth?"

"Yes, to a healthy baby boy. She named him Antonio after that no good father of his. As soon as they cleaned up the baby and took him out of the room, doctors and nurses began rushing in. That's when they asked me to leave. Arsenio, they were ankle-deep in blood!" explained Ana with great concern. She had intended to remain calm for her husband's sake, she didn't even come close to achieving her goal.

"Arsenio, please go speak to someone. We need an immediate update on Ofelia," suggested Luisa.

Arsenio and Carlos approached the receptionist's desk to inquire about Ofelia. Before getting to the desk, Arsenio saw a doctor down the hall and turned in his direction.

"Carlos, please go back so you can accompany the girls. I'll get the information we need. Thanks."

"Doctor," called out Arsenio, motioning for him to stop.

"Doctor, my daughter is giving birth and her mother has just informed us of complications. Would you please update us on her condition?"

"I'm Dr. Corrales, I would be glad to help. What is her name?"

"Her name is Ofelia Cruz."

Dr. Corrales stepped behind a partition that separated the front desk from the hallways leading to the elevators. The phones on the wall facing the restrooms connected to all the wards within the hospital. The doctor picked up the blue phone and received an update.

"Sir, I didn't catch your name," said Dr. Corrales.

"My apologies, I'm Dr. Buendia, professor at Havana University." Arsenio added his profession so as to not be mistaken for a medical doctor.

"Dr. Buendia, your daughter has lost a great deal of blood. When women give birth, the blood vessels in their uterus where the placenta was attached, open. Bleeding is normal during child labor, in some cases women bleed excessively. We call this postpartum hemorrhage (PPH). The only way to replace the lost blood when the bleeding is excessive is through a transfusion, Ofelia lost thirty percent of her blood. She's getting a transfusion now and will be fine."

"So we have nothing to worry about, Doctor?" Arsenio needed some extra assurance.

"Nothing at all, you'll be home changing your grandchild's diapers in no time. Your daughter will be correcting you every step of the way as if that were your first diaper change. Happy New Year, Dr. Buendia. It was a pleasure meeting you."

"Thank you, Dr. Corrales. Happy New Year."

Arsenio made his way back to Carlos and the ladies.

"Ofelia is fine, I spoke to Dr. Corrales who told me she is getting a transfusion. She lost more blood than usual, but everything is under control. We'll probably get to see her in a couple of hours."

"Thank goodness. You see? We truly are blessed," said Ana.
It was 1:52 am
January 1st, 1959

The sun peaked through the curtains, indicating the end of night. Its rays, particularly strong for that early in the morning, represented strength and vigor. Energy arriving from our mother star in less than ten minutes serves its purpose in warming our planet, and grants us the necessary strength to go about our day.

At first glance it appeared to be a day like any other, upon closer inspection it was obvious that nothing could be further from the truth.

Arsenio awoke first. He was making his way to get some coffee when he heard celebratory bustle, three orderlies wearing superfluous grins were gathered by the supply station discussing the latest news.

"Gentlemen, what's the good news? Are you still celebrating the new year?" inquired Arsenio.

"Much more than that, sir."

"Please let me share in your excitement. What is it?"

"Batista fled last night like the coward he is, we now have new leadership to move us forward."

At this comment, his friend added:

"President Castro will take us places."

"He'll take us places all right, straight to hell! Gentlemen, a president is elected into office, he doesn't become president through instilling fear in people's hearts and by flooding the airwaves with propaganda and empty promises. Fraudulent elections and terrorist tactics add to the illegitimacy of his takeover. He is a thug in fatigues!"

Arsenio stormed towards the bathroom to wash his face, his blood pressure must have been through the roof. He walked back to Ofelia's room, not wanting to disclose the news on such a joyous day for the family.

"Ana, how long have you been awake?" asked Ofelia as she stretched and yawned.

"I've observed you sleeping for almost an hour, I didn't want to wake you," she responded as she cradled Antonio in her arms.

The nurse took Antonio from Ana and handed him to Ofelia. The new mom was all smiles, she was going to be a terrific mother.

"Thank you, nurse."

"My pleasure, Ofelia. Would you like to feed him later?"

"I'd love to!" She replied wide-eyed and enthused.

There's nothing like being a first time mother, thought Ana.

"I'll return later with the bottle, enjoy your treasure." It was obvious the nurse enjoyed her profession.

"Ofelia, he is gorgeous. I think he looks a lot like you. What do you think, Luisa?" asked Ana.

"Yes, especially the pudgy nose and the hazel eyes, even though eye color can change after a few months," mentioned Luisa.

"I can't tell if he looks like you, all I know is that he's a great looking baby. He is very alert for a newborn, they say that indicates a high level of intelligence. I'm sure he will take a few of my courses someday," said Carlos with a grin.

"I can see this one heading off to work with his cane and false teeth years from now, teaching Antonio," added Luisa, as she elbowed him in the ribs and laughed.

"Arsenio, you are uncharacteristically quiet, my friend. This is a joyous occasion, join in our celebration."

Carlos knew there was something wrong, he could read every wrinkle in Arsenio's face. Arsenio's physiology served as his traitor whenever he wished to conceal his emotions.

"All is well, my friend. Ofelia, you have no idea the joy this baby brings me. It is great to have a new family member," said Arsenio.

"Thank you so much, I love you all like family." Arsenio's comment meant the world to her, there weren't many people she could count on, she felt very lucky to have them."

"What a joyous day, one we will never forget," remarked Ana, bursting with enthusiasm.

If only she knew, thought Arsenio.

The celebration outside got louder. The orderlies had either shared the news or the employees had gotten a hold of the morning paper. Either way, Arsenio knew what the commotion was about.

"Arsen, vamos a tomar un cafe," said Carlos, noticing his friend needed a coffee more than anyone else.

"Carlos, you know I hate that nickname," said Ana with a smirk.

"That's right, though spelled differently, arson means "*someone who likes starting fires*" in English. I won't do it again, Anita."

"Now, let's go, Ar-SEN. Carlos playfully ran out with Ana in tow, swinging her arms as she attempted to hit his shoulders.

Arsenio caught up to Carlos and accompanied him to the main lobby.

"Spill the beans my friend, what's wrong?" asked Carlos as they approached the coffee stand near the main entrance.

"You'll see in a minute, I'll treat you to some strong coffee and we will sit down to read the morning paper together."

From a distance, Arsenio caught a glimpse of the El Pais headline:

Batista Flees the Country

"Two black coffees and two copies of El Pais, please. Keep the change."

Arsenio grabbed both coffees, the papers, and headed towards the nearest couch.

The second most prominent headline read:

Cubans Celebrate the New Year and Batista's Departure

By the time they sat, Carlos had read the headlines.

"Arsenio, no!"

"While everyone celebrated last night, our world came to an end. The speed with which we must act is great," emphasized Arsenio, his eyes transfixed on his paper.

"Is that the celebrating that was taking place in the hallway upstairs?" asked Carlos.

"Are they blind?" he continued.

"Castro has made many promises to the poor and has fooled many wealthy citizens as well. We, as political science professors, understand what lies ahead. We foresaw a train wreck and lacked the proper tools and manpower to prevent it, how sad," exclaimed Arsenio.

"God help us."

They sat drinking their coffees, reading about the events that took place while Cuba celebrated the new year.

Ofelia's doctor requested at least one night's stay, maybe two. Both families left the hospital at four in the afternoon on New Year's Day. They promised Ofelia they would return the next morning with the children.

On their trip home the ladies couldn't stop talking about the baby, neither Arsenio nor Carlos had yet informed them of the news. The gentlemen's silence in the car was rare, they would always talk when together, especially when they were with their wives. Seeing them in the front seat without uttering a word bothered Ana, she knew something was wrong.

"Thank goodness we're almost home, I'm going straight to bed," expressed Ana.

"We intend to do the same," added Luisa.

Arsenio broke his silence by making an observation.

"The street ahead is closed, we will have to take a detour."

"I wonder what it is," said Luisa.

As they crossed the street where they usually make a left turn, they noticed people in the streets with signs, jumping up and down as they yelled:

Castro in, Batista out

The chant was loud and continuous. Debris covered the street with no visibility of what lay underneath. A metal garbage can in the far corner had been set ablaze, these people were enjoying themselves in their little corner of the world. Was it just this little corner, or had this wildfire spread to the point of no return?

"Gentlemen, is there something you need to tell us?" asked Ana, with fear in her voice.

"Let's get home first," suggested Arsenio.

"Arsenio, go down three blocks and make that left, it will take you to the other side of Prado. Hopefully that area hasn't been affected," said Carlos with a hopeful tone.

"Traffic is light because of the holiday, but these closed streets are affecting the little traffic there is. I haven't seen any police officers," observed Ana.

"They probably closed off the necessary streets, took off, and hoped for the best," said Luisa.

"Arsenio, that's the street coming up."

"Closed off, we either continue or turn back."

"I'm getting scared, we all live on the other side of town. I don't like what I've seen in the streets, this could get very dangerous for us. This is class warfare, we will end up on the losing side," mentioned Luisa.

They were all tense, focusing on getting out, feeling like caged animals with no escape.

"Listen, we'll try a few more blocks and turn back should we have no luck," said Arsenio.

He thought he had travelled every street in the city, but the only street that remained open was a dark, narrow street he had never entered.

"Arsenio, even in broad daylight that street looks darker than the others and not very safe," mentioned Ana, hoping her husband wasn't thinking of crossing to the other side of town using this route.

"Ana, we are running out of options! This city is going wild, I've never seen anything like this. What else do you want me to do?" Arsenio responded, raising his voice.

Carlos interjected, "Arsenio, calm down."

"I'm sorry Anita, I shouldn't have yelled."

"Honey, just get us out of here. What you decide is fine with me," said Ana with a look of terror in her eyes.

"Luisa is right, it *is* class warfare. We are driving a luxury car down a street with a riotous mob surrounding us, it doesn't look good for us."

"The people with the signs see us as the enemy. We are the wealthy elite who have been keeping them down all these years, at least that's their perception," said Ana.

Arsenio made the left turn onto the narrow street, immediately realizing his mistake. It was a one-way street with buildings at both sides, people hanging out of windows, breathing in the air, and enjoying the entertainment the coup d'état was providing. A group of young men walked in their direction in the middle of the street. They spotted the car and knew that it didn't belong, this street was theirs, it didn't belong to the aristocrats who lived on the other side of the city.

"Grandpa, you read the news? I'll be living in your house before long," yelled one of the young men. Their pace towards the car quickened as Arsenio attempted to make a U-turn.

"We're finally going to get our share! My father died working in those sugarcane fields, and we are living like pigs with nothing to show for it. It's our turn!"

Arsenio put the car in reverse, there were six or seven men in front of the car. The one yelling at him threw a rock and shattered the windshield. Ana and Luisa yelled.

"Arsenio, drive! Get us out of here, for God's sake!" Both Ana and Luisa were sobbing uncontrollably, they didn't see a way out.

He swore he could hear his heart beat as he did battle with the steering wheel, Carlos felt useless sitting in the back seat. They knew getting out of the car meant certain death, three of the boys held baseball bats and the others had rocks.

Arsenio completed the U-turn and accelerated blindly, unable to see clearly because of the shattered windshield. He felt a thump against the front bumper, followed by a young man's yell. He continued to accelerate as a barrage of rocks rained upon the car. As they made the turn the windshield caved in, causing Arsenio and Carlos minimal injury, but giving Arsenio full view of the road ahead of them.

Half a mile away from danger, Arsenio began driving at a slower pace, in awe of what had just happened. They were finally on their way home.

Silence permeated the car.

Chapter Seventeen
The Letter

The letter could turn out to be innocuous, a formality that would clear up when meeting with the officials on the assigned date. He shared the contents with Nora and even though she was upset, he calmed her down and asked her to take it a day at a time.

"Guillermo, all I'm asking is that you discuss the letter with your brother. I really think we should seek legal advice just in case," suggested Nora.

"A lawyer? As if I were a common criminal? Nora, you know me better than that. I have nothing to hide, as a matter of fact I think we're building this all up for no reason. It's probably nothing to worry about."

"Dear, the new government is what scares me the most. I've heard that some of the things they've done the first eight weeks in power would instill fear in even the strongest. Speak to Arsenio," pleaded Nora, with urgency in her tone.

"All right, I'll speak to my brother, but not a lawyer."

"I'll invite them over for dinner tomorrow night, is that all right?" he added.

"Fine, as soon as possible. You're scheduled to appear in front of the committee five days from today, we have no time to waste," responded Nora.

By nature, Guillermo handled adversity well. He was a rock, unlike his brother. He did not reveal the fear that lingered in his soul so as to not frighten his wife any more than needed. Ever since the bachelor party from the previous year, a few layers of valor had been stripped off his armor, political chaos was softening his outer shell much like an ever-flowing river breaks apart sediment on its journey to the ocean.

Ana and Arsenio arrived at Guillermo's and Dora's house the following evening at eight o'clock, unaware of the letter's existence.

"Brother, come here for a bear hug!" exclaimed Arsenio, as his older sibling opened the door.

"You think you can put the squeeze on me? How mistaken you are." Guillermo laughed and smacked Arsenio on the back.

"Anita, Arsenio, how good to see you," remarked Nora as she dried her hands and walked towards the door to greet her guests.

"Come in, let's sit and chat. The chicken will be ready in forty minutes, let's relax until then."

Her plan was to casually work the news about the letter into their conversation to elicit a natural response from Arsenio and Ana. Only then could she accurately gauge the seriousness of the situation.

"Ana, how's that lovely grandson doing?" asked Nora.

"Never more beautiful, growing by the day. He turned two months yesterday. Time doesn't stand still for anyone, does it?"

"Not for a single soul, my dear," responded Nora, with more on her mind than she cared to consider. She stepped into the kitchen and returned with four wine glasses and a full bottle.

"Maybe it will slow down just a bit with that concoction you are holding," quipped Ana.

"This is my idea of a party, family and a bottle of wine," said Arsenio.

"Ana, when do you and the children leave?"

"Our flight was rescheduled for April 15th, I'm starting to get everything in order. It just scares me to leave Arsenio behind, but we have to sell the house."

"I heard that the sale fell through, I'm sure you'll find a buyer soon. Owning a business makes it more difficult for us, we should meet you in New York within a year's time," exclaimed Guillermo, as the contents of that letter occupied his thoughts.

As they sat comfortably, sipping their wine, Nora graciously worked the letter into the conversation.

"Arsenio, let me show you something."

"Absolutely Nora, what is it?"

"We received this letter a couple of days ago, I'd like to run it by you to see what you think." She reached for the letter and handed it to Arsenio.

"This letter refers to the group who rented your place for the bachelor party last year," observed Arsenio.

"Yes, government officials have questions about those men. The thing is, I know nothing about them," stuttered Guillermo.

"Did those men ever mention their political affiliations?"

"They were communist, if nothing else they are probably pro-Castro and in favor of the revolution."

"That makes sense, I think you have little to worry about," said Arsenio.

"That's exactly what I told him," sang out Nora with a tune of relief.

"Honesty is not your greatest virtue, my dear." Guillermo kissed his wife and danced to her tune, his look had completely changed.

They enjoyed the rest of the evening, sharing anecdotes and attempting to block out the madness that surrounded them.

The streets were flooded with rainwater from the previous evening's storm. Havana's drainage system was effective, but spring storms were sometimes too much for it to handle. It stopped raining approximately one hour before sunrise, there were few things as beautiful as a tropical sunrise following a storm.

The knock was no louder than that of a friend's who was coming over to dinner for the evening. It was an odd hour but Guillermo didn't think anything of it. As soon as he opened the door three armed soldiers entered. The couple was taken aback, they dared say nothing. Within minutes they made their rounds, acting as if they were looking for something. They left the house with Guillermo and Nora.

By the time Guillermo made his way to the front lawn in handcuffs, the sky was a stunning blue with white puffy clouds creating a beautiful contrast. The physical beauty of the country had not changed, other aspects were quickly turning this tropical paradise into a living nightmare.

The sight of his wife of over twenty years following in tow under the same predicament brought heartache and fear to the few neighbors observing the spectacle that early in the morning. They knew Nora and Guillermo well, most couldn't help but wonder how and when these changes would affect them or someone near and dear to them.

"Sir, why are you arresting us? We have done nothing wrong," implored Guillermo.

"Guillermo, what's happening?" asked Nora.

"My love, don't say anything. I'll call Arsenio and he'll assist us in straightening all this out. This is obviously a big mistake," assured Guillermo.

"Stop talking, I will knock all you teeth out next time you or your wife utter a word!" yelled soldier 13. He was standing to Guillermo's left, situated between him and Nora.

This silenced them both but Nora's tears continued.

The five entered the jeep the soldiers had driven to the house, it was a tight fit on the drive back to the station. Where police officers had been a few months prior was now occupied and run by the army.

They entered the building, gloom exuded from its walls and floors, dread lay heavy in the air like dense fog on a humid night.

"Take these two to desk #4," said the man whose job it was to assign "booking soldiers" as prisoners entered the station.

The gentleman being interrogated at desk #3 had been answering his questions in a low tone until something set him off.

"Revolution? Revolution? This is a revolution of pigs! Pigs who will do everything to the detriment of hard working citizens. ¡Que viva Cuba libre!" yelled the man, still in handcuffs.

"Shut up, we will not put up with counter-revolutionaries!" shouted a soldier holding a rifle. He stormed over to desk #3 and twice slammed the butt of the rifle into the side of the man's head. The man fell to the ground on his knees, blood gushing from his wound. Another soldier pulled him by the handcuffs in an attempt to get him to stand, he immediately fell. Both soldiers dragged him outside as he left a stream of blood in his path. A few minutes after they were out of sight, two gunshots were heard in the distance.

The silence after that was deafening.

"Now, let's get started. Don't worry, not all interrogations end up like that. Cooperate, and all will be well," said soldier 21 wearing an arrogant smirk on his face, having power over others intoxicated him.

"Mr. Buendia, what is your place of business?"

"Guillermo's, a café on the outskirts of Havana," said Guillermo, holding his head high. He would not let intimidation affect the man he was. As far as he was concerned, his integrity was still the same. He would not convey fear, they would not get that pleasure from Guillermo Buendia.

"Are you the owner?"

"Yes."

"How often does your wife work with you?"

Guillermo hesitated, he understood the significance attached to this question. If he was honest he would implicate his wife in whatever accusations they had against them. He had a good idea they already knew the answers to all the questions, lying would be much worse.

"She works with me most of the time, Nora is my right hand at the café," reluctantly responded Guillermo.

"Are many bachelor parties held at your café?"

"Hardly any," responded Guillermo. Now he knew where this line of questioning was leading.

"Mr. Buendia, do you recall a bachelor party that took place at your café a year ago?"

"I remember it well." Guillermo did not fold in the face of adversity. He was a proud man with valor to spare, always facing difficult situations head-on.

"What can you tell me about those men?"

"They were a group of about thirty, out to celebrate their buddy's final days as a bachelor."

"What were they wearing?"

"What do you mean?" Again, Guillermo had an inkling as to what the soldier was referring to but he didn't want to offer more information than necessary.

"Was one gentleman dressed in fatigues?"

"Yes."

"And the others?"

"Civilian clothes. Sir, with all due respect, please get to the point. My wife has sat here quietly as I've honestly answered all your questions," Guillermo said with a dry mouth. The thought of the man at desk #3 flashed across his mind reminding him of how quickly things change around here.

"Mr. Buendia, the point is that you are accused of assisting six of the men at that bachelor party with counter-revolutionary activities," stated soldier 21 with a look of satisfaction. This was another notch in his belt.

"Sir, please let me speak to them. We can see them together if you wish, they will help clear my name." Guillermo knew they meant business, he feared for his family's safety.

"I'm afraid it is too late for that, they were executed yesterday. Justice here is served swiftly."

"Oh my God!" blurted out Nora as she began to weep.

Justice? What kind of justice is executing someone days after accusations have been brought against him? Guilty by association? God help us, thought Guillermo.

"They were there only once, sir. I assure you." Guillermo did not want to raise his voice. The man by desk #3 may have saved his life, if he would not have been executed, Guillermo would be yelling by now.

"Your trial is set for Thursday, three days from today," said soldier 21 with the calculating tone of a robot.

"Trial? Trial? But sir..." Guillermo stopped himself from uttering another syllable. He understood that if he had any chance of survival, silence was his best friend.

"Guillermo, I will call Arsenio as soon as possible," said Nora as two soldiers led Guillermo away in the handcuffs that had been placed on him earlier that day.

"Don't worry sweetheart, all will be well," whispered Nora.

Nora's inner-strength was taking over, this was no time to break down, she needed to stay strong for her husband. She was released hours later, more composed than expected considering what had transpired that fateful day.

Thursday morning Guillermo met his government appointed defense attorney, they had three hours to prepare his defense. All was done within the confines of his cell, the soldiers on guard granted them the luxury of a small table and two chairs, leaving little room to stand. The government had not allowed Arsenio to hire an attorney for his brother.

"Mr. Buendia, I am Mr. Rivas. I will represent you in front of the judge. The accusations against you are serious, I must know everything that transpired between you and those six gentlemen."

Guillermo spoke for twenty minutes, he included every detail he could remember. He emphasized the fact that he had neither seen those men before nor after the bachelor party.

It took Mr. Rivas less than two hours to gather all the material needed for the "case".

Mr. Rivas said his goodbyes and the soldiers removed the table and chairs.

Guillermo sat in awe, he wondered whether Mr. Rivas represented him or some *other cause*. The speed with which he had gathered all "necessary" information was staggering, he had no doubt it was all a façade.

The mock trial lasted less than one hour. Guillermo walked out the same way he had entered, in handcuffs.

What had taken Guillermo and Nora decades to build up crumbled within hours.

He would serve ten years of hard labor.

Chapter Eighteen
Defense Committee of the Revolution (DCR)

Concentrated efforts by Arsenio and a select few in the community to free Guillermo from prison were thwarted by powerful forces, making his brother's destiny clear as water, a fate no different than that of a skydiver in mid-flight whose parachute does not open.

Arsenio could do little to rectify the criminal behavior perpetrated on his brother by an unrecognized government, the appeal process had been abolished leaving little recourse. Having nowhere to turn did not equate to giving up, Arsenio's primary concern was his brother's lack of freedom, he would do anything to gain that freedom back for his lifelong friend. All his energy was directed at saving his family from the ill effects brought on by criminals in uniforms.

On this day, his family was flying to New York. They experienced dual emotions, fearing the unpredictability of the future and feeling grateful for their economic situation, one that afforded them the luxury of relocating to a country known for democracy and freedoms currently lacking in their native land. Not everyone was in a situation to make such a move. The Buendia Family took things well considering everything they endured. Separating was difficult, a necessary step in attempting to reestablish normalcy in their new home, while never abandoning hope of returning to their land of palm trees and white sandy beaches.

"Ana, the flight departs in three hours. You know we must be there early, my love," said Arsenio with all the composure he could muster. His fabricated, calm demeanor could fool most, but not his wife.

"Honey, I have my bags packed and the children are ready. Please tell me we don't have to go. Better yet, purchase a ticket for yourself and join us, forget the house." It was not just rhetoric, she was sincere. Ana would trade the value of their house for her husband's safety without hesitation.

The children were quiet the day of departure, they had thoroughly prepared for this day with guidance from their parents. Rehearsals had been many leading up to the main event.

"Anita, maintain your focus. The house is up for sale, as soon as it sells I will join you in the States. My most precious possessions will be safe within a few hours," said Arsenio with a reassuring smile.

"And mine is staying behind with his life threatened by thugs in power!" She was furious, her concealed emotions were surfacing. Ana understood, however, the importance of keeping them in check for the foreseeable future.

"Anita, come here." Arsenio hugged her tightly, kissed her, and whispered something in her ear that brought her a little relief:

"You and the children are my life, I will be with you in three months. If the house hasn't sold by then, I will transfer the deed to Nora. With the cash we sent Aldo a few months ago, we can start over again in New York. We will be just fine, I guarantee it."

"I really needed to hear that," said Ana.

"I mean every word," he added.

"I know you do. I love you!"

"I adore you, kiddo," said Arsenio. He had used "kiddo" as a term of endearment for as long as he could recall.

The drive to José Martí Airport took longer than expected because of unanticipated closures and detours. It had gotten to the point where detours became an everyday part of living in Havana. People were better off not questioning changes, many citizens were making the mistake of freely expressing their opinions at a costly price.

Arsenio parked the car and took the luggage from the trunk, he dreaded the final minutes when the clock would come to a standstill as they waved their goodbyes. He needed to conceal his feelings, the fear he felt of never seeing his family again consumed him. His strength would help his family endure the hardships of surviving in a new land under difficult circumstances.

After Ana and the children checked in, Arsenio kissed them and reassured them that this was temporary. In three months, if not less, they would reunite in New York.

They had installed a new checkpoint at the airport to ensure that only passengers could cross over to the point of departure.

"Arsenio, should I give you my wedding ring?"

"Keep it, you have a better chance of getting it through now. Things will probably be stricter when I leave in a few months."

"Honey, please keep all your thoughts to yourself. Remember what happened to Ingrid's husband, such a wonderful man who's in prison for speaking out against the government. They'll grant him a mock trial like they did with your brother and nobody will ever hear from him again."

" Shhh…. Ana, keep it down. Please calm down, none of that will happen to me. I promise."

"Remember to take good care of Ofelia and the baby, she is especially vulnerable now. I will miss them so much!" expressed Ana.

"Of course, my dear. Ofelia is like a daughter and Antonio is our grandson. I will try to convince her to leave with me."

He turned to his son.

"Angel, you're the man of the house, kiddo. Take care of your mom and sisters. Understand?"

"Understood, Pops. I love you."

"Love you more." The kind of heartache Arsenio felt was more painful than any physical pain he had ever experienced, including his accident from a few months before.

"Who are my two princesses?"

"We are," replied Maria and Barbara as they rushed to his arms.

"Daddy, don't go," requested Barbara. Maria had told her to be strong but she couldn't help it. Barbara began to weep.

"Chata mi niña. Look at me, I will see you before you know it. Be strong, we will all be together soon."

Ana and Maria, who were on the verge of crying, wiped away their tears and said their final goodbyes as they walked away. They knew their special man would be with them in less than 90 days.

They crossed the point of no return. Final security was beyond Arsenio's view, all passengers' belongings were carefully scrutinized, security was their primary concern – or so they claimed.

The first thing they did at final security right before boarding, out of view from Aesenio, was take Ana's wedding ring off her finger.

On returning home, Arsenio paid Ingrid a visit. They had been neighbors for over fifteen years, if she was in need he wanted to help. He and Octavio had never been close, but in times like these it was important to work together. He pulled into his driveway and walked three houses down to theirs.

Arsenio rang the doorbell hoping there was nobody home, he was emotionally drained and should have waited to visit another day. She hesitantly opened the door until she realized it was Arsenio.

"Arsenio, you heard about my Octavio?" She surmised the news had carried over to his household, for he didn't visit them much.

"Yes, Ingrid. I'm here to offer any help possible, my brother is in a very similar predicament."

"Please come in, stay for a while."

She was a woman in need of company and reassurance. They were in their early sixties, a couple with three grown children and seven grandchildren living out their golden years. Their current situation was a terrible shock to all who knew them.

"Take a seat, would you like some lemonade? I just made some," mentioned Ingrid as she pointed to the couch.

"I would love some," replied Arsenio, thinking that speaking to

Ingrid during these difficult times could serve as therapy for him.

The last thing he wanted to do with his brother in prison and his family on their way to New York was go home to ponder their predicament in a large, empty house. Ofelia had left to visit a cousin for a couple of weeks, he was afraid that she wanted to become independent, leaving her old life behind. Breaking all ties with her and the baby would be very painful to him, and devastating to Ana.

"Here we go, tell me what you think." Ingrid handed Arsenio a glass of lemonade.

Arsenio took a sip, it was a little sweet for his taste but very refreshing. "Delicious, Ingrid. Thank you."

"Are you prepared to discuss what happened with Octavio or should I return at a later date?" asked Arsenio.

"Let's talk, I'm doing him no favors by sitting here without sharing his story. Maybe I will be able to figure out what this is all about. Arsenio, our world has turned upside down without rhyme or reason. What is going on?"

"You must take it a day at a time, *we* must take it a day at a time. Now, tell me what happened."

"Well, let me premise it with this. Have you heard of the Defense Committee of the Revolution?"

"Word is starting to get around, tell me what you know," said Arsenio.

"The Defense Committee of the Revolution, also known as DCR, is a committee implemented by the communists to weed out anti-revolutionaries. Their goal is to have one committee member per square block, each member's task is to report anybody who is against the revolution."

"Yes, I've heard that, Ingrid. Since they are at the beginning stages, the arrest numbers are great, they're getting many people off guard. What happened with Octavio?"

"I'm not sure you know that Octavio retired from full-time

employment a couple of years ago. He continued working for the same company a couple of days a week, mainly to stay busy."

"I wasn't aware of his retirement. He worked for Woolworth's as an executive, didn't he?"

"Yes, may that company never close. They have great benefits, at least at the executive level. Octavio always told me that they treat their employees well at all levels. Anyway, one day he was discussing the changes in our government to a colleague, someone he doesn't know well. It just so happens that his colleague is a member of the DCR."

"What did Octavio say?"

"He made the mistake of mentioning that he knows Castro's government is communist and that they are going to ruin this country." Ingrid let out a sigh and a few tears.

"Arsenio, they knocked our door down and took him out in handcuffs like a common criminal at three in the morning. This happened three weeks ago. Like a criminal! All for expressing his beliefs."

Ingrid started to shiver.

"Take it easy, we will do what we can for Octavio and Guillermo, and all will be well. I promise."

Arsenio was starting to doubt himself, he was no longer sure he would be able to follow through with all of his promises – guarantees that lacked the assuredness people had grown to expect from Arsenio Buendia.

"Arsenio, whatever you do, don't express how you feel to anyone. You must promise me that."

"Two promises in one day? Yes, I promise." Arsenio winked at Ingrid, trying to do his part to help calm her nerves.

"His trial is next Wednesday, I'm scared to death."

"Pray for the best and expect the worst, I always say. We must be strong, Ingrid. Hopefully someday soon we will all wake up from this nightmare."

Arsenio stood and hugged her.

"Thank you so much for stopping by," said Ingrid, sounding defeated.

"My pleasure, I will keep an eye on you. Ingrid, don't give up, you know where I live, come to me for absolutely anything you need, *anything*."

"I will, God bless you, Arsenio."

"Thank you, you too."

Arsenio walked back home, looking lost for the first time in his life. Not since the passing of his mother many years ago had he felt this anxious, he was a high wire performer without a net.

In all his years he had never been so frightened.

One could easily sit on a handful of chaises that remained and contemplate the history of this dilapidated hotel in the outskirts of Havana, considering the fact that this once remarkable building was now a shell of what it once was. Some of the bright paint remained on the wall, the rest had peeled off from years of neglect and seawater crashing up against the hotel with the dozen or so powerful storms that would cross Havana's path every year.

The swimming pool was drained the year the hotel ceased operation, Batista was not yet in power when it closed. Word had it that management embezzled hundreds of thousands of dollars, draining the hotel of much more than its pool water.

The interior staircase served as a conversation piece, bringing many to compare the hotel's staircase to that of the Titanic's, with its intricate detail and winding railings. The front desk was pure mahogany, matching the stunning backdrop that served as mail slots, one for each guest. Every room had an ocean view, elegance did not lack in its heyday – this hotel, now a phantom of what it had once been, aimed to please high-end clientele.

The twenty women standing inside the waterless pool were oblivious to the historic significance that accompanied the hotel, all they knew was that they were prisoners inside a swimming pool - prisoners accused of anti-revolutionary activity. Soldiers were ordered to gather women the DCR targeted. As hundreds of people were gathered, space became limited. It was the brainstorm of a young recruit trying to impress his superiors that they begin putting the excess women into the swimming pool of "*The Palace*", the mock term frequently used for this lifeless hotel.

"What are they going to do with us?" asked a young woman with ponytails. She was wearing pajama pants and a sweater, indicating she had been taken from her home in the middle of the night.

"I don't know, but I pray they don't fill the pool with water, I can't swim," said an older woman, struggling to speak through her tears.

"They took my husband away and condemned him to ten years of prison for something he didn't do and now this," she added.

"Don't worry, we'll be fine. They will eventually let us go," said the younger girl, trying her best to believe her own words.

"Thank you, honey. I appreciate your kind words. What's your name?" asked the older lady as she forced a smile.

"My name is Emily, and there's little that can keep me down. If they don't put the ladder back soon, I'll climb out of this Olympic pool and get it myself. What's your name?"

"I'm Nora, I've seen you before in my café."

"Yes, I knew I recognized you from somewhere. You own Guillermo's?"

"Yes, my husband and I own it."

"Nora, why was your husband arrested?"

"Probably for the same reason I'm currently standing inside a swimming pool talking to you. Can I trust you? I don't know who's trustworthy anymore," said Nora, looking Emily in the eye.

"I was dragged out of my house in my pajamas at three o'clock in the morning and am standing inside a swimming pool with twenty other women! Lady, if you don't want to trust me that's fine with me," said Emily, with frustration clearly present in her tone. She tried to stay positive at all times but had an explosive temper.

"Why don't you both shut the hell up? They'll end up executing us on the spot for being too loud!" exclaimed a tall, bulky woman standing a few yards away from Emily and Nora. She too wore pajamas.

Nora motioned to Emily to walk away from the screaming woman. Here she was, claiming that being too loud could endanger their lives, and she was yelling at the top of her lungs.

"Follow me, we need to get away from this crowd."

They walked to the far end of the pool where few had gathered. It was an Olympic sized pool with no shallow end, the soldiers had dismantled the ladder and lowered each newly arrived prisoner one at a time, one soldier holding her from each arm. Two men with rifles observed as the transfers from the vans to the pool took place.

"I'd like to apologize for insinuating you couldn't be trusted, we are obviously in the same predicament," said Nora with great humility.

"Emily, tell me your story first and I promise I'll share mine."

"Fair enough, my friend. I attend Havana University and am currently studying accounting. As you know, there were protests on campus and a number of students were arrested."

"I know it too well, Emily. I read about the demonstrations, it takes a lot of courage to demonstrate and fight against the changes taking place." Nora did not want to reveal too much, considering the environment and the government's effective use of the DCR, she could not be too safe. She excluded her brother-in-law and nephew from the conversation altogether.

"Thank you, but I don't consider myself courageous, I'm doing what comes naturally. Does it take more valor to sit on the sidelines doing nothing while your world falls apart or to step in to fight against an evil you know is negatively affecting those you love? It is man's natural instinct to fight for freedom and survival, for that matter it's an instinct belonging to the entire animal kingdom."

"Emily, I couldn't agree more. What inhibits a bigger movement is hope. That is a trait with a double-edged sword, it can benefit or prevent people from taking decisive action. When you hold on to hope for too long, doors begin to close. It gets to the point when you are enclosed with no way out. Many Cubans hope this thing blows over in a couple of years, maintaining that belief hinders them from appropriate action when warranted."

Nora continued speaking, keeping her eyes on the armed guards. They stood their positions as the drivers made their rounds to the police stations for more prisoners. What the women did not know was that the soldiers were conducting mini-investigations to determine whether they should live or die. From the point of arrest to release or execution, as few as six hours could elapse.

Their conversation could have had them shot on the spot. Women in the pool distanced themselves so as to disassociate themselves from them and their potentially lethal topic of discussion.

Emily pondered Nora's comment before continuing. "I live on the poor side of town, not too far from your café. I've always compensated for monetary wealth with spirit and positive attitude. Very few things get me down. My biggest flaw is my trustworthiness, my faith in people is what did me in, that is why I'm standing here with you today."

"My neighbor and I have always gotten along on a superficial level until a few weeks back. She looks a bit weird and dresses in all different colors, so I had never approached her before. She invited me over for coffee and for the first time I felt a bond, my thinking was that a friendship could develop from this. We kept each other company for hours, discussing everything that came to mind. She and I have a lot in common, from opera to our passion for movies."

"Sounds good, what happened?" inquired Nora.

"After the coffee we turned to vodkas, the discussion turned to politics, and I opened up to her. You know how they say liquor is a truth serum? That goes double for me..."

"Is she a member of the DCR?"

"Two plus two equals four," said Emily as she held up four fingers.

"What's her name, that's a person I must avoid."

"Eva."

"Eva? Eva? Oh my goodness, Rainbow Girl!" responded Nora in shock.

"Nora, how do you know Eva?"

"She frequented our café, Eva is the reason we are both standing here, Emily," added Nora in disbelief.

Nora thought back to the day the group of gentlemen came to book the bachelor party, Eva was there. She was probably there the night of the bachelor party, come to think of it Eva was at the café all the time.

She got a chill, understanding now why her husband was serving ten years in prison.

By Nora's estimate, she had been in the pool for close to eight hours. With the noon sun almost upon them, the women were starting to peel off a layer of clothing to use as protection from the strong Caribbean sun. Two additional guards arrived and gave them each a 20-ounce cup of water - that was all they had consumed since arriving to *The Palace*.

"There's a van with newly arrived prisoners," whispered Emily.

The driver stepped out and motioned to the guards, they swung their rifles onto their shoulders and walked towards the van. The driver opened the rear doors, and a new batch of women followed him towards the pool.

"Ladies, listen carefully, following my instructions could save your lives. Those who do not do as they are told will not live to regret their foolish actions."

All save one were weeping uncontrollably, keeping their mouths covered so as to mute their despair.

"Why aren't you crying, little one?" asked the driver of the van.

"Because I don't fear you," she responded with emphasis and valor. This "prisoner" was no taller than five feet three inches with courage for ten.

"You don't fear us, you say?"

He looked at the other soldiers and began to laugh. They all joined in, mocking the courage the young lady demonstrated through her words.

"Gentlemen, what should we do with this brave, young lady?" asked the driver, not expecting a response.

"Do you fear *anyone*, little one?"

"My Christian name is Wilma."

"I'll rephrase that. Do you fear *anyone*, Wilma?"

"I love God and *fear* his wrath, as should you. It is never too late to receive forgiveness from the Almighty. Repent and he shall forgive you."

"Is that all you have to say, Wilma?"

"That is all."

Wilma's preaching had visibly upset the driver, she had the nerve to tell him what to do – a female, counter-revolutionary prisoner, nonetheless.

The driver's eyes were fixed on her, his look of contempt unmistakable. There was a part of her he envied, the courage she had just demonstrated was admirable and extraordinary, his bravery came in the form of a gun.

All eyes were on Wilma and the driver, anxiously anticipating the next move. Nora silently prayed.

"If you do not fear me, than this should be of no consequence to you, for it is only an extension of who I am."

Before anyone had time to react, Wilma lay in a pool of blood, eyes wide open and lifeless. The driver had pulled out his gun and shot her in the head. A few of the women yelled, afterwards silencing each other realizing the danger in expressing fear to men who thought so little of life.

Minutes after the execution, the driver called out four names.

"Emily Santiago, Jessica Gomez, Caridad Sanchez, and Nora Buendia step to this end of the pool. Come quickly!"

The ladies did not know what to think, but reacted without hesitation knowing that chances of survival increased by responding to orders.

They walked towards the driver and the other soldiers who awaited them. The two soldiers carefully lifted Nora, Emily, and Caridad out of the pool.

"Jessica Gomez, walk here immediately," demanded the driver.

"What is it you want?" asked Jessica, believing the other three women had made a mistake by following their orders like sheep.

"Come out of the pool to find out."

At this comment Nora began to shake in terror, she prayed, knowing she wouldn't live to see another day.

"Why, so I can become another one of your victims? I will meet my maker on *my* terms, life is precious and worth fighting for." Jessica was choked up, for she knew she was about to meet her fate.

Jessica had not seen the soldier hiding behind the bushes when she knelt behind a group of women. The soldier took one shot, hitting her in the head. Blood splattered on those near her, once again creating commotion and fear among the women in the pool.

"It's a shame she didn't follow orders," said the driver with a smirk.

He gazed at the three ladies standing by the edge of the pool, enjoying his power over them, thrilled at the sight of women willing to give him anything in exchange for their lives. Jessica had turned the tables on him, through her fearlessness she gained power - that is something he could never permit.

"Ladies, we have concluded your investigations. You are free to go."

Was she dreaming, had the driver just told them they were free to go?

Nora couldn't believe it. She looked at the other two ladies and began walking towards the gate as the soldiers observed, motionless.

"Hurry up or I'll change my mind," said the driver.

They didn't stop running until the pool was completely out of sight.

Had Jessica followed orders, she too would have lived to see another day.

Chapter Nineteen
Young Pioneers

W hen their mother received the school's call, she turned pale. Her children had always obeyed without question; their work ethic, handed down from their parents and grandparents, was exceptional. Santiago's father would always say - *idle time could never be reclaimed*. Maribel and her brother Luis had both entered second grade the previous summer, both were exemplar students throughout most of the school year and had received numerous academic awards in the first grade. Santiago and Alicia Nuñez were very concerned over the upcoming meeting, their children seemed to be fine at home, neither their behavior nor their routines had changed. Both parents were highly educated and well informed on education reform implemented by the new government.

What bothered them the most was the lack of details regarding their scheduled 1 pm meeting, the woman from the school said the children were not "following directives" - that could mean a number of things, to which directives did she refer? How serious were the infractions? Under the new government, would their children's actions affect the entire family?

Maribel and Luis were ten months apart, everyone mistook them for twins. The day of the meeting Alicia prepared everything early, she needed to make sure they arrived on time, both she and Santiago were anxious.

"Luis, your clean shorts are on your bed. Use the spare shirt in your closet," yelled Alicia as she ran around getting everything ready. She couldn't leave the house unless the beds were made and everything was tidy.

"Mommy, where are my overalls?" asked Maribel.

"Same place as always, honey. Check your top drawer."

"Got it!" Maribel was the sloppier of the two, Luis did a good job of keeping his room organized, he needed to know where everything was at all times, a trait he acquired from his mom.

As mom finished making the beds and dad dressed, the children prepared for inspection. Santiago served in the military for six years under Batista, he decided against reenlisting because of the combat occurring in the mountains between Castro's revolutionaries and Batista's military — Alicia begged him to sit this one out, reminding him how much she and the children needed him. Having been in Batista's army added another reason for living in fear, the new regime was trigger-happy with those known for deviating from the controlling party's political ideologies.

"Honey, the children are ready for inspection," cried Alicia.

The little ones got a kick out of this daily routine, Santiago and Alicia equally enjoyed it. It served them well, teaching them discipline would help them achieve heights others may fall short from attaining. Santiago believed in building a foundation for his children.

"Success follows good discipline," he would always say.

They stood next to each other facing Dad, their near-perfect posture not like that of average second graders. Luis wore sanguine shorts with a matching handkerchief around his neck, a white shirt, and black shoes. Maribel's red overalls matched her brother's shorts and handkerchief, her white blouse matched his shirt. She wore white socks that almost reached her knees, and black shoes.

"Ready for inspection, Daddy!" yelled out Maribel with a smile on her face.

"Shhh...soldiers aren't supposed to yell like that," said Luis.

"Looking sharp, soldiers! Are you ready for school?"

"Yes, sir!"

"Will you learn much today?"

"Yes, sir!"

"Good. At ease, soldiers!"

Maribel and Luis spread their legs and relaxed.

"I love you, Daddy!" said Maribel.

"Me too, Dad," added Luis.

"Come here, that's an order."

Santiago opened his arms as they ran to him. He gave them a tight hug not wanting to let go.

They entered a sea of red as the school guard led them through the playground towards the main office. Every student wore the new required uniform; on viewing these youngsters all dressed in red, anti-revolutionaries visiting the school couldn't help but think of all the blood shed in the past few years for the sake of the revolution. Playtime was clearly over as the bell rang, causing a conditioned response within the students in the yard. Within seconds they lined up, each "regiment" ready to return to class. Discipline was obviously one of this school's strong points. Santiago couldn't help but wonder - at what expense?

"They line up well, just like our soldiers. What do you think?" asked the guard with a gleam in his eyes, he seemed very proud of what was being accomplished with the students.

"Impressive indeed, I hadn't seen such straight lines since..." Alicia shot Santiago a stern look as he bit his tongue. They had agreed to reveal as little as possible about their past.

"Since what? Did you serve during the revolution?" excitedly asked the guard.

"I will be joining this summer, I can't wait to defend the revolution that will finally bring equality to all," added the guard.

Santiago ignored the last comment, he only responded to the guard's initial question, "No, I didn't serve. I was referring to the lines we had when I was in school."

"Oh. But you are not too old to serve, aren't you tempted?"

"Yes, I'm tempted, but I would never leave my wife and kids behind," he said, attempting to disguise his lie to the best of his ability.

"I can understand that, sir. Here is the main office, take a seat and the principal will be with you in a few minutes," said the guard as he entered the office and motioned to the couch.

Dr. Villanueva had the secretary call in the couple less than ten minutes after arriving in the office. The school principal led them into her office and closed the door.

"Mr. Nuñez, Mrs. Nuñez, kindly sit. I've called Luis's and Maribel's teacher and a student teacher into this meeting, they have both observed the children's defiance.

"Dr. Villanueva, I assure you that whatever misgivings you may have about our children, they have always obeyed laws and regulations and have been excellent students," said Alicia.

"Mrs. Nuñez, let's wait for the teachers to discuss the concerns at hand, I wouldn't want them to miss anything. I assure you of one thing, it is a serious issue, otherwise we wouldn't have called you in."

For the second time in less than an hour, Santiago bit his lip and said nothing. He realized they were living in a completely different world now, besides, he would get his opportunity to speak soon enough.

Mrs. Fernandez and Ms. Avilez walked in and sat on a sofa adjacent to the principal's desk. The principal and both teachers faced the couple as the meeting commenced. Mr. and Mrs. Nuñez still wondered what the issue at hand was.

"My dear parents, we have called you in today to discuss certain indiscretions exhibited by Luis and Maribel," pointed out Dr. Villanueva.

"I will let Mrs. Fernandez begin by giving a specific example," she said.

"Thank you, Dr. Villanueva. As you folks know, we are under

new leadership in this country. It is a leadership we firmly endorse. As a leader within our community, our school has acted ahead of most by making changes that demonstrate certain ideologies other schools have refused to adopt as of yet. Do you follow where I'm going with this?" asked Mrs. Fernandez.

"I'm afraid I follow all too well," responded Santiago.

"Mr. Nuñez, this is not something to fear, it is a change we must all wholeheartedly embrace."

"Yes, that's what I meant." Bite number three, at this rate Santiago will have a swollen lip by late afternoon.

"Anyway, in the mornings we have our opening exercises: our school pledge, our government pledge, and morning announcements. Luis and Maribel refuse to cite the school and government pledges," said Mrs. Fernandez, her chin high in the air, exhibiting a straight posture.

"What are the contents of the pledges you are asking them to recite?" asked Santiago.

Mrs. Fernandez handed Santiago and Alicia a copy of each pledge, she had been prepared for Santiago's question. Her smug attitude filled the air, asphyxiating Santiago - he prayed he could get through this day without doing something he would later regret.

They sat, reading both pledges as they restrained themselves, refusing to believe what this country had become in such a short period of time, unrecognizable from what it once was.

The school pledge contained phrases such as:

Young pioneers
Equality for all
The rich owe us

The government pledge mentioned:

Revolution - 4 times
Fidel Castro - 3 times

Santiago took a deep breath before continuing.

"Is this what you are teaching our children? You are inculcating them with communist propaganda instead of teaching them to think for themselves?" Santiago was beet red, he could not contain himself.

"Mr. Nuñez, comments like those are safe behind these closed doors, but you must refrain from speaking out like that to just anyone. It could cost you dearly," advised Dr. Villanueva.

"Please get me a cup of water," requested Santiago.

"Absolutely, Mr. Nuñez."

"Gloria, please bring a pitcher of water and some glasses," called out Dr. Villanueva.

After Santiago calmed down and had his water, Dr. Villanueva continued speaking with an air of arrogance as they both sat and listened.

"We have young pioneers in this school, children who will carry the torch that's been instituted by the founders of our glorious revolution. As pioneers they will lead others into a new way of governing, leading with foresight that few other countries dare to implement," preached the leader of the school.

"There will be no dissent in our school, any student who refuses to acquiesce will be reported!"

"Dr. Villanueva, my husband and I guarantee that there will no longer be any problems in that, or any other respect, with our children. We will take these copies home and they will be reciting both pledges tomorrow with as much fervor as the other students," interjected Alicia, speaking before giving her husband a chance of verbalizing anything else.

"Very good, then. It was a pleasure meeting you both," said Dr. Villanueva.

"Gloria, if any students come to see me have them wait, I'll be on an important phone call for the next half hour," demanded Dr. Villanueva.

On their way out, Ms. Avilez caught up and called the couple over to the side of the school, under a palm tree with nobody else in sight.

"Mr. Nuñez, I'm doing my teacher training in Mrs. Fernandez's class. You seem like a nice family, I wanted to warn you to not say what you said in there to just anybody."

"Why are you risking your job and freedom for us, Ms. Avilez?"

"Please call me Chary. The answer to your question is that I've already lost someone I love dearly because of this, he moved to the United States and I don't know if I'll ever see him again. I help others because I can empathize having experienced repercussions brought on by our new government. Anyway, I've probably said too much already. Take care."

"I'm sorry about your loved one, but I'm sure if you try hard enough you'll be able to join him someday," responded Santiago.

"Nice meeting you, Chary. We must go now," said Alicia, praying to God she would never experience anything like that again.

They arrived home at 2:30 pm, had dinner at 5 pm, the children learned both pledges by 7 pm, the family went to bed at 10 pm, Santiago was in a six by four cell by 2 am.

He had said too much to the wrong person.

Chapter Twenty
Lost Cause

Through all the turmoil and oppressive laws implemented under the new regime, Carlos tried to maintain as much normalcy for his family as possible while keeping his eye on the prize. His house was on the market with little success thus far, but he was hopeful. Arsenio's had been on the market for months with only two offers, both deals falling through.

The passports were ready, Luisa and Mario would soon join Ana and the children in New York, while Carlos stayed behind to wrap up their financial affairs. The house must be sold and all accounts closed.

"Carlos, now I know how Ana felt having left Arsenio behind," mentioned Luisa.

"Don't get cold feet now, we have it all planned out. You and Mario will be in New York with family in three weeks. I will make you the same promise Arsenio made Ana, if I can't sell the house within three months, I will transfer the deed to someone close to us and join you and Mario. I promise," affirmed Carlos.

"The longer you wait the more dangerous it becomes. Material wealth is not worth the risk, let's just leave together with whatever cash we can take. I don't want to leave without you," expressed Mario with tears in his eyes. He loved both parents deeply, but his relationship with his dad was very special.

"I appreciate those sentiments, Mario. You've always had a heart of gold. Give me some time, I promise things will work out," said Dad.

"My love, I have faith. Everything will turn out just fine," echoed his mom.

"Of course it will, my beauty." Carlos kissed his wife and gave Mario a love tap on the head.

"Ouch!" remarked Mario, with an exaggerated demeanor and groan.

The three laughed for minutes. They were losing their country, but their family was intact. That is what mattered most.

"When will I be able to write to Angel? I want to know how he is doing in New York," mentioned Mario.

"Mario, we have spoken about this a number of times, mailing international letters now is dangerous. We don't know whether agents are reading those letters before they leave the country. Remember, Angel's uncle is in prison for associating with emigrants, Guillermo was guilty of nothing else. Angel and his family emigrated to the United States, we can't write to them now," explained Carlos.

"Dad, let's go for a walk, just the two of us."

"Deal, let's go."

Both father and son were in a great mood, they were best friends, always making the most of being together. Carlos believed that the simple things in life ended up being the most meaningful - taking a walk downtown for no particular reason with his son was one of these. Luisa couldn't be happier knowing the type of relationship Mario had with his father.

"Here, let's get a milk shake, son," said Carlos, pointing at his place of choice.

"Chocolate shake at Woolworth's? You sure know how to live it up, Dad! Count me in!"

When Carlos teamed up with his son, he turned twenty again, and they thoroughly enjoyed each other's company.

The simple things in life

They approached the building adorning the iconic red letters spelling Woolworth's, the store referred to by the locals as the 5 & 10. Brown chairs made of fake leather sitting on red poles looked worn, a couple were in need of service and could not be used, but this was heaven to Mario and his dad. If they had been dining at one of Havana's finest restaurants it wouldn't have made any difference, they were together, acting like themselves, and having fun.

The simple things in life

"I don't know why we even look at the menu, we always order the same thing," said Carlos.

"Two chocolate milk shakes and two egg salad sandwiches. The bill adds up to $1.10 and we always leave $1.75 on the counter," added Mario.

"Your mother says we buy too much crap, but when we're done eating let's take a look around, something will probably grab our eye. Maybe we can buy your sisters a hula-hoop and some play-doh, I've read that kids love those new toys, they're selling like hot cakes now," suggested Carlos.

They looked at each other and smiled, Carlos and Mario were quickly forgetting their troubles, and a father and son trip to Woolworth's was all it took.

The simple things in life

"There are a number of Woolworth's in New York, son. We can continue our tradition of getting shakes and egg salad sandwiches with Arsenio and Angel," said Carlos as he sipped on his chocolate shake.

"That sounds outstanding, Dad. I really look forward to that, you know Angel is like a brother to me."

"That's the same way I feel about Arsenio, friends like those are hard to come by, they are no doubt family to us."

Mario gleamed at the thought of going to Woolworth's with his brother in New York. He was starting to feel that everything would turn out just fine.

The simple things in life

After their escape to Woolworth's, Mario and his dad did something they rarely did alone, they went for a walk on the beach without shoes, feeling the sand underneath their feet and the refreshing Caribbean water up to their knees.

Havana is known for glorious beaches, neither Carlos nor his son frequented those beaches as often as they should have. Today they were making up for lost time, taking advantage of each other's company and the splendor they call home.

"Dad, how are we going to get ahead in the United States without speaking English?"

"Mario, I'm not saying it's going to be easy, but people who do not fear work can make it anywhere. A good education combined with a strong work ethic will see us through. We will all learn English within a couple of years and be as successful in our new home as we have been in our native country."

"You make it sound simple."

"It will be a difficult ride, but the solution to such a drastic change is actually simpler than many think. Work hard and never give up, that's the recipe," said Carlos as he gave his son a smile and a thumbs-up.

"You're a great man, Dad. I love you!"

"That means a lot coming from you, son. I love you to the moon and back!"

It is the cumulative effect of these simple moments in time that makes life worth living.

No attempts were made to enter the dwelling through traditional means, no ring of the doorbell or knock on the door was attempted, leading the owners to the conclusion that no good could come from this intrusion in the middle of the night. Two soldiers armed with rifles entered after knocking down the door, their two partners with holstered pistols followed and stormed up the stairs. Luisa was the first to awaken in a state of fright.

"Carlos, there's someone in the house!" Luisa's yell could be heard throughout the house.

"Wait here, I'll go check," he responded, choked up with emotion as so many thoughts rattled off in his brain. He didn't like what his sixth sense was telling him about the current situation.

As he left his bedroom to see whom the intruder was, Carlos saw Mario dragged out of his room by two soldiers.

"What the hell is going on here? Release my son immediately! Now!"

Carlos began running towards the soldiers, coming to a sudden halt after hearing his wife's voice.

"Carlos, stop! They will kill us all! I don't know what is going on but I'm sure we can clear this up," said Luisa, summoning as much courage as possible.

"Listen to your wife, Dr. Diaz, she is wise indeed. I have enough bullets in this gun to kill all of you, and I will not hesitate in doing it," said one of the soldiers, holding Mario's left arm to ensure he wouldn't try to escape.

"Dad, what's happening? Why am I being arrested? I didn't do anything," implored Mario, glancing at one of the soldiers. As he said this the other soldier slapped him in the face as a warning.

"Let me go! I haven't done anything, you communist pigs!" Mario fought them off, causing them to tighten their grips.

"Mario, I beg of you, shut up!" pleaded Luisa, seeing her son tormented by all this. She concealed her true emotions until Mario could no longer see her.

"Hang tight, son. Your mother and I will get dressed and go to the station to clear this up. Don't say anything else. Understand? Be brave, all will turn out just fine."

Carlos entered his bedroom after the soldiers left with their only son and wept uncontrollably, he could hear Luisa sobbing hysterically in the bathroom.

Their orders were clear, arrest everyone who was speaking out or had ever spoken out against the revolution. Penalties were harsh, all must face severe consequences.

Methods employed for finding anti-revolutionaries were many, among them performing audits of arrest records - if properly entered, the records indicated the crime, and protestors were their primary targets.

Half-dressed, Carlos and Luisa made their way to the local station to see what charges were being brought against their son, neither one spoke on the car ride over. Luisa's tears made her unrecognizable even to those closest to her. On entering, they immediately noticed the transformation in personnel, changes in dress code from police uniforms to army fatigues were noticeable, as were the unkempt beards everyone seemed to have. The beards turned Carlos's stomach, having seen Che and Fidel sporting theirs in photos that appeared in newspaper articles.

"Excuse me, we need to find our son, Mario Diaz. He was dragged out of our house forty minutes ago, I'm sure it's all a mistake," said Carlos as he approached the front desk.

"Are you accusing us of being incompetent?" asked the man behind the counter, wearing a beret that matched his uniform.

Carlos could tell this was not going to be easy, humility was the tool he needed to use.

"No sir, my apologies. Could you please help me locate him?"

"Mario Diaz, you say?"

"Yes, sir."

"He's still being booked, Mario is accused of leading an anti-revolutionary demonstration last Fall. He will not be released, a judge will determine his fate next Wednesday." The official spoke with the calmness of someone ordering his lunch at the corner restaurant .

"His fate? His fate? Carlos, what does he mean?" Luisa threw herself on the ground, pleading on her knees.

"Sir, I will do anything you want, he is our loving son. Please name the price, I beg you, please do something for us!"

"Name my price? Are you attempting to bribe a government official? We are government officials doing what's best for the people of our country, therefore we cannot make any exceptions! Get out of here before you are both arrested as well!" He pointed to the guard by the door who escorted them towards the exit.

There was only so much crying and thinking Mario could do, he was stuck in a dark, humid cell with another prisoner accused of the same crime. For all he knew, they would meet their maker on the same day.

"What is your story?" Asked the plump young man with the wavy hair.

"I'm not sure we should be discussing this," responded Mario.

"At least tell me your name."

"My name is Mario. What is yours?"

"Saul."

"Listen, Saul, nothing personal but I'd rather keep conversation to a minimum. I hope you understand why."

"I understand just one thing, that you think there's a way out. Newsflash, my friend, there's only one way out - the firing squad. These people mean business," said Saul, putting up a transparent front.

"The way you speak leads me to believe two things, you have given up and you don't fear death. Your aloof manner disturbs me, especially considering what's at stake," responded Mario.

"How can you fight it? Who could win against this regime that has stormed its way into our capital and taken control through brute force?" asked Saul emphatically.

"Saul, I'm just going to sit here in peace for a while. Not knowing the answers to you questions, I'd rather give my mind a break and not attempt any responses. We will not be able to win behind these cells anyway, that's realism."

"Just one last question, Mario. What would be your last words? If it gets to that."

"I know exactly what my final words would be, hopefully I will not have to utter them as I draw my last breath. I'd rather not share them with you at this time, I'm hoping for a happy ending, Saul."

"Same here, my friend."

Mario woke up the next morning with an awful backache and what appeared to be a rash on his arms and legs, the mattress on the floor must have been fifteen years old and no more than two inches thick. He sobbed as silently as possible not wanting to disturb his cellmate's slumber.

Minutes after a guard brought what they called "breakfast" to their cell, Saul woke up. They ate their small shares as quickly as possible to avoid tasting the food.

"I see the bugs bit you last night," said Saul.

"What?"

"Those marks you have on your arms are from bedbugs in the mattress," added Saul as he pointed to Mario's left arm.

"You've got to be kidding me! I guess I'll sleep on the floor tonight."

"You're a rich boy, huh? From my side of the tracks, bedbugs are a common occurrence. I feel like I'm immune, you're fresh meat," said Saul with a sardonic laugh.

"Don't mock me for being rich or intelligent, in this cell we are equals," pointed out Mario.

"Correction, we are far from equals, I am better equipped to deal with adversity than you, and my entire life has been training for this struggle. Also, I am probably as educated as you, my friend. Higher education does not always equate to higher income levels, there are other factors involved, I was one of few from my neighborhood protesting against the new regime. Most living in poverty think they will end up getting their fair share, they have something else coming."

"I couldn't agree more with that sentiment, Saul. This regime has already fooled many into believing they are the poor person's salvation, the façade continues, hurting those who get in the way and most through no fault of their own," remarked Mario.

The following day, less than forty-eight hours after Mario's arrest, eight accused of anti-revolutionary protests stood before a judge in yet another mock trial, their "defending attorney" had been assigned two hours before the "trial".

It took the judge less than forty minutes to decide that of the eight only one would walk free that day. The judge claimed there wasn't enough evidence to convict this particular prisoner, many said a *person of power* pulled strings to get this young man off. His release was an aberration, when people heard of this young man's release they were thrilled, in the few months in which this deplorable regime had executed hundreds, this was the only release ever granted. The young man's parents picked him up, thrilled to be taking their only son back home with them.

On the day of the execution, four soldiers assigned to gather the prisoners followed a predictable pattern, picking up each individual, cuffing him, taking him out of his cell, and moving on to the next one. All the while, two of the soldiers stood outside each cell holding their rifles ready to shoot, not caring where the executions were held; if the prisoners gave them a reason to shoot, they would happily oblige. Knowing their outcome was certain, most prisoners behaved with tremendous valor, not revealing their inner fears to these revolting sponsors of death.

"This is a brave, quiet bunch," said soldier 1 as he led the group of seven to the courtyard.

"Nothing like last week's group, remember the one who shit himself on the way out? What an awful mess," exclaimed soldier 2 as they all enjoyed a good laugh.

"Maybe we can keep these and convert them, they would make great revolutionaries," mentioned a third soldier.

"Never, asshole! I'd rather die." yelled out one of the prisoners as he spit in that soldier's face.

Soldier 1 calmly turned towards the prisoner, lifted his rifle, and took one shot to his temple. Another soldier dragged the fresh corpse off to the side, they would deal with that later.

The rest of the march went off without incident, two soldiers in the front led the remaining six prisoners as the other two soldiers followed the morbid parade.

Two large, wooden doors led to the open courtyard surrounded by concrete walls twelve feet high. It resembled the interior of a fort from Cuba's glory days as a Spanish satellite, used to successfully defend itself against foreign enemies. The executioners kept no secrets, the grounds and walls were stained with blood from previous atrocities.

The six prisoners were lined up against the prison wall, each was offered a cigarette and a blindfold. All but one accepted, he was too proud to take anything these pigs had to offer. The chunky one with the curly hair was weeping like a child.

"Get a grip, man. Leave this world with some dignity," whispered soldier 4. He wasn't like the others, soldier 4 didn't take as much pleasure in performing his duties.

"I beg of you, let me go, I'm innocent of all charges. Please!" begged Saul.

At this, the prisoner next to him told him something to try to calm him down.

"Saul, this is exactly what they want. Don't give them the satisfaction of groveling, die like a man."

"Mario, I don't want to die," he whispered back.

Saul ran towards the nearest guard and tackled him, his proximity to the guard caused hesitation in the other soldiers, preventing any gunfire that may have instantaneously occurred. Saul wrapped his handcuffs around the soldier's neck and squeezed as hard as he could, if he was going to die today he would take someone with him. The soldiers standing in the courtyard were stunned by this unexpected event, they performed to the best of their abilities, trying to contain the situation. One soldier held the other five prisoners in position, the executioners stayed put, and the other two soldiers aimed at Saul, waiting to get a clear shot without injuring their comrade.

Saul continued to wrestle with the soldier on the ground, never letting go of his neck. His fate was sealed once the soldier stopped breathing. Saul's body was riddled with bullets. Two soldiers coolly strode towards their handiwork, as both bodies lay in the center of the courtyard, blood splattered, serving as a fresh coat over the previous stains.

"Show's over, let's get back to business, gentlemen. We only have a hand-full of prisoners today, but we have thirty-eight executions scheduled for tomorrow. We can't afford to fall behind," said the leader.

The five remaining prisoners lined up against the prison wall, drawing all the courage they could from within, understanding the inevitability of their situation, begging their Lord for forgiveness, and praying for eternal life.

One of the prisoners could barely stand, the terror in his face hidden behind the blindfold and his urine-soaked pants served as a reminder of the inhumane treatment this new regime was imposing on its citizens.

One soldier walked around a second time offering blindfolds, Mario thanked him but turned it down once again. He respectfully requested a few seconds before the shots were fired to say something, they turned down his request.

All five were lined up, the firing squad readied itself, as Mario yelled out a few final words:

"*¡Que viva Cuba libre!*"

Their aim was right on, within seconds their lifeless bodies lay on the ground.

Mario died a hero, his faith in God and love of country helped guide him through those final hours.

Many more would die similar deaths opposing tyranny, fighting back a tsunami with levees only six feet high.

Chapter Twenty-One

Time Stands Still

The *For Sale* sign was on display for less than four days before someone snatched up the amazing deal. Arsenio's 1956 Pontiac Bonneville Convertible, with an original price tag of $5,400, a higher sticker price than some Cadillacs, sold for the bargain price of $900. He had driven it 16,400 miles and took great care of his pride and joy. Cubans with some cash on hand with no intentions of leaving the island were bargain shopping from those who had no choice but to hold fire sales.

In his final preparations to leave the island, Arsenio closed all of his bank accounts leaving him $1,200 on hand, which was enough to hold him over until the sale of the house. Ana and the children were in possession of the rest of their money in New York. Should the house not sell, he would keep his promise to Ana and transfer the deed over to Nora so he could join his family in New York.

"Dr. Buendia, I wish I could give you more for this lovely car, but my budget is $900. I'm glad I could help you out by purchasing the car from you, I wish you the best of luck," said the buyer.

"Thank you, my friend. Enjoy the car in good health," responded Arsenio, not telling him what he truly thought about this transaction. He knew that this particular buyer had recently purchased three other cars with the intention of selling them for a profit.

At least this leaves me a total of $2,100 until the sale of the house, thought Arsenio. That was a cushion he could live with.

After the sale of his car, he called Nora and asked her to stop by for a while. Since Guillermo's arrest, she had opened the café much less than when they were together, her depression made it difficult to move some days. Arsenio looked after her as much as he could.

The doorbell rang and Arsenio opened the door.

"Nora, it's always good to see you. Please come in," said Arsenio as he hugged her.

"Hello, Arsenio. I came over because you insisted, I really felt like staying home," said Nora in a whisper. Her tone and demeanor broke Arsenio's heart.

They all felt the loss of Guillermo, having been sentenced to ten years, Arsenio could only imagine the impact on a spouse, someone who was accustomed to living with that person on a daily basis for so many years.

"It's good for you to get out, Nora. I'm glad you decided to come over, there's something we need to discuss."

"Arsenio, as I told Ana before she left, there is no way I would be able to leave the country without Guillermo. She mentioned the possibility of leaving to New York with you, I appreciate the gesture but my final answer is no."

"No, I need to discuss something else with you. Let's get comfortable in the library so we can talk."

They went to Arsenio's library and sat across from each other.

"As you know, I've been trying to sell the house with little success thus far. My guess is that people are afraid of making major investments with the future of this country as uncertain as it is," said Arsenio.

"Have there been *any* offers?"

"Only two, and both fell through right away."

"Arsenio, tell me what I can do to help, I want you to get out before it's too late."

"Actually, there is something you could help me with. If the house doesn't sell in the next two months, I would like to transfer the deed to you. There's nobody I trust more than you. If the house sells in the future, I will give you 20% for having helped me out."

"Arsenio, I'm insulted that you would offer me money for helping you out. You're family and I'm glad to assist."

"I knew you'd agree and I also knew you wouldn't accept any money, so I won't fight you on that. Thank you so much, Nora. I would never want this house, which holds so many wonderful memories for us, to go to the wrong people," said Arsenio, fighting off tears.

"We're all in the same boat, Arsenio. Everything will eventually play itself out. Hopefully this regime will not have control for long, I'm praying for American intervention."

"Don't hold your breath, they have their hands full right now out east, Vietnam could pull them in and it could get really ugly in the near future for them."

"That won't prevent me from praying. God help us."

The conversation for the rest of the evening consisted of everyday topics, those discussed by people who have just met each other, not by family members experiencing trials and tribulations unprecedented for Cubans of their generation. Their pain was deep, their losses many, and their mental anguish close to unbearable.

Just when he thought things couldn't get any worse, he received a certified letter from the government. Arsenio could feel his heart stop for a second, he couldn't help but imagine that it was a letter like the one Guillermo had received a few weeks before. He quickly opened the envelope, pulled out the letter, and began to read, his eyes couldn't move fast enough across the typed words:

Dr. Buendia,

It has come to our attention that your family left the country and that your house is up for sale. We can only hope that your intentions are not to leave the country permanently, as it would be our loss to have such an accomplished citizen as yourself cut ties with Cuba.

Considering the circumstances and our mission to create equality among all, bank accounts exceeding $1,000 are immediately frozen and ownership of all properties will automatically transfer over to the state.

Within thirty days of receipt of this letter, an Inventory Specialist will come to your house to take inventory of all items. From that point on, the house and all the things within it no longer belong to you.

You must also transfer the 1956 Pontiac along with ownership papers.

Should you have intentions of joining your family in New York, that can only be accomplished with your Inventory Checklist in order.

Thank you for your cooperation,

Wilfredo Cabrera
President
Realignment Committee

Arsenio was floored, he had not expected the new government to seize properties this soon, he always thought there would be time to sell before leaving. Where would he turn? Nora had problems of her own, Ofelia had moved out with Antonio, and Carlos wasn't communicating with anyone; he and Luisa had gone into isolation after Mario's tragic death.

"How can this be happening to us? How? How?" He yelled, over and over again, at the top of his lungs.

"Is this what we get for being good citizens? For caring about others? For always doing our duty? Is this all?" Arsenio continued yelling, shaking about randomly, hitting his head against the refrigerator a few times.

Maybe physical pain will diminish the mental anguish I'm experiencing, he thought.

He stayed home for over two weeks, ate just enough to survive, and slept fifteen hours a day. Arsenio lost twenty pounds - his facial hair made him look unrecognizable. A man who was known for keeping up appearances through proper grooming and fancy suits now looked like a vagabond, his behavior was erratic, and his vocabulary unlike that of Dr. Buendia's.

His brother was in prison, his best friend's son dead, his best friend on the verge of lunacy due to the loss of his only son, and *he* had lost everything - including his family if he didn't find a way out of this hellhole.

Arsenio Buendia lost the will to live.

Soda cans and empty wrappers littered both floors of the house, especially the bedroom and living room. The refrigerator was empty, save for a little milk and some eggs, he had subsisted on dairy products for a week, not wanting to go grocery shopping or to any restaurant.

Ants made their home in some food Arsenio had accidentally dropped on the kitchen floor days before, the infestation worsened by the day.

He hadn't showered in days and wore the same clothes for almost a week, having no energy or reason to dress up anymore. Arsenio briefly contemplated suicide, though his Catholic upbringing immediately dispelled that idea, thoughts of his family 1,300 miles away helped deepen his depression.

It was the morning that he regurgitated in his sleep due to drinking some bad milk that Arsenio realized he had to make a move, this self-pity and relinquishment of life was not helping his loved ones, he needed to be stronger. *A man proves himself by getting up every time he falls* is something his father repeatedly said throughout his childhood, now was the time to apply that lesson.

He showered, shaved, and dressed. Arsenio went to his library, took out a pen and pad, and commenced to work on a game plan to pull himself out of this precarious situation. He completed the following list:

To Do List:
1. *Buy back the Pontiac*
2. *Purchase one way ticket to New York*
3. *Contact Carlos and Luisa to say goodbye*
4. *Visit Guillermo in prison (if permitted to do so)*
5. *Leave Nora as much money as possible*
6. *Complete the Inventory Checklist*
7. *Fly to New York*

Arsenio knew where the owner of the Pontiac lived, it was almost two miles from his house. As soon as he ate something at the corner restaurant, he started to walk towards his destination, not looking forward to completing the tasks on his list, but understanding there was no other option.

As he approached the buyer's house, Arsenio's heart beat faster. He only had $2,057, needing money for food and his airfare. He just wondered what it would cost him to repurchase his own car so he could hand it in to the government. Arsenio pondered that thought for a minute.

He needed to repurchase his own car to hand it in to the government.

Ludicrous

Arsenio rang the doorbell, he hoped the gentleman was home so he could be done with this. No response. He rang the doorbell again, knocking hard as he rang. Still no response. His knuckles hurt from knocking. Arsenio walked away with plans of returning later.

"Sir, may I help you?" yelled the owner of the house, seeing Arsenio's backside as he walked away from the house.

"Yes, I must speak to you," responded Arsenio as he turned around and headed back towards the front entrance.

"Dr. Buendia, what a surprise to see you here. Please come in," he guided him to the parlor, which was set up with four chairs, a center table, and a sofa in the corner.

"Please sit, what would you like to drink?" asked Mr. Torres.

"I'm sorry, sir. I'm afraid I don't even know your name," mentioned Arsenio.

"I'm sorry, that was awfully rude of me. Mario Torres, just call me Mario."

"I see, if you don't mind I'll call you Mr. Torres. I'm here on business, you see," responded Arsenio, taken aback by the man's first name.

"Do you have another car you want to sell? I would be happy to take it off your hands," said Mr. Torres with a smirk.

"No sir, quite the contrary. I need to purchase the Pontiac back."

"I see."

"Of course, I would give you extra money for the car."

"Of course," mimicked Mr. Torres.

"What do you think would be a fair price, Dr. Buendia?"

"I will give you $1,000, a $100 profit for having had the car only a few weeks."

"No, that won't work, you see."

"Mr. Torres, I must give the car to the government to meet my family in New York."

"So you admit to being a traitor, to leaving your country when it needs you the most? We are in a transition period in order to improve so many things that need fixing, and you decide to leave?"

Arsenio bit his tongue, as he had done so many times before. "Please tell me what you think is fair, I'd like to work something out."

"It's a fine looking car, I believe it has a little over 16,000 miles, and is less than two years old."

"Please give me a fair price, Mr. Torres," pleaded Arsenio.

"This is only because you sold it to me only three weeks ago - $3,500."

"What? I sold it to you for $900!"

"Yes, because you were desperate, as you are now. I'm a business man, I don't run a charity, Dr. Buendia."

"I don't have that kind of money."

"What kind do you have? Cut to the chase, how much can you afford?"

"No more than $1,500."

"Impossible. Have a good day."

"Wait, let me think. I'll be right back."

Arsenio stepped out to the front entrance and prayed, he prayed for guidance. He was truly desperate, and for once in his life was clueless. He entered the house, trusting he would do the right thing, knowing God would not abandon him.

"Mr. Torres, please consider my offer."

"I *have* considered it, Dr. Buendia. My final offer is this, give me $2,000 for the car and drive it away, or leave my house and never return.

Arsenio's back was against the wall.

"Here, Mr. Torres." Arsenio pulled out $2,000 in $100 bills and handed it to Mr. Torres. He had $57 left, no money for the airfare, and he would be homeless in ten days.

Of the seven items on the to-do-list, he completed one. Arsenio didn't see how he could get around to any of the remaining six.

"Nice doing business with you, here are the keys," said Mr. Torres, as he waved in a mocking gesture.

Arsenio drove home and went straight to bed. It was two o'clock in the afternoon.

The Inventory Specialists appeared at Arsenio's home three days early, he was mentally prepared for their visit, knowing their methods of operation. Arsenio decided to hide only one thing from them, understanding the consequences should they ever find out. The Rolex Ana gave him for their anniversary meant the world to him, and he knew that she paid cash for it, so there was no trace of its purchase. If he could keep it from them until they left, he would get to keep his prized possession.

It's strange, these people storm into houses for some things and act cordially at other times. Animals that they are, communists can sometimes pass for respectable human beings. Their choreographed motions are one thing, avoid looking them in the eye, the beast within is unleashed through a look they possess. This is the look Arsenio Buendia needed to put up with on the last day he would ever see his lovely home, with the balcony facing the ocean, the backyard where all his children's birthday parties had been celebrated, and the kitchen where Ofelia and Ana had cooked all those special Noche Buena meals.

The doorbell rang and Arsenio immediately opened the door.

"Good day, Dr. Buendia. We are here to complete the Inventory Checklist. I am Mr. Alfonso and my partner is Mr. Avila."

"Yes, gentlemen. I expected you a few days from now but luckily I am here. Come in." Arsenio's head was spinning, treating these two thugs like human beings was one of the most difficult things he had ever done. God help me, he thought.

"We're glad to hear that. Here is what needs to be done. You must show us everything around the house as we check off all items on our checklist. We already have a good idea of what should be here, if we notice anything missing, you will be brought up on charges. At that point a judge will determine what consequences, if any, are appropriate. Do you understand?"

"Perfectly well, sir," responded Arsenio.

"Excellent, this should be painless. We will be out of your way in less than an hour, you may sit here and wait for us."

Painless? Painless? These pigs destroy our lives and they have the nerve to call it painless? Thought Arsenio.

Mr. Alfonso showed Arsenio to the sofa, as if he were the one visiting. He followed Mr. Alfonso and sat for almost two hours, patiently waiting.

"Mr. Buendia, good news. We have searched the entire house and everything seems to be in order. Let us have the car keys and all copies you may have of the house keys."

Arsenio handed him the keys.

They stepped into the portico, exited onto the front lawn, and walked to the corner. Arsenio took one last look, focusing on the balcony; he had wonderful memories attached to every room in the house, but that balcony was very special to him. Ana announced each one of her pregnancies to him sitting on that balcony, so many hours spent sitting and enjoying the ocean view from that balcony, the many times his children spent playing on that balcony, all the good times he spent with Carlos on that balcony – yes, aside from his library, that was the most special area of the house to him, a balcony on which he will never set foot again.

"Good day to you, sir," said Mr. Alfonso one last time.

"Thank you, good day to you," responded Arsenio, with the most natural smile he could produce. He walked away holding a small suitcase with nowhere to go.

Arsenio waited an hour before returning to the rose garden to retrieve his Rolex.

With $3 in his wallet and nowhere to go, Arsenio was homeless and in danger of going hungry soon. He found a corner where he could brave the outdoor elements, an area he had known for years. This was the treasured corner his family claimed every year for the Carnival. Memories of the carnival from the previous year danced in his head like so many chorus girls he had seen in nightclubs before. And now it was all gone, never to return. He was now living there, in a street corner, begging for money. Through no fault of his own he had lost everything he owned.

Ludicrous

After a few days of living there, he set a routine for himself. Arsenio slept as best as he could from sunset to sunrise, hiding the Rolex on his left wrist. There was no longer any need to look at the watch. He figured it was safer to wear it than to put it in his luggage, his bag could easily be stolen in the middle of the night. He begged from sunrise to sunset, took breaks in-between to eat, and went to the bathroom after every meal to wash up as best as possible.

His routine of begging and eating continued, everyday, three times a day. When lucky, he would eat three meals a day. Each day blended into the next, almost as if time were standing still, there was no longer a need to look at a calendar or a watch, the sun served as Arsenio's guide. The chains of bondage no longer imprisoned him, he did as he pleased, went where he pleased, and he was free from demands – not his director, not his wife, and especially not the passing of time could any longer dictate his actions.

Those duties are what he missed the most, he longed for his old life.

One day Arsenio saw Lily and Adolfo, walking hand-in-hand. He immediately hid, not wanting them to see him like this. Sometimes he wondered *"what if"*...but no, he would always stop himself. *What if* are cursed words when used conjointly, second-guessing your life, especially when most of it goes fulfilled with good family and friends. It is what it is, as the saying goes.

He stood, shaking his can full of change, hoping for better days ahead. His plan was to save enough money for his airfare to New York. At this pace it didn't look good, he needed the little money he got for food, there was no surplus.

"Money for a meal, money for a meal..."

Clickety clack, clickety clack.

A nickel here, a penny there. So many people would pass, avoiding eye contact, not acknowledging his existence.

Ludicrous

It doesn't matter much who you were before becoming homeless, what properties you owned or what titles had been conferred, after only a few weeks you begin to look and act the part of a homeless person, a vagabond with nothing to do and nowhere to go. Passersby look right through you, if they bother to look at all. Your past does not count in this world - Arsenio's new cosmos.

"Money for a meal, money for a meal…"

Clickety clack, clickety clack.

When receiving change from the generous, he rarely looked up. Arsenio would nod and say thank you. This one particular day, not knowing why, when he heard the change drop in his tin can, Arsenio looked up…

He couldn't believe his eyes.

Were his senses deceiving him? Could this be possible? What should his next move be?

"Dr. Buendia, is that you?" asked a man wearing an army uniform.

"It is I," responded Arsenio, not feeling much like Dr. Buendia these days.

"How did this happen? Where is your family?" The young man sounded concerned, at least on a superficial level.

"Well, my family is in New York, I'm trying to join them. I've lost everything to the government, *your* government."

"*My* government? We are going to accomplish great things, Dr. Buendia, just wait and see."

"Please allow me the right to disagree. Gerson, remember the lunch date we had at my house? I really enjoyed that."

"I did too, Dr. Buendia. I'm sorry it's come to this for you," said Gerson, with a genuine look of disappointment. The tables had turned, leaving Gerson with mixed feelings — he now had the power, that feeling intoxicated him. On the other hand, Dr. Buendia had been good to him and offered him kindness when nobody else would.

Gerson looked around to ensure they were not being watched.

"Would you reciprocate for my good deed from a year ago? I need $200 for food and an airplane ticket to New York."

"What, for nothing in return?" asked Gerson, with a grin on his face.

"Sir, I took you off the streets, gave you a meal, and attempted to make your situation better. Is that not reason enough to help me out when I'm down?"

"No, I need something in return."

"I have nothing to offer."

Arsenio shifted to the right, feeling a cramp coming on. He left his left wrist exposed, revealing his Rolex. Gerson saw the watch.

"You know what, I owe you, so here's what I'm going to do. In exchange for that watch, I will give you the $200 you have requested as repayment for your generosity."

Gerson knew what a quality watch looked like, this was top notch.

Arsenio knew there was no possibility of negotiating, his opportunity had arrived, the door was wide open, he must step in without hesitation.

"I suppose that sounds like a fair deal," responded Arsenio, with hope in his tone.

"By the way, how's my son?" asked Gerson.

"Your son? How would I know?"

"Rumor has it you've done a great job helping Ofelia with Antonio. That is another reason I'm helping you out."

"Ofelia named Antonio after his father, you can't be his father," said Arsenio, recoiling in disgust.

"Dr. Buendia, I'd like to formally introduce myself. I am Gerson Antonio Fonseca, on my leisurely outings at night I use my middle name."

Arsenio sat a few seconds, taking it all in. He found no need to respond.

"Give me the watch, here are your $200. The sooner you leave *our* country, the better."

Gerson took the watch and placed it on his wrist, beaming with joy. He looked at the time and stated, " Arsenio, it's half past noon, if you rush you might make the three o'clock flight to New York."

Gerson walked away with a swagger.

Half past noon, pondered Arsenio. Once a day, for the rest of his life, he would look down at his watch at twelve-thirty in the afternoon and think of this moment in time — forever engraved in his mind.

Minutes later, Arsenio stood up, packed his things, and began his trek towards the airport. Ominous clouds threatened, the waves would soon crash against El Malecón creating the mist his family enjoyed so much.

CPSIA information can be obtained
at www.ICGtesting.com
Printed in the USA
LVHW021800280822
727047LV00009B/468

9 781478 760634